THE SUBJECTS

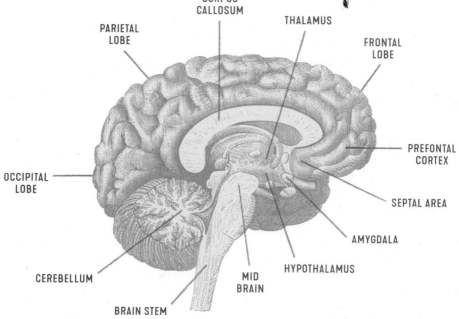

CORPUS
CALLOSUM

THALAMUS

PARIETAL
LOBE

FRONTAL
LOBE

PREFONTAL
CORTEX

OCCIPITAL
LOBE

SEPTAL AREA

AMYGDALA

HYPOTHALAMUS

CEREBELLUM

MID
BRAIN

BRAIN STEM

ALSO BY SARAH HOPKINS

The Crimes of Billy Fish
Speak to Me
This Picture of You

Sarah Hopkins' first novel, *The Crimes of Billy Fish*, was shortlisted for the Commonwealth Writers' Prize and highly commended for the ABC Fiction Award. Her third novel, *This Picture of You*, was shortlisted for the Barbara Jefferis Award. She works as a criminal lawyer in Sydney.

sarahhopkinsauthor.com

THE
SUBJECTS
SARAH
HOPKINS

TEXT PUBLISHING MELBOURNE AUSTRALIA

textpublishing.com.au

The Text Publishing Company
Swann House
22 William Street
Melbourne Victoria 3000
Australia

Published by The Text Publishing Company, 2019

Book design by Jessica Horrocks
Images by iStock
Typeset in Sabon 11.25/17.5 by J&M Typesetting

Printed and bound in Australia by Griffin Press, part of Ovato, an accredited ISO/NZS 14001:2004 Environmental Management System printer

ISBN: 9781925773781 (paperback)
ISBN: 9781925774535 (ebook)

A catalogue record for this book is available from the National Library of Australia.

This bound proof is printed on paper certified against the Forest Stewardship Council® Standards. Griffin Press holds FSC chain-of-custody certification SGS-COC-005088. FSC promotes environmentally responsible, socially beneficial and economically viable management of the world's forests.

QUESTION 1

In answer to the first of their questions:
what was the nature of the facility?

I say it was a school.

Transport

What I could see outside was nowhere I'd ever been. Fields of dry stubble, train tracks beyond them. Clumps of blackened trees. Inside, a new-car interior and the driver's headphones leaking a tinny treble of white noise. When I tried the window it wouldn't open. I wasn't surprised; in the movies, the windows never open.

Questions started to form but didn't take hold. The events of the morning, the pounding on the door and her mad, bleary eyes; the courtroom, the man standing at the back. All of it flashed past with the fields and the trees, scattering somewhere in the outback sameness. At some point it occurred to me to slide over to get a view of the dash. It was 4.24 pm, and outside it was 24 degrees: a synergy of time and temperature. Reassuring. I had no control over where we were going, but somehow it was the right road. I sat back.

A little later, a heat haze rose out of the black tar ahead, and rising out of the haze I saw a figure. A man? A man waving his arms. I leaned forward as the van approached him and tapped the driver's plastic shield. Could he see it too? The driver didn't turn, and then the man on the road stopped waving and disappeared, just the shadow of a tree branch and a clump of roadkill.

I looked back to double check. Right: *it never happened*. And the rest of it? From the moment I woke up, the banging on the door. *It never happened*.

Except it did. The courtroom—the dark suits and stern faces.
The objective seriousness, the supply of drugs…
Vulnerable school children…
The level of sophistication and the public harm.
The fact that I was a vulnerable child myself—my 'sorry history'—was no excuse.

My lawyer did her best. She got all flushed as she painted the dead-set tragedy of my home life.

'Where is his mother now?' the judge interrupted. He looked too young to be a judge but he talked like an old man.

'At home, your Honour. Her condition is such that she doesn't leave the home.'

That cut two ways. On the one hand the absence of a fully functioning parent explained why I was such a fuck-up. But it also meant the prospect that it would change any time soon wasn't great. That is where the judge seemed to land.

'You are an extremely intelligent boy, Daniel. The reports all tell me that. It is a gift, and I find it very sad to see how you have chosen to use it.' He turned away from me and back to the lawyer. 'We are talking about a *very* sophisticated and *very* lucrative

4

operation here. This was an established pattern of behaviour that put the health and welfare of dozens of children at risk.'

'Yes, your Honour, but today he is pleading guilty and that demonstrates—'

He didn't let her finish the sentence. He had 'formed the firm view'—I'm not sure how—that my early plea indicated indifference to my fate rather than evidence of remorse.

He was half-right. It wasn't remorse, but I did care. The thought of going into juvenile detention made me want to peel off my skin. I told the lawyer I wanted to plead guilty and get it over with because I am one of those people who can't have a blade hanging over their head and go on pretending it isn't going to fall. They are the same people who eat the bad stuff on their plate first—always have, always will. I knew how it was going to turn out. I'd done it. I knew I'd done it; they knew I'd done it. I'd done it before and I'd done more and worse and the likelihood was I'd do it and more and worse again. True fact. Hard as it was, there was only one way forward: suck it up, swallow, move on.

The judge launched into a loud and lengthy sermon about the need to send a message. Not just to me, but to all the young people like me, the whisper of deterrence in the ear of our future selves...

(I mean for fuck's sake. Show me a kid who stopped in his tracks and veered a different way because of something a judge said one time. This is just bad science. Real consequences—certain and known consequences—barely weigh in, let alone the double maybe of what *might* happen *if* you get caught. Actions are determined by immediate, front-and-centre reasons to act; and I had plenty of reasons to take money from kids looking for pharmacological assistance. So, sure, lock someone up because you want him off the streets for a while. Just don't couch it in all the bullshit.)

Anyhow, the upshot: today there was no alternative. Full-time custody. I was going in.

And then I wasn't.

Behind me there were muffled whispers and the judge started looking over my head. I turned around and saw, standing at the back of the courtroom, a man with a pale grey suit and a mop of black hair combed in a side part. I'd never laid eyes on him before, but he smiled at me and nodded at the judge and the judge raised his eyebrows, like it was part of a secret code. And all of a sudden, the wind changed direction.

'Very well,' said the judge. 'I can see merit in that.' This was in reply to nothing anyone had said. 'We just need to be satisfied that he is not currently on any form of medication.'

'We have that information,' replied the man in the grey suit. 'He was taken off clonidine in May.' The accent was foreign, but very slightly, and not from anywhere in particular. A bit of east and west.

The judge peered down at me again like it hurt his eyes to do it and, without looking at me a second time, made a hurried pronouncement placing me on an order for twelve months under section whatever, my release conditional upon compliance with blah blah...And so forth.

'Daniel, do you understand what I have said?'

I nodded.

'You are not free to go home, Daniel. I have ordered that you enter a residential program to address the issues underlying your behaviour. You will be taken directly from the courthouse to the location. What this means is that you are a lucky young man. Please don't forget that.' Leaning forward, he repeated it slowly. 'A *very—lucky—young—man*...Do you understand that, Daniel?

I said I did; I understood.

And the blade didn't fall. I slid into the back seat of a van, with a driver who was not the man in the grey suit, on my way to find out what 'lucky' meant.

I'd slid deeper down into my seat and drifted into sleep, and when I woke up my mouth was dry and my head was an old sore and when the window still wouldn't open I banged it with the palm of my hand. More than once. It was me and the world again, and though we'd never been on this particular road, the feeling was familiar, the bond between us unchanged. I banged the window again, then the driver's shield, and I told him I was going to keep banging until he pulled the fucking car the fuck over.

It was more effective than I'd anticipated. He flicked his head-phones out and slowed the van—to give me an earful, I thought. But no, right there and then, the van turned off the road. Not because I banged. Because we had arrived.

Intake

A white-pebbled driveway cradled on either side by plump eucalypts and greenish fields. At the top of the driveway, a sandstone building.

In another story, an orphaned cousin would come up with a lot of ways to say it was big and pretty. I'd read books like that and I always skipped those bits. I wasn't going to let myself be fooled by a few blocks of sandstone. As we got closer, I could see that behind the sandstone was another building—curved concrete; purpose-built. But no fence, no wire. Not a bar in sight.

A very lucky young man.

I sat up and craned at the dash—6 pm and 22 degrees, which didn't give me a lot to work with, a single prime factor—then the driver swung his long legs out the door and, as he stretched his arms to the sky, the front door of the building opened and a guy stepped out. A flop of blond hair, fine-rimmed glasses; a white short-sleeved shirt, striped cotton pants and sandals. He was smiling but he didn't walk towards the van.

I climbed out. Turned back to the driver. 'What is it? This place?'

He shrugged and passed me my backpack. 'You know as much as I do.'

He looked like he wanted to say something else. His voice was soft and something made me regret the window-banging and wish he wasn't going to get into the van and drive away. But he did, and I watched him go.

When I turned back, the blond man was gone, the door still open, leaving me with the impression that whether or not to walk through it, the decision was mine.

Inside was what looked like a doctor's waiting room. The blond man stood next to a reception desk, still smiling, but bravely, like he was bracing for something. Close up, his face was pockmarked and his roots were black.

'Could I take your height and weight?' he asked.

I shrugged.

'Sorry.' He extended his hand. 'I'm Greg.'

'Daniel.'

'Yes.'

I was about to give him some rough numbers when he guided me to a set of scales with a white measuring rod mounted on the wall behind it. He made a note (176 cm and 63 kg), then directed me to help myself from the water cooler.

'I shouldn't think he'll be too long.'

I didn't ask who it was I was waiting to see or tell him that I had a cracking pain in my head and was hungry enough to eat his eyeballs.

The room had three doors: the outside entry, the one through which Greg left, and another one on the opposite wall. My guess was that I was waiting to see someone sitting behind the third door, and that Greg was standing on the other side of his with one of those new slimline taser guns somewhere in his stripy pants. (That was the go in those days if you worked with the bad or the mad: non-lethal self-protection at your disposal.) Still, I was surprised to be left alone. That didn't seem like normal procedure.

I sat in the chair facing door three, scanned the ceilings for CCTV (none that I could see), and drank three glasses of water. 176; 63. I busied myself with that for a while, mashing it up and finding a sequence, before landing back on the unsatisfactory facts—I was 16 years old and 176 cm. The man sketched in my memory with the label 'father' had predicted I'd have 'real height'; the fact that I hadn't grown in two years wouldn't have worried me otherwise, but it was the only talking memory of him I had.

Would he have cared whether I'd blitzed a test or scared away the tenants or managed (by whatever means) to save $23K by my sixteenth birthday? I had no idea. I just knew he'd thought I would be tall. Then I doubted whether he'd said it at all, whether it was just something I'd got from the TV.

Anyhow, 176; 63; 16: they were my numbers and here I was. As the pain in my head eased, I placed them inside the food pyramid info-poster on the wall in positions that might best reflect the relative size of the angles, then paced across the room a couple of times and checked an empty drawer in the reception desk. My options exhausted, I opted for the second door, Greg's door.

I was wrong. Greg wasn't on the other side of it. When I describe what was there—in terms of understanding the impact of what I saw—keep in mind that in my day-to-day, up until this point,

I was one of those people who know the lie of the land. People, places, situations didn't surprise me; rainbows didn't shoot out of thunderclouds. And this—what was on the other side of the door—being but one of a number of surprises in a single day... at a limbic level, it resonated. There was a shift, a stirring of the dopamine; that's all I'm saying.

I stood alone—no Greg, no taser—in a circular corridor surrounding a large internal courtyard. The entire inner wall was made of glass, so that in the fading light I could see right across the courtyard and around the whole arc of the corridor. There was a series of closed doors over two storeys with timber stairwells at opposite ends. The sheer scale of it, and the contrast with the ordinary little waiting room, not to mention all the rooms in all the mean buildings that came before it—the windowless bedroom, the fluoro-lit kitchen, the damp-stained classroom—it was as though I'd stepped into another world. It was a concrete Tardis with a core of natural light and, at its centre, three fruit trees in massive, milky-white planter pots. I found out later they were pear trees.

Later, I read the descriptions in the transcripts, the intention behind the whole design. But even that day—the moment I laid eyes on it—I understood there was symmetry to the structure that was intended to influence those inside it. The impression was fluid and full of future promise, as if one day the whole building would take off into the sky. And of course, the trees: *pyrus nivalis.* It was summer now and they were in full leaf, shading the slatted benches and casting dappled shadows over the pebbles, but I'd soon see for myself that the real show was in autumn when the leaves turned purple and gold and began to fall.

Later, when counsel assisting the inquiry stopped interjecting and let Dr J speak, that is what he talked about—a full page of transcript on why he picked the trees: the abundance of the spring blossom and the softness of the silver-green leaf but, most important of all, the fact that it would for some time stand bare— life and death, growth and renewal.

'Put your cross on a mantel,' he said. 'I will plant my pear tree.'

Looking at it all for the first time, I had to give myself a moment to take it in. My chest emptied as I began to weave the setting into a mental narrative: *I belong here, in a purpose-built home for lucky young men, shaded by a branch in the courtyard and surrounded by others like me. Slow build to crowd scene and we are marching with the fervour of purpose (it doesn't matter what that purpose is, the point is that we have one). A soft-focus filter in the pinky golden sun and there am I, front row, centre left, blending into the crowd...*It started to build into a beautiful crescendo—*all of us, side by side*—when something drew me out of it.

A question: where were they, the others?

Setting aside the lure of light and space, I looked around me again and all I could see were the empty corridors. I heard foot-steps, but saw not a soul. Then the sound of a slamming door. And bang—I could feel it creeping back, the real story. I was caught. This was not prison, but it was my prison. I had been plucked out of my life and placed in the unknown, the empty corridors and the courtyard and the waiting room, nothing more than a trick of time and light.

Somewhere there is a report I haven't found that kicks off with a baseline: status of Daniel G pre-intervention. It will read that I was oppositional defiant or ADHD. Some such description, plenty to pick from.

My input is that standing and viewing my new surrounds that first day, I hoped for something different but feared it would only be the same.

Hope and fear, slot that in somehow.

'Did you need something?' Greg, with a hand on my shoulder. Strangely gentle; just fucking strange. I shoved his hand away and stepped back with the urge to get the hell out of there. I guess he read it, nodding his head like he understood. 'It's okay,' he said. 'He's ready for you now.'

Back in the waiting room, Greg tapped on the third door before opening it.

I stepped inside. In front of me was a desk covered in framed photographs and, at the other end of the room, a pair of wing-backed chairs. Seated in one was a man holding a piece of paper close to his face like he was straining to read it. The curtain was partly drawn, leaving a lamp—a cloudy glass tulip—as his source of light, and the rest of the room, including me, in relative darkness.

'Daniel,' the man said. 'Come and sit.' The quiet voice was familiar, the lilting accent. When he pulled the page away I saw that it was the man in the grey suit from the back of courtroom. The jacket was gone now, the striped shirt sleeves pushed up his arms and wedged on an impressive pair of triceps.

I never liked to be told to sit. It meant you'd done something wrong or you were about to be forced to dredge up something you wanted to let lie.

'My name is Dr J. We met in a roundabout way in the court-room this morning.'

I nodded. I did not sit.

'You must be famished,' he said, asking Greg to bring us some food. And after Greg had left: 'So, what now?'

I waited for him to answer his own question but he didn't, instead directing me to 'please have a drink'. Beside him on a small table was a glass jug with pieces of lemon floating in it and two glasses. He filled them and passed one over. The drink was sweet

13

and very cold and smelled like the jasmine growing on the bus shelter outside our flats.

'It might be more comfortable if you took a seat.' His eyes were dark and far apart. They moved down to the seat on offer and then back again to meet mine in an entreaty that was both gentle and firm. The chair itself—I didn't wait to be asked again—was an armchair covered in worn green velvet. It felt good enough to sleep in.

When I finished the drink he handed me the piece of paper he'd been reading as I entered. I looked down at the page in my hands. The first line was in bold and read: *As between Daniel G and the School.*

'What is it?' I asked.

'It is a contract.' That trace of an accent. Even when he spoke his lips remained in a half-smile.

I looked back to the page. The next line was a heading: *The Conditions*, and under that it was blank (rendering the document, as far as I could understand, meaningless). 'Where do I sign?' I said.

He smiled more fully. 'Let's you and I draft something first. Think it over for a day: what you want of me, and what you are prepared to give…'

About that time Greg reappeared with a tray of finger sandwiches, put them on an empty table with two plates and left without speaking. Dr J motioned for me to help myself, and I piled my plate high with two of each mystery filling. When I was sitting down again and eating, he helped himself too; we ate for a few minutes in silence. I can't really explain why I was relaxed enough to do that, only to say that I was hungry and the fancy sandwiches were as good as cake and I was comfortable in my velvet chair. Nothing bad had happened yet. Maybe if I could just let things slide for a while and wander around the luminous corridors, how could it hurt? It didn't mean I was falling for the 'let's you and I' bullshit; I only had to go back to this guy's coded conversation in the courtroom to know where he sat in the scheme of things. It was a skill that throughout my almost seventeen years had served me well: how to peg people. Teachers, lawyers, customers…if you gave me ten minutes, I could tell you who to trust.

I started: '"The School." The judge said it was a program. You say it's a school now?'

With his mouth still full he shrugged and nodded simultaneously.

'What happens if I leave?'

He put the rest of his sandwich back on his plate. 'What would happen to you if you left?' He appeared genuine in his need for clarification.

'If I woke up in the morning and walked out the door.'

He shook his head. 'How would I know?'

'I mean, do you call the cops?'

He gestured towards the piece of paper now sitting under my plate. 'There is no fine print in there, Daniel. It is blank, a clean slate, as we call it.' His eyes held firm again and I noticed that his face was without symmetry: a high forehead and a severe side part, the left eye larger than the right, so that the bushy eyebrows were uneven, one a little higher and more arched. His nose deviated to the left with a pronounced bump at the bridge, and at the right corner of his full lips there was a small raised purple scar.

The face was a roughly drawn map of a shadowy place you wouldn't want to linger in too long; but his physique, that was something different. His collar was a little tight. Above it, an Adam's apple rose and fell as he swallowed. And then his triceps. You could watch them as he moved, and the little muscles down his forearm, the blue-green veins beneath skin that was a fine, poreless olive. No excess, nothing wasted, nothing wanting. If I'd

15

been that way inclined, it might have been arousing. As it was, I just found something reassuring in his physicality.

'This is what they gave us,' he continued, pointing to a folder on the table with the tulip lamp. 'The file that travels with you. I have only read the cover sheet but if you prefer me to read more I will do that.'

'I'd prefer it if you gave it to me.' Part-joke, but he didn't get it.

His reply was straight-faced: 'That wasn't one of the options.'

Now, as I recall this, I see the Doctor was responding as he did to most things—in his peculiarly literal way, any of the subtleties of nuance or sarcasm sliding through to the keeper. But that day as he spoke, I took it as his declaration of authority, and it threw me immediately onto the attack.

'Like it's going to make a difference if I want you to read it or not,' I said. 'Like you haven't read it already. I'm not an idiot. I don't know who you are or what this place is. I just want to know what I need to do to get signed out...'

(I hear it: these are not the words of a boy filled with hope and fear. But I tell you, they are precisely that.)

At some point while I was speaking he dropped his eye contact and reached over to make a note on a piece of paper on the table, ceasing to react in any way to what I said or to the anger in my voice. Again, now I can read it—this was his habit: for lack of relevance, a speaker would lose his attention. In his mind our interview was complete. For the time being he did not need anything else from me; I may as well not have been speaking at all.

'And now,' he said as he continued to write, 'if you're happy to stay with us tonight, I'll get Greg to show you your room.' I hadn't noticed Greg come in but he was back, standing behind me. 'And tomorrow morning after a good sleep you can find your feet. Let's meet back here when you're ready, how does that sound?'

16

The answer in my head was that I had a business to get back to and I wouldn't still be here at the end of tomorrow, but I was exhausted and played along, said goodnight and followed Greg out of the room. We walked through the waiting room and into the corridor.

Now it was darker there were lights at the base of the big pots in the courtyard that made the pear trees glow. There was the sound of quiet voices, which I traced to the back of a pair of straw-coloured heads sitting out of the light between the planters. With their hair cropped short, I couldn't tell if they were boys or girls.

I stopped. It looked good out there. Private.

'The sisters,' Greg said. 'They're having dinner. Do you want to meet them?'

I did but I couldn't. I needed to sleep. I needed to sleep, then I needed to wake up and obtain the information necessary to make a plan.

During the inquiry a decade later, the Doctor was asked under cross-examination about the file he pointed to in his office that first day, and in particular the absence of a single entry during my seven-month stay. His response was that he could not add to the file because he hadn't read it in the first place. Then came pages of long-winded and cryptic questioning by the counsel assisting as to how he had conducted assessments in light of such an omission, culminating in this:

> COUNSEL: I take it then that you had no regard for the conclusions of every other professional involved up to that time in the lives of these students? Every doctor or teacher or therapist, you thought it right to disregard? Are you familiar, Dr J, with the term 'God complex'? You didn't feel you were playing God, just a little bit?

After years of laying the blame with him, I re-read the answer a number of times and I smiled like an older man recalling a fond childhood.

> DR J: No, I did not. Keeping with your metaphor, I was not playing God; I was trying to block out the noise so that I could hear him.

Amenities

The starting point, as I understand it now, was a mindset. A mix of sorry circumstances and clever architecture meant that in spite of our innate mistrust of institutions, within the first twenty-four hours of arrival each of us at some point had the same thought: whatever this place was, being here was a good thing. Light-filled corridors and a jug of lemon water were our introduction to the concept of a benevolent universe. But the clincher for me was the shower.

When Greg opened the door to my room and said goodnight I saw, across from the double bed with the sky-blue doona, a sliding door. On the other side of it was a bathroom—a toilet, a basin and a shower. Inside the shower, I kid you not, standing on a little wire shelf, a pump pack of citrus-scented body cream. I tapped the tiles to check for another entry point before daring to believe that there was only one door and it was mine. (It is a simple truth: give a sixteen-year-old boy his own shower and you are giving him a 1.2 square metre pleasure zone.)

A bathroom attached to a bedroom. I didn't even know there was a word for it. In that instant, without learning anything more about my place of banishment in the arse-end of nowhere, the question beating in my brain went from how quickly I could get out of there to how long I could put up with whatever weird shit they were going to throw at me. It wasn't like I hadn't known weird in my life, and really, I reminded myself, normal didn't have a lot going for it.

I slept for fourteen hours. When I woke up I was relieved it wasn't a dream. It took me seven seconds to get the shower to a perfect warm. When the screech of monkey laughter came over the sound system I didn't know what it was telling me to do. I wiped the fog from the mirror and leaned in close to take a long look and to see if anything was different.

You need a plan.

It was a thing for me, having a plan—for me and for my mum, Mary. Without one we were prone to panic. You can get to hell and back, Mary said, as long as you have a plan. There was Mary to think of, alone in the flat...My throat constricted as it flashed up, a week back: a ball of bruises on the kitchen floor, one eye closing up. I had uncurled her, pincered a half-smoked joint to her blood-cakey lips (who could argue?), and she asked where I'd been, like it was any other day, like I was any other son.

'What's our plan then?' she'd said. We had signals, for when I should leave or when I shouldn't come inside. A tea towel on the fridge door.

'Hang it on the fridge.'

'Which one?'

'The blue stripes.'

There were other plans, less relevant to the danger at the door, like what shelf she should put photo albums on in case the plumbing went again, or remembering to keep insect spray by the bed for the ants—my mother casting a net full of holes around a treacherous universe. She liked to go over them, her plans—repeat them, or parts of them, like a drill, off by heart, in her sleep: the blue stripes, the second shelf, the bedside drawer—projecting herself into a different version, where simple precautions would avert disaster. With the strategy crafted, she'd tick a mental box. Job done. I never heard her utter a word of complaint about anything that was actually happening.

She smiled and nodded as she closed her eyes. 'Make a plan.'

However illusory, line up at the post, make a mental map. Decide. A tea towel on a fridge door. There was no reason to think it would work. And looking into the mirror now, there was nothing different about my face. Then it fogged up again and I couldn't see anymore. I resolved to give it a clear week, whatever it was they threw at me, then reassess. It wasn't much of one, but that was it; that was my plan.

The monkey laughed a second time and I opened my door to the glare of a sunlit corridor. Through the glass, I was looking directly at the upper branches of the pear trees and, through the leaves, into the opposite corridor. There—with his face at the glass looking back at me—stood a fat guy. When our eyes met he started walking in my direction. I'd never been mean to fat kids but I'd seen plenty of other people be mean to plenty of fat kids and I'd seen fat kids who were mean fuckers too, classic victim-turned-perpetrator, the worst kind.

This one looked at me sideways as we drew together at the stairwell.

'You looking for someone?' A little voice, high and reedy.

'Ah, I'm not sure—Greg, I guess.'

He shook his head. 'You don't really see Greg again. I dunno what he does all day. I'm Tod. You should probably just come with me.'

'Where are you going?'

'The kitchen.'

'I need food.'

He cracked a smile. 'I can help with that.'

At the bottom of the stairs was a big white-tiled kitchen, pristine except for a stack of bowls and a pile of banana skins in the sink. At the end of a long, stainless-steel table sat a round-faced girl with messy hair and muddy skin. She was reading a cereal box and did not look up.

Tod ignored her and opened a double-doored fridge which was chock full of milk and orange juice, cartons of eggs and jumbo packets of cheese. One end of the counter was covered with bowls of apples and grapes, and lining the whole length of it were honey jars. There must have been twenty of them. I didn't ask; I just watched Tod as he started cracking eggs with one hand into a bowl. He was clearly chuffed to tell me that he was making me an omelette with feta cheese and spinach, and some of the herbs that grew in pots in the garden; double-chuffed when I told him I'd never had an omelette before. I wondered to myself why he was so fat if he ate food like this. I guess he intuited my question.

'I get lessons now, from Magnolia. She's a mad cook. Columbian. I didn't used to eat this sort of stuff. I've lost twelve kilos in three months, if you can believe it.'

'Well, sure,' I said. 'Anyone can be fatter.'

22

I wasn't trying to be funny but the girl snorted and looked up. She had amber-brown eyes. Golden, almost.

'Daniel—meet Rachel,' Tod said.

We got as far as a nod when two other girls swept in. I recognised their heads from the courtyard. The sisters. Fair and freckled; similar but not the same. They glanced at me in unison before sitting down opposite Rachel.

'How did you sleep?' one of them asked her. And when there was no reply: 'Any dreams?' It came with a smirk.

At which point Rachel was on her feet and out the door in a blink. The sound of her spoon dropping into the empty bowl hung in the kitchen.

Satisfied, the sisters made toast and were spreading honey when another boy entered. He stood at the bench for a minute watching me eat before approaching the table.

'Hello,' he said. 'My name is Alex.' Dark hair. His eyes a gentle green.

'You want some eggs?' Tod asked. Alex shook his head.

I checked the time. It was midday. 'I think I'm meant to go see the doctor guy.'

'Things start late here,' Tod said. 'And they know where we are—there are cameras. You just can't see them.' I looked around. He was right; I couldn't see any.

'Did he give you your contract yet?' It was Alex.

I nodded. 'What's that about?'

He looked back at me like he wanted me to answer my own question, like he suddenly wanted something from me. Everyone seemed to be waiting on the answer, even the sisters, but when the silence went on too long they shrugged and left.

I motioned to the door. 'Why are they here? What did they do?'

Tod seemed glad I'd asked. 'Imogen and Grace,' he said.

Smiled. 'They shaved their heads and set up a scam charity for rare childhood cancers. Made thousands of dollars through online donations. Very clever.'

'And you?' I asked. 'What about you?'

The question was for both of them. Tod was the one to answer: 'Same as you, same for all of us. A better option.'

We all let that hang for a while. I didn't ask for any more information but Tod eventually offered it up.

'I hit my teacher in the head with a hole-puncher. His right eye's screwed.' Seeing the glint of surprise, he stared me down. 'Had me pegged for a gentle giant?'

Here in the culinary bosom of fatty Tod, I didn't want to argue. 'Cook like that,' I said with a final mouthful, 'I don't care if you blinded your whole class.'

The omelette had a creamy middle and crispy edges and I could have eaten another seven, no problem, but when I eyed off the remaining eggs, Tod shook his head. 'There were four in that omelette; you don't want to eat more than that.'

The reasons to like Tod were building. For all I knew, he was part of all this, someone's little helper, but when he told me I shouldn't eat more than four eggs, I didn't feel the need to play the firecracker and scare him away. The truth was, I was strangely touched. The only other person in my life to ever voice even a fleeting interest in what I ate was Mary. Tod, after his twelve short weeks with Magnolia, presented as a more competent guide.

Over the loudspeaker came the monkey again, and out in the corridor the sound of footsteps and chatter.

'I guess I go see him now,' I said.

I must have looked worried. Alex leaned in. 'It's a trip,' he said.

'And where do you guys go?'

They said Helen's class and I asked what subject.

'There are no subjects,' Alex offered. 'It's kind of free-flowing. A group thing.'

My inner alarm sounded. 'Fuck that,' I said. 'I don't do group.'

Tod stood in the doorway, filling the whole thing up. 'Neither do I. It's not *group* group.' And when I didn't move he shrugged, unapologetic now. 'It's just…it is what it is on the day.'

If it wasn't group, I thought, it was God, God or some version of it. The scenario was already building at the back of my mind: gone was the pink sun and the crowd scene. Instead it was a happy-clapping Greg with the Doctor doing deals in the dim light.

It all fell into place—the fancy building, the wholesome food. That's where the money came from; God is big business, especially Our Saviour of the Mansions, out here in the middle of nowhere. I knew what this God looked like, too. Mary and I saw him on morning TV, sitting on a white sofa surrounded by pot-plants and talking about sacrifice and salvation.

With eyes in the back of my head, I peeled off into the waiting room, wondering if it would be my first and last day, if soon I wouldn't be running down a long straight road trying to find some train tracks. I liked the trees, I liked Tod and Alex, and I fucking loved the pump pack, but not enough to sell my soul.

And then I had my first session with the Doctor.

Personal Health and Development 1.1

Standing at the wood-panelled door, I heard voices inside and so I waited.

When eventually I knocked and entered, the Doctor was there alone, sitting at his computer. We had no set appointment, but still he looked at his watch and nodded, as though to confirm I was expected and on time. He ushered me away from the desk to the wingback chairs near the window and before I sat down he reached out to shake my hand. It was awkward in itself; more so as he kept hold of my hand and stared at me, like he was searching for something and dissatisfied with what he was finding.

On the table to his side was the jug of lemon water. The contract was next to it, in the same place we'd left it.

'Shall we start with that?'

I half-laughed. 'I don't know. I don't really get it.'

'No, you don't understand it yet.'

Sometimes it was hard to tell if he was correcting you or agreeing with you, or just translating out loud. But my point in being there was not to work that out. All I wanted to know was that this whole business of the contract wasn't going to lead me down some weird, secret corridor.

'Why don't I begin?' he said. 'This is our contract. Let's start with an easy one. We ask that you participate each week in at least two hours of video games. That is not a limit, but a minimum.'

I took it for a sweetener and asked him what was next.

'The second condition I'd like to include is your in-principle consent to co-operate *with me*.' He looked at me again like he was trying to burn a passage into my brain and I did the thing I do when people try that on: turn my focus to their hairline so I'm not looking at their eyes. He kept talking.

'I don't mean turning up to class on time, or doing anything in particular that anyone else here asks of you. What I mean is that if *I* ask you to try something different you listen, and consider it, and if it's within the realm of possibility, you'll give it a go—you won't close yourself off. I can't ask for a mental shift, but just in practical terms, if you know what I mean. To the extent that is possible...'

I had expected something a little more silver-tongued. As it was, I had almost no idea what he was talking about, and he seemed frustrated at his own inability to articulate it. Whether intended or not, it put me on a more level playing field than I'd anticipated.

'Maybe you could give me an example,' I suggested.

'Yes, good idea. I have one I'd like to start with. You are right-handed?'

I nodded.

'For the next, say, seven days, would you—*to the extent that it's possible*,' (it was a phrase he repeated a lot) 'use only your left hand.'

I played along. 'For everything?'

There was no trace of a smile. He was serious. 'I have some tape I can stretch across the fingers of your right hand so it is harder to use. Of course we won't include that level of detail in the contract—simply your in-principle consent...'

'...to give it a go.'

'Precisely—to keep an open mind, I like to think of it that way.'

The condition was noted and he smiled, genuinely pleased, as if it was a game and he'd won the first hand. 'Your turn.'

'You mean I get one?'

'You get as many as we agree to.'

I had to think for a while. 'Is whatever I say to you our secret? Are you that kind of doctor?'

'Yes. I'm a psychiatrist. With that, there is a doctor–patient confidentiality, of course.' He was waving it away, a more signif-icant question of his own forming. 'You asked about leaving yesterday. Tell me, why do you want to leave?'

I shrugged. 'To get out of here.'

He cocked his head as though that made no sense at all. And then: 'The primary reason you have for leaving is so that you can go home to be with your mother, is that right?'

I shrugged again.

'That is because you want to be at home to protect her.' There was no tip-toeing around the subject as others had done. And when I didn't respond: 'You don't have to worry about that. Greg made inquiries, about your stepfather...'

'I don't have a stepfather.'

'Apologies. Your mother's partner. He is in prison interstate, for a minimum twelve months. You will be home by then; we won't keep you that long.'

I spent a moment piecing it together: what he knew, what he thought he knew. Satisfied, I moved on, content to take up the direct approach. 'If you're serious that I get to ask for something, how about this: you agree to tell the truth—about me, I mean, once you've worked it out, what's wrong with me, you know, whatever condition it is I have.'

He responded immediately. 'I can tell you that now: you don't have any condition.'

I laughed. 'That's not what they say.'

'Tell me, what do *they* say?'

'I dunno. You name it.'

He smiled. 'That's precisely what I'd like to avoid doing. But let's try it: give me an example.'

I was eleven when I was first told there was something wrong with the way I responded to things, and fourteen when I was told to start taking pills to fix it. There was a lot to go on. 'All right. There was one called oppositional disorder. I definitely had that.'

He nodded, small rapid movements like he was processing something. 'You'll have to listen carefully. Oppositional defiant disorder...You ready?'

I nodded.

From here he spoke slowly, as though he was dictating and giving me time to write it down. 'Tick as we go: over a period of at least six months, at least once a week, you display a minimum of four of a series of symptoms. That series includes anger or irritable moods, or being argumentative or defiant or vindictive (that just means 'mean')...Careful here, not two or three of these symptoms, but four. If you have three you don't have it; only if you have four. And if you have four of them but only for five months then you're out too. That pretty much sums it up, I think. It's a very popular one at the moment.'

I had a thing for numbers. Sometimes when people were talking to me the only thing that would make sense was when a number came into it, like a clear voice on a crackly phone line. But these numbers weren't speaking to me at all.

'What do you think?' he finally said. 'Do you fit the bill?'

By the time he got to this last question he seemed to have such contempt for what he was saying that he couldn't even hold eye contact with me anymore. Instead, he was looking at a tiny bird on the window ledge.

'A finch?' I knew birds. Mary liked them. She put bowls of birdseed outside the windows.

'Yes, agreed,' Dr J replied. 'It is a finch.' At which the bird hopped across the ledge and flew away.

'So all this, you think it's bullshit, a joke?' I said.

He took a while, then nodded, just once. 'I do. But not the funny kind.'

I had been playing dumb, of course. I remembered everything every doctor had ever said I had:

- oppositional defiant disorder (as above. I'd googled it; he wasn't telling me a lot I didn't know)
- disruptive mood dysregulation disorder (the child psych after I was suspended: she showed me sets of facial expressions 'from neutral to full intensity,' and said I was slow to recognise fear. The treatment would be about 'relabelling my perceptions'; antipsychotics were an option. That was it for Mary: we were out of there)

- PTSD (a police youth liaison officer when I wouldn't tell them what I'd seen)
- ADHD (well, doesn't everyone?)

And now, Dr J: you don't have anything. It was appealing to me, what he was saying. It always felt like the others were talking about someone else. Now we went around in circles: 'So can you tell me what is wrong?'

'Nothing is wrong.'

'But when it is bad...'

He leaned in. 'Think of when you are "bad"—what it feels like, the level of control you have.' He gave me a minute. 'If I were to say to you there is no illness affecting you, but rather, and bear with me, you are possessed by a demon. You've seen movies like that?'

I nodded. Plenty. The old classic: the devil-girl's 360 headspin and *your mother sucks cocks in hell*.

'Okay, so the demon has infiltrated your body, and when you are *bad*, as you say, what you are thinking and feeling has nothing to do with you; it is the demon. If for a moment you could accept those things...?' He paused. I shrugged. Why not? 'Then I want you to close your eyes and think about this thing, this demon. Don't tell me, but just think about what it looks like, how big it is, where in your body it sits. What sort of creature is it? Imagine its head, its body...'

He gave me another minute. I was thinking shiny and dark, hard-shelled, slow-moving.

'Do you have it?'

'Sort of.'

'Okay that's fine. Now I have another question, the only question I want you to answer.' He tilted forward. 'Do you want to be rid of it, Daniel, or do you want it to stay?'

I remember thinking in that moment that this one was smarter than the others. I remember looking at a black and white photograph on the wall, trying to think of ways to deflect the question. The photograph was a landscape: soaring granite cliffs and a soft patina of light over a forest at the edge of a lake, and behind it all a blackening sky. The cliffs were reflected in the water, a mirror image, like a photograph within a photograph. I noticed then at the edge of the lake closer to the forest there was an object rising out of the water, a clump of shadowy bracken. It marred the beauty and I wanted to move closer to make it out, because now that I noticed it, it was all I could see.

'Daniel?'

I turned back to him. I held his gaze and he mine. The answers to his questions, the shape, size, where it sits...In my mind I held up my closed fist: *so big.* My other hand I placed flat against the centre of my chest: *here,* and then over my gut and the back of my skull: *and here and here*...There is no face, no head. My fist-sized demon—hard-shelled and slow-moving—had its own faceless functions: toxifying the lungs, secreting bile through the guts. It had its own defence system. A simple answer to a question was no threat to it, but at least it was being asked a question. No one had ever spoken to it before. Still, I shook my head at him. 'Why do I do what I do? You tell me that.'

He nodded then, like it was too easy. 'I don't know what you do yet, but when I do, yes I can tell you that.'

'I want it in the contract,' I said.

'What is that?'

'I want you to tell the truth about me. And then I want it to stay between us.' There it was, the second condition. And the third: 'I want to be able to leave whenever I decide to leave.'

32

He wrote them all down.

'And for mine,' he continued. 'If you agree to meet here at this time every week for a minimum of an hour. Are you happy with that?'

Sure, but let's be clear (the cult thing was still at the back of my mind): 'To talk, just like this.'

'Just like this?'

The Children of God, the Family of Love. It didn't matter how good the shower pressure was. 'No weird stuff.' And when he looked up, blank-faced: 'No touchy-feely.'

He took it in his stride. 'No, no touchy-feely. In fact, no touchy anything, with anyone here. Let's add that?'

I acceded. Never having achieved a real-life enactment of my shower scenes, it didn't seem much of an ask. (I couldn't see Rachel showing any interest, and I had a hunch the sisters were lesbians.)

'Anything else?' he asked.

'I go to classes and watch videos. I eat. I see you. That it? What about medication?'

He shook his head. 'No need for that. It's been at least three months since the last prescription.'

This was a final piece of information I was happy to share: my raised middle finger to the quacks. I didn't realise it at the time, of course, that in disclosing it, I was putting us on the same side, us versus 'them'.

I shook my head. 'I never took it in the first place.'

There were only a couple of times across all of our sessions when I saw him genuinely taken aback. He looked at me for a while to digest what I had said. 'If you could explain that to me... That was not what I was told. You didn't take the medication?'

'That's right.'

With this information he jumped from his chair and walked

behind his desk and then back again, now smiling conspiratorially. 'What did you do with it?'

He was forgetting why I was there. 'I kept the pills, and I sold them.' It was my first act of supply, before diving into the dark web.

'And you just told the doctors that you were taking them?'

I nodded.

'That's lovely that is…For how long?'

'A year and a half. A bit more…I said they made me calmer, more able to manage.' I kept it real: I went up and down. They messed with the dosage.

'So you *never* took it?'

'Well, later. I tested stuff I sourced from the web, a pill here and there—just so I knew what I was selling.'

He waved that away as irrelevant. For the next few minutes he appeared to be engaging with a different audience. Walking around again, he wagged a finger in the air, shook his head, rubbed his chin and then squinted at various objects around the room (including my face). At one point he exhaled abruptly and started to clap. 'Yes, yes, yes,' he said, and then closed his eyes and smiled, and stayed like that for long enough for me to wonder if I should just get up and leave.

I didn't. I was enjoying myself. I had never told anyone about any of this and to witness the impact was giving me a sense of my own significance.

Finally he sat down again, as though returning to the room.

'Tell me one thing,' he said, now solemn. 'I understand that you sold them later on, but that first time, when the doctor prescribed you the medication. Why didn't you take it?'

I hadn't considered that question since I made the original decision, but the answer came clearly back to me—why it hadn't crossed my mind to take the drug.

'You know the kind of school I went to, loads of out-of-control kids,' I began. He had folded his arms to listen, sitting back in his chair, as though for this he had all the time in the world. 'There were a few of them who went to the office at lunchtime to get their pills because their parents used to forget, chaos at home, all that, so off to Mrs Jennings in the office they went. Some of them calmed down a bit, some of them got wilder. We all knew who got them. They knew we knew. They were the mentals; that's what we called them.'

Momentarily he looked sad—for me, for the mentals. And then he nodded. 'You're not what I expected,' he said. 'You know, Daniel, I might do something I'd never normally do, with your permission: I'd like to make some further inquiries.' He reached over and picked up the contract. 'And perhaps if we could hold off on signing this until then.'

What was notable for me was that I was deflated by the fact we were not signing our contract, and that already I felt a desire not to disappoint him. I accepted his offer of a mandarin even though I didn't want one. (It was something he did every time I sat there with him, offer me a piece of fruit from the bowl on the sideboard.)

'So are you going to tape my hand?' I held it up, but he waved it away like it was not his suggestion but mine, and a silly one at that. When I asked if we were done, he gave me a look as though it was for me to decide.

'Do you have any other questions?'

The tone was more procedural than inquiring, more an opening for 'where are the toilets' than 'what the fuck is this place'. In light of that, I said I didn't.

•

After I left, I started heading back to my room but stopped at the door to the courtyard. It was bathed in an orange afternoon light. I went out, sat on the bench and started to think how I could put some more flesh around my plan. Yellow-bellied birds tussled above me in the branches of the pear tree as the door to one of the study rooms opened.

Rachel appeared and stood in the corridor for a minute looking down at the floor. Then she raised her head up, like it took a particular kind of effort, and her gaze landed right on me, the boy staring at her in the courtyard. For a long second she held it, with no effort from either of us to acknowledge or communicate.

At some point Imogen and Grace appeared out of the kitchen. As they approached Rachel, and oblivious to my presence in the courtyard, they stopped and leaned in to say something to her, one cupping her mouth to Rachel's ear; smirking as she pulled away. I couldn't make out what they said, or Rachel's reply, only the ripple of anger that crossed her face before they went their separate ways, the sisters arm in arm.

Left alone, the incident I'd just witnessed played again in my mind. The look on Rachel's face, the sort of words I imagined were behind it...I caught myself, surprised at my level of curiosity. Pulled myself back to ponder my plan. A couple of days suddenly didn't feel like a long time, or long enough to make a fully informed decision. I closed my eyes and opened them again to a colder light, to the voice of my mother in my ear: 'What's our plan, then?'

It is a sort of plan, Mary—to hold off on making a plan.

I undid a button on my shirt using my left hand, easy enough, but no matter how many times I tried, I couldn't do it up again.

Mary made this trill-like noise sometimes, in response to something I did or said. I don't think she meant to; hers never came with words. It was a bit like the sound of Nina's cat when it collapsed

36

into its perfect patch of sun. I heard something like it just then. Maybe it was the birds welcoming in the night, but I took it how I wanted, and nodded back.

It will do for now.

It is better to stay away.

Biology

The next morning I followed Tod into my first lesson with Helen K.

There she was, sitting on the desk with her feet on the back of a chair, her eyes cast out the window with the look of someone much further away. Cowboy boots, worn pale suede like a shorn cat, and the cheesecloth shirt that hugged her A-grade rack. She had pale skin and frizzy hair and wasn't really my idea of pretty, but before she even opened her mouth I knew she'd be playing a lead role at shower time.

With Tod and me, there were twelve of us, and on each desk there was a tablet—one of the newest hybrid models, an eight-inch variant, thin as air—and a very schmick headset. I managed to slide into my seat without anyone paying me much attention, picked up the headset and looked it over. When I say schmick, I mean I'd never seen anything like it before—a double-banded headpiece made of rubber and a super lightweight metal.

'Go on, try it.' She had come off her desk, was standing next to mine. Waiting for me to put it on (it fit like a glove), she reached out her hand and introduced herself. 'Hi there. I'm Helen.'

Her voice was warm and gravelly. Again it gave me pause: the teacher and the technology, the glass walls and the pots in the courtyard, the bathroom in the bedroom. Not so very far away there was a bunk with my name on it in a juvenile prison.

Helen raced through the new-boy intro to the rest of the class. Next along from me was a boy called Fergus with a forehead of Himalayan acne and in front of him, Alex from the kitchen. In the row behind sat the three girls—Rachel and the sisters, and behind them, a back row of boys. There were five of them. I caught the names of a tall guy who shaved his head, Glen, and two Bens. The shorter Ben held up his tablet so I could read the screen. The letters were fluoro green and big enough: *FUCK OFF PEDOPHILE*. This spurred on Glen and the other Ben, who came up with:

Ur Asexual

Where's my penis >

Standard stuff. What followed was less standard.

'Okay,' Helen said, 'we're good to go. Headsets.'

With no further coaxing everyone went quiet and put them on, back-row boys included. Everyone doing what the teacher said to do.

I was curious enough to play along. Through the headset now came lots of nice noises increasing in volume: birds and waves, chimes, a wind instrument, a few strings.

Tod saw my quizzical look and motioned for me to lift out my earpiece.

'Noise-blocking, surround sound,' he whispered. 'Good, isn't it?'

Helen scanned our faces, gave the thumbs-up, and motioned for me to scroll. I did, and the nice noises ceased. An image appeared on the screen, some kind of mythological figure that reminded me of my ancient history textbook. I checked around and everyone was looking at it like it was something interesting, so I did my best. For lack of relevance, I had not hitherto been a fan of ancient history. Draw a circle around what you need to know, that was my school motto. Modern history scraped in. I could see it was something I should try to get my head around—how fucked-up people managed to fuck up everything for everyone else: the Holocaust, the A-bomb, the Khmer Rouge, Tiananmen, Rwanda. Boko Haram wasn't even on the syllabus but occasionally I'd do a quick net trawl to see what they'd been up to. Anyhow, the ancient figure now on the screen had three heads. One was a lion, then a guy with a face like God and last a dragon with wings and snakes for fingers. If such a creature had ever existed I would have been interested in taking a closer look; as it was, I scrolled on.

There was still no audio. I took out an earpiece. 'I can't hear anything.'

Helen said that was okay; when I was meant to have sound, I would have sound.

The next image was more my thing: a boy with a neck thicker than his head and a bulbous growth the size of my fist protruding from his left cheek. I tried briefly to imagine what that would feel like then scrolled on. Number three was a ring, and inside the ring a bullseye pattern of concentric circles, graduating from pale grey in the middle to a minty outer orbit. It looked like a pretty pattern, but I clocked it from the start as an agar plate. There were a few more, other creatures and patterns and bad heads and then, at the end, a blank screen and the nice noises again.

For the first ten minutes or so the class sat in silence, scrolling. Maybe this was what I was signing up for—to react, to be watched. Maybe they were monitoring our responses to the images like the old psych flashcards: *what is the first thing that comes into your mind?* Maybe, I thought; maybe not. And maybe I don't care. I didn't have anything to hide anymore; I didn't have to stay under any radar (never excel, never fail). I started to feel some relief about that, because it had taken its toll, the oscillating between personas. Turning up the dial on 'weird explosive kid' when the standover boy senses your weakness. Edging closer to a group when a teacher tags you as the outsider. Not too clever, not strikingly dumb. Always in fear of being noticed, caught out...It was all starting to fall away. It didn't matter anymore.

My attention had turned back to the teacher when there was laughter from the back row. The bigger Ben was using the stylus to scribble over one of the images.

'You want to share?' Helen asked.

When he held it up there was a group guffaw. It was the boy with the bulbous growth, only now it had multiplied so the face was a montage of mutations and towering pustules, a giant penis sprouting out of his ear. It was pretty good. The guy could draw.

Helen was gracious, the blue cheesecloth shirt with the sleeves pushed up to make room for her clunky bangles, her hair pulled into a tangled nest on the top of her head: cupping her chin in her hands as she considered her reply. When it came it was just one word:

'*Virulence.*'

We all sat blank-faced as Alex chimed in. 'I saw a guy on You Tube once,' he said, his voice soft, melodic, 'who had a similar thing encrusting his forehead. It looked like bark on a tree.' He went silent. We waited. Finally he added, with the solemnity of a TV newsman: 'They cut it off and it grew back faster.'

Helen clapped. 'The question is why does it grow back? How does it conquer the immune system? The answer is?'

Silence.

'*Virulence*. The power of mutation. Nothing can hold it still. Think about what we can take from that. Thanks, Alex. Someone else?'

No one.

Helen motioned for us to remove the headsets. When she spoke again, she seemed to be projecting her voice to a more distant audience. 'From the start,' she said.

I scrolled back to the first image: the three-headed guy.

'Proteus. The sea-god who could see everything—past, present and future. Men travelled from far and wide with questions. When he refused to answer they became desperate, violent…'

She scanned each of our faces and, ignoring the WTF expression on mine and the fact the sisters were hand-signing between themselves, she nodded and continued.

A hand shot up from the back row. 'Can we just start now?'

She smiled. 'Give me three minutes.' I wasn't sure what they were going to start but the timeframe seemed to be accepted.

Helen continued. There was a lot to watch when she told a story. Her hands shaped imagined landscapes and her eyes darted all over the place. It was a performance, the tone all wrong for a class of twelve delinquents, and yet it wasn't. I slid down into my seat, more scared for her than anything: how could this type of earnestness survive?

'But Proteus could elude them. Proteus had the power to transform.' This she imparted with a meaning-of-life zeal, making me wonder whether this was history or religious education and I was right about the cult thing, whether Helen hadn't escaped from somewhere, whether this light-filled building was not an outback temple to an ancient sea-god. (The God of Mansions, the God of Dirt—'There's as many gods as you want,' Mary said, 'whatever you care to believe.')

'One day, King Menelaus became shipwrecked on the same shore. Proteus was asleep with the seals. When he refused to tell Menelaus how to get home the king took hold of him and didn't let go. Proteus turned into a snake, into water, into fire, but Menelaus held on.' (I don't know how you hold onto fire or water either.) 'And when the cycle was complete and he returned to the form of man, all that was left was to speak the truth.'

And Menelaus found his way home, end of story.

'Hallelujah.' It was Rachel. Her tablet was turned face down, and after she spoke she dropped her head into her folded arms and didn't surface for the rest of the lesson. (It was more of the same in class the next day and the one after that. Inside of class the whole first week it was the only word I heard come out of her mouth. *Hallelujah*. That seemed fine with Helen K, and it was no surprise to me—Rachel and the antisocial stuff. Same with the other Aboriginal kids at my old school and the blackfellas in the flats who you crossed the street to avoid. The old ladies who sat out front never did much harm but they got lumped in with the rest. Nina said they got given too many handouts. I am pretty sure Nina was on the pension too, but she held fast on her reasons to begrudge them theirs.)

End of story for the boys in the back row meant they could put their headsets back on and start playing video games. Two of them left to go to the 'games room', apparently with Helen's blessing. The sisters slid out right after.

That left Tod, Alex and me for the last slide. I was right about the agar. The image was swarming bacteria. Helen hit the whiteboard and started drawing dots in a tunnel:

'The opportunistic pathogens in the human intestine. How do they survive? How do they thrive? We were talking about this yesterday...' I wondered if that meant she had explained some of the concepts then too, but suspected this was how she rolled, jumping around any which way. I started to settle into the idea that she was a bit mad. Good mad, not spooky mad and mercifully, no God involved. She kept drawing, turning the dots into a diamond weave (six a side, no variation).

'If there's nothing to fight them, if the host is weak, they link together and form a raft, a swarmer cell.' One big diamond made up of twenty-eight small diamonds and no room for any more dots or diamonds, at which point she stopped and smiled, that awe-struck look again, more like a child than a teacher, and from the back of her throat pronounced the secret weapon: 'Virulence!'

The point being, I was starting to work out, that the slides were all linked by a common thread—Proteus and the growth sprouting out of the kid's face, the bacteria—and in finding the link, we were linked too (at least those of us left listening) in a subliminal and pointless joint enterprise.

What we were meant to be learning day to day was anyone's guess. Reading the transcripts years later, I was interested to learn that part of Helen's brief was to teach us English. That was not made clear to us. During her classes we did not, for instance, open a single book. No mention was ever made of good grammar. This was put to her by the counsel assisting the inquiry, to which she responded that they had only a brief window to work with the students, and that inverted commas were not high on our action list.

As I read on I imagined her cupping her chin in her hands like she did in class, then letting her fingers creep over her eyes the way she used to when we were missing the point.

COUNSEL: And instead, Ms K, lesson after lesson of random, unrelated stories and experiments...

HELEN K: I think if you did your research, you'd find they were neither random nor unrelated.

Nor of course were her stories just stories.

More a chemistry boy myself, during the next part of her biological exposition on the colonial structure of the bacteria I zoned out with Rachel and took a closer look at the uber-tech headset. The rubber was still warm in my hands, and on the inside of one of the headbands I saw my initials on a white sticker. Further down, a stamp: Made in Pakistan. When I zoned back in, Tod was telling a story about his own gut flora: how at age fourteen his meds started messing with his blood sugars and he began to gorge himself into a state of gargantuanism. (He wasn't sure what the meds were for, only that he'd stopped sleeping and started acting up.)

'Within a year I went from chubby boy to school fat kid.'

But he wasn't a head-butting insomniac anymore so they kept him on the pills. Eventually his fatty acids secreted into a place they weren't meant to go, with the result that he started smelling like bad milk.

'Bad milk, a very bad smell, everywhere I went, and I couldn't wash it off, no matter what I did.'

This was more my area: the pills. Risperidone, Zyprexa, Seroquel—they were all in my inventory, a strong trade with the Year 12 high achievers who started flipping out at exam time because they couldn't sleep, couldn't concentrate. I made a mental note to get Tod's contact details before I left; he'd be a perfect source and the doctors would be gagging to get him back on the meds when he got out of here. As long as he was happy to trade them on...

I was starting to think about the logistics of that when Helen K clapped her hands, this time nice and loud:

'Agar,' she said, rolling the *r* and half-laughing, a private joke between her and the man in her mind. 'Let's get some agar of our own!'

Everyone seemed to know that meant moving to the courtyard with the pear trees, for those who wanted to, and ongoing games or sleep for those who didn't. As Tod had a session booked with Magnolia, it just left Alex and me outside with Helen. For the rest of the afternoon we stood at a trestle table covered in swirling agar plates, taking swabs from various parts of our bodies and incubating our own bacterial colonies, both of us focused and quiet like kids making a fort out of pop sticks.

The next day we came back to check them. While mine remained a sad little dot, Alex's plate was covered in pale, pox-like fuzzy circles—a bona fide biohazard.

'What orifice did you swab to come up with that?' I said.

It was the first time I saw him crack a smile, our first one-on-one conversation and the beginning of the second most important friendship of my life.

'Superior virulence,' he said.

We stared at it for a while, the virulence. I found a face in the microbial blobs, an open mouth leeching in horror (when there are no numbers I find faces), and he started telling me about a protein that can mutate and destroy a part of your brain, how once it does you can't sleep anymore, and it gets worse and worse until you get double vision and become delirious and start hallucinating.

'There was this guy once, it was so bad they tried to induce a coma but his brain still refused to shut down.' Alex had the slightest of lisps—a dragging of the *s* that sometimes disappeared altogether, adding to my sense of an underlying fragility. He looked at me tentatively now, like he was waiting for a contribution to the discussion. When I didn't have one he jump-started another:

'You like Helen's story yesterday? The one on the beach?'

I shrugged. 'What kind of bullshit is that?'

'Yeah, made no sense. What even happened to that guy?'

'He got home, didn't he?'

'No, I don't mean the king. The one in the picture, the shape-changing man.' He was waiting for me again. Any last trace of a smile disappeared. 'I mean, once he tells the truth, does he die?'

Proteus. He'd read the story as I had read it: the shipwrecked man as an assailant; his actions—pinning the sea-god to the sand—as a violation. I was unused to peers connecting on any level other than the comical or commercial, and this one had a way of holding eye contact longer than the moment deserved. A directness in his gaze that put you under the microscope.

'Let me rephrase,' he eventually said when I had no answer for him. '*Should* he die?'

Again, I hesitated.

'Go on, just yes or no. Don't give me a reason.'

'No.'

Sometimes he'd flinch as you spoke. It was barely perceptible, but I could see it, as I did now. Like a pinprick. Like he was hearing or seeing something no one else did.

I made a go of changing the subject and asked him what landed him here.

He smiled again. 'Good question.'

I waited.

'I sprayed stuff on buildings.'

I shrugged it off. 'Street art...'

He shook his head. 'Not sure you'd call it art. I can't draw for shit.'

'Yeah, but they sent you here for that?'

He nodded. 'As I understand it, yes.'

Making no effort to extrapolate, he picked up the small plate from the bench and peered at the fuzzy growth. 'Nom nom nom,' he said, like the cookie monster, and before I realised what he was doing, he sucked the full plate of bacterial contents into his mouth.

I never said it was a long conversation. But it was noteworthy.

After he left, I sat down on the bench and stared at my reflection in the glass: me and the pretty trees and pots. Wherever you sat, surrounded by glass, you could see yourself reflected. Putting Tod's story together with my own, each of us was there because of a wrongdoing, saved only by the presence of Dr J in the courtroom. I had sold drugs to fellow students, Tod had almost blinded his teacher, but Alex—what had Alex really done? I never pressed it with him. It was only later, reading the transcript, that I came to learn the extent of his crimes. He was telling me the truth: he spray-painted birds on the walls of bank buildings. He was caught and cautioned and then caught again, this time for drawing guns on the door of the police boys club. He was ordered to serve the community by cleaning it all off. He didn't. He painted penises on a Catholic primary school and didn't clean them off either, and more, and again, until he left them without any options. His crime was that they didn't know what to do with him; they didn't know how else to make him stop.

I've since wondered if it was a warning, that first conversation, that first question. *Should he die?* I have wished many times I had been less equivocal in my response; that I had screamed him down.

Geography: Biophysical Interactions

When I sat in that first class with Helen K, I'd assumed that there were more students in other classrooms. I was wrong. Our cohort was twelve in total. Soon I would learn there were others, other children in other places, but it was only when I sat down at a computer last week to find my name that I got a true sense of the scope.

There it was, my very own dashboard: metrics reduced into graphs and grids—performance measures and targets, a timeline of key events over my forty-seven years of life. Until that moment, the scientist in me had felt that human existence was in one sense wasted because it went unobserved. Wrong again. It turned out someone was paying attention.

•

The first field trip came at the end of the week.

After four days at the School I had accepted that students were confined to the building and the courtyard. Around us were grey-green paddocks glimpsed through long and narrow windows in each of the classrooms, with no way to access them; all interior doors faced inward, to the courtyard. Apart from Dr J's waiting room, the emergency fire doors were the only way to exit. It was just something I noted—having made my plan to wait and see, I wasn't much bothered with what was outside.

When I came into the kitchen on the Saturday, Tod hurried me through my bowl of chia porridge and then out into the corridor where the rest of the students had assembled outside the furthest emergency door. After a minute or so of waiting, it clicked open. On the other side of the door was Helen K in a wide-brimmed hat, standing behind a table piled with small backpacks and handing them out to the students.

The doors, the trips, the backpacks—none of this was ever explained to me; I never got a list of house rules. If you didn't manage to get to the kitchen for breakfast by 11 am, it closed, door locked. It opened again between 1 and 3 pm, and then again between 7 and 9 pm. The hot water got turned off between 11 pm and 5 am, the same hours there was no access to the games room. If you asked a question, they'd give you an answer, but it was never laid out. You felt your way. What I couldn't work out, and what perplexed me more than the rules themselves, was why this group of supposed delinquents was so compliant. The ensuite bathrooms and the video games and the fridge stocked full, sure—I could see there was no reason to riot—but there had to be more to it. The field trip was the next piece of the puzzle.

'Where are we going?' I asked, the last to get a backpack.

Helen smiled. 'Wherever you want to go,' she said, like she

was bestowing some great gift. 'Be back by dark.'

In front of me was a gate to a yard. The others had left it open and hadn't waited. They were all walking now in separate paths across a massive field. At the end of the field was a tract of bushland that went all the way to the mountains. Apart from the car trip, this was my first real chance to scope my natural surrounds, standing on a patch of earth that spanned beyond the mountains to a line that blurred into cloud, and between me and the line, close-up and distant patches of colour and shade, less real, but still it was all somehow beneath my feet.

So where to?

Wherever you want to go.

The boys from the back row had stopped on a flat bit of paddock to toss a ball around; Alex and Tod had taken off towards the bush, boys with a purpose. Behind them was Rachel—without a pack and also without shoes, and last, the sisters. My decision to follow came not from an instinct to explore, but an instinct not to get left behind.

I trailed by fifty metres, maintaining my distance, until Rachel stopped in her tracks just as she reached the bush and turned to face the sisters. It was sudden, confrontational. I couldn't hear what she said but by the time the sisters caught up with her, I was within earshot.

'Knock, knock, who's there?' It was the taller one, Grace (she was slightly younger; there was less than a year between them).

Then Imogen: 'Crazy fucking psycho bitch.'

Grace: 'Crazy fucking psycho bitch who?'

When they saw me coming they put the punchline on hold and disappeared into the bush.

Rachel looked at me for a moment like I was a curious new species. Furrowed, her eyebrows almost joined up.

'You think they just want to be friends?' I said.

She almost laughed. 'I think they are serial killers.' Then she shrugged and something harder came into her eyes, something untouchable. In spite of the sisters' efforts to infiltrate, she could shut them out. The sisters, all of it. In the lessons and around the school...Rachel was the first out of class. She slept a lot. She stared into space. A couple of times I'd caught her smiling at some thought inside her head. And now, as the words left her mouth, she had spun around into the bush and disappeared. The girl was hardwired to deflect, I thought as I peered after her through the trees: a rogue cell cluster up against the toxic pathogens.

Left alone, I questioned whether to go on.

A bushwalk. That was something people did, I told myself. They got special boots and broad-brimmed hats and went on weekends or whatever. Sometimes they got lost and rescued and had to thank the emergency services. One died once, a Korean woman who went off on her own, and I remember thinking what sort of fucking idiot takes off on a solo trek. Until this day I couldn't say I'd been on any kind of walk in anything that would qualify as bush. At the end of the park I used to hide in there was a bunch of trees; when you rubbed the leaves in your hands it smelled like toilet cleaner. They were decent trees, well-spaced, and they stood straight like trees are meant to.

From a distance, as I walked towards the bush on the day of my first field trip, I had expectations of something similar. From a distance, from the outside, the bushland presented as an entity within a landscape, a shapely mound of green positioned as a breaker between paler pastureland and a greyish rocky mountain, promising, in my mind, shade, life, protection. But from the first step under the canopy I saw it for what it really was, what was hidden from view: its bones and its spindly innards, a dishevelled mess of gum trunks sloping all over the place in a grab for a place in the sun, matted bracken and burnt-out logs, a battleground of ragged survivors.

There was no clear space to walk, no path, no order. I tried to tie it into a narrative: *boy on mission, boy in obstacle course—lightfooted, stepping up and over, never stumbling. The others gathered and waiting on the other side in a golden place...*Then I hit a landmine—a hole covered over in twigs—tripped over and landed on my arm, a deep scratch sprouting bubbles of blood. I wasn't on the ground ten seconds before I felt the bite on my ankle—a pair of ants on my sock line big enough to eat. I jumped up. There, not a few inches from me, what I'd thought was a boulder I now saw was a clay tower infested with the fat little fuckers. That thing I said when Mary tried to tell me something was good: *this is the opposite of good.* I repeated it now as I picked up a rock and threw it, ducked when it hit a tree, rebounded and almost took me out. The tide of bad adrenaline peaked with the realisation that no track meant no track back. It got blurry and I went in circles for a while before stumbling into a clearing of sorts where I paused, stood my ground, waited.

I heard a twig crack, footsteps. A figure coming through the trees...I hoped it was Rachel but it wasn't. This one wore boots. It was the boy with the acne. Fergus.

'You look fully freaked,' he said.

'Yeah, I'm okay. Which way is out?'

That was all I wanted to know from Fergus, but he sat down, took out a bag of sandwiches from his backpack and started eating. With a mouth half full of ham and tomato he started shaking his head. 'I had the weirdest friggin' dream last night.'

I did what I do in the face of unsolicited sharing; I said nothing.

The message wasn't received.

'I've had it before. I keep getting the same one. I'm in like a trench in a battle and right in front of my face is this wall of mud and it's like full of cut-off arms and legs with no bodies. The Doctor reckons I'm like tapping into the dreams of my grandad. He's dead. He was in a war, like a hero…'

It went on. There was a gurgle of phlegm in his voice. I stood up and he stood up too and when I started walking he followed and kept talking. I stopped him mid-sentence.

'Fuck off,' I said. Habit. I picked my people; with an operation like mine it was the only way it worked.

He either didn't hear or pretended he didn't and kept walking along beside me. I got way too close to his pus-filled face when I said it again. Louder this time; also something about breaking his fingers. Then I walked alone towards the light.

When the trees cleared I was back in the white glare. In front of me was a creek, a bit ganky. Not far down it ran dry, and up a way too, after which there was a rise, a rock face which was as far as I could see. I found a patch of grass next to a boulder blanketed in pale lichen (no ants) and sat down again, took off my shoes and my shirt and ate my sandwiches. Without registering that I was tired, I leaned against the rock, closed my eyes and almost instantly fell asleep.

I was blasted out of it some unknown time later by a desperate cry, like someone groaning in distress or in physical pain.

I didn't move.

Out of the corner of my eye I saw something beige and fur-covered with overgrown toenails. A hoof. Two. I remained motionless and so did the hooves. Terror, that was my first reaction. I would be trampled or kicked to death; maybe eaten.

Slowly, I trawled the courage to turn my head and look up from the hooves to the legs; the body. When I reached the woolly coat, it was with some relief that I realised I was looking at a goat. The neck was long and slender, supporting a strangely small head with a face like a camel. The creature was standing alert, a metre and a bit high, pointed ears pricked forward, fluffy tail raised. Big doey brown eyes partly covered by an outcrop of longer, flopping fleece on top of the tiny head, staring right at me.

My fear ebbed away. It was not humanly possible to be afraid of this pair of eyes. I stared back, and we stayed like that, me and the little goat, for what seemed like minutes. A peaceful standoff. Its ears fell flat and it made a clicking sound inside its mouth. I mimicked it the best I could. I didn't want to move now because I didn't want it to run away. A feeling of calm washed over me, an endorphin rush, like a nice diazepam. For a second I even wondered if I was still asleep; it was that smooth. I didn't have any other thoughts, just this channel flowing between me and my goat. You couldn't pay money for that.

But all good things. The sound of steps approaching, heavy through the trees: the goat let out a squeal like a girl screaming and sped away at an awkward and endearing gallop, while out of the trees, puffing and pink-faced, stepped Tod.

Looking me over, he told me to be careful. 'You'll get burnt.' And when he saw my indifference: 'Even when it's cloudy, as long as you can still make a shadow.'

He looked like he was intending to walk on, but reconsidered and, like Fergus before him, plonked next to me and took out his food pack. No sandwiches, just boiled eggs and carrot sticks. He was 'off wheat'. He'd lost another kilo over the last eight days.

'Dr J wants to take away my scales. He thinks I'm starting to fixate.'

Like Fergus, but unlike Fergus…

'Are you?' I asked.

'You've got no idea how fucked it is being fat.' He was sick of the gym room. He needed to get out here more, into the wide open sky. 'I need to change my contract…You signed yours yet?'

'We're still working on it.'

He squinted a little when I said that. 'Get it right. Once it's signed, that's it; he won't let you change it.' The last bit he mumbled, more to himself than to me. This wasn't the Tod from the kitchen, but I didn't expect it to be. This was a different set of conditions, I understood that.

I changed the subject. 'I saw a goat,' I said.

'Just by himself?'

I nodded.

'That's the good goat. They reckon it's got some kind of brain damage. Goats don't normally come near you.' He finished his egg, got up and started walking away, up the creek. I called out: 'Where are you going?'

'Swimming,' he shouted back.

I followed. Unexpectedly agile, Tod kept up a cracking pace. Scrambling up the rocks behind, I guessed this was his survival mode, or a workout, one of the two. He was a way ahead of me so he disappeared when he reached the top. As I neared it, I heard voices. And it came into view: the creek widened into a waterhole, framed on one side by a jutting rock platform and on the other by a willow tree, the tips of its branches dipping in the water. The water itself was muddy brown at the edges, clearer as it deepened, and in the centre, a dark and velvety green.

And there, floating in the bed of velvet, was Rachel.

What happened next was unexpected. I stepped closer to the edge…Girl floating in creek. Star-shaped limbs, a halo of waving

56

hair, eyes closed. Just beneath the surface, the outline of her body and rising above it, through black singlet fabric and with a buoyancy all of their own, her breasts, in the flickering wet light like they were communicating with me somehow. It was the most perfectly intimate thing I had ever seen and my physical reaction shocked me. It was not mild. You would better say extreme to off-the-charts, like the peak of synthesised MDMA, stomach churning, scaling through light-headedness and nausea to a release of cranial and muscular pressure, and finally, euphoria—which is by its nature short-lived.

Tod, struggling to pull his shirt over his chest, started to emit a series of grunts, and Rachel's body turned at the sound and slid beneath the surface. When she resurfaced, she looked at me. I almost jumped when she spoke.

'You swimming?'

I said nothing. Possibly, I gaped.

'You should.'

I would have done pretty much anything she wanted. I stripped down to my shorts, suddenly conscious of my pale and weedy body. Stepping in, the rocks sharp underfoot, the water muddy and cold, I clenched my teeth and dived under. Came up hyperventilating.

'It's not that bad,' Tod said, laughing.

I held back on the obvious retort about blubber and swam around to warm up. I stopped when I heard clapping coming from above. I looked up: Alex, standing on a branch of the willow tree that extended part-way over the creek. He was wearing boxer shorts and, it seemed from a distance, a shirt with a pattern. As he sidestepped out over the water, I saw that it wasn't a shirt; the images were on his skin, tattoos—half a dozen birds in upward flight forming a diagonal line from left shoulder to right thigh, the last half-covered by his shorts.

He wasn't holding on to anything anymore. As he raised his

arms in the air, pretending to dive, I could see his ribs jutting out; he was painfully thin. Even with the branch bending under his weight he was five or so metres above us. Directly beneath him, only a small area of water looked deep enough to jump into safely, and even there I wasn't so sure. I glanced at Tod who looked on like he'd seen the show before. Annoyed, tolerant; tense but not anxious.

'Isn't it too shallow?' I said.

Rachel answered. 'It's not my spinal cord.' She shrugged, but the words came out too forcefully for someone who didn't care, and I noticed she didn't look.

I said nothing more, just moved closer to the edge to give him room. He stood a moment, almost graceful, then launched into the air. In the millisecond of flight I caught his expression—the joy of weightlessness. He hit the spot in a massive splash and seemed to come up okay but when I saw his face I thought he was in pain. He went under again and came up smiling.

For the next while, the four of us stayed in the water, me wading my way closer by millimetres to Rachel but trying not to look in her direction. No one spoke. It went so long like that, I wondered if there was some kind of unspoken rule about it (a term in their contract?) but either way I was beginning to find it a bit excruciating.

'Has everyone seen the goat?' I said.

'Yeah.' Tod took it up where he'd left off earlier. 'The next property is a farm. There's a lot of them there. Sometimes they let them over here to graze. But that one seems to be here for good.'

'Do they eat them?' It was the question on my mind.

Alex said they did in India.

'Not just India,' said Tod. 'Goat curry. It's the most consumed meat in the world.'

It wasn't much but at least group conversation as a concept was no longer off the agenda. We were out of the water now, drying off, eating the rest of our rations, all except Alex, who wasn't much of an eater. He lay spreadeagled on the muddy ground, his birds rising and falling with his breath. They were just outlines, like a child's drawing, unfinished. He told me later he had done them himself with a home-kit. 'Stick and poke. Wasn't too bad.'

I asked Rachel how she walked barefoot through the bush. She'd put a T-shirt on and had a towel around her waist but I was close enough to see the goosebumps on her skin; the faint scars on the underside of her forearms.

'You got to be light-footed, that's the only way to do it. We walked barefoot all over the place when I grew up,' she said. 'There were bits of glass and bone crunched up in the dirt. That's what we walked on.' There was no natural flow to her dialogue; a pause weighed heavily between sentences as she seemed to consider whether or not to continue. It made you wait for every word.

Tod came in. 'What kind of bone?'

'Stray dog bones.' She was talking to Tod, not me, but for this last bit she looked at me: 'I don't mean like the ones they chew. I mean dead dogs. Their bones.'

Whether she was throwing it out there in a 'don't fuck with me' way or it was an effort to connect, there was a message in it and the message was for me. And I wanted more.

Tod took us in another direction. After a minute's silence for the dead dogs scattered on the floor of Rachel's childhood: 'So where are *you* from, Alex?' he asked, overly enlivened, a mocking enactment of the social ritual of conversation.

Alex was from a small coastal town. 'A little piece of paradise,' he said. It sounded more sad than sarcastic.

'You grow up there?' I asked.

'Nah. Me and my dad moved there after Mum went AWOL.'

Rachel asked if he missed it and the lightness leached out of his eyes in a single word. 'No.'

There was more chat about postcodes. Tod was in no hurry to get back to his. I told them I had a view from my kitchen window out across the city.

We went quiet for a while, then I cut to it: 'So why are we all here?'

I had assumed that this had been discussed among them at some other time—in the kitchen, on a field trip. But from the silence they retreated into, it was safe to say I was wrong. It was like the line between us had been cut, and I found myself working hard to build it up again. I went back a step, talked through what happened in the courtroom, and in my first meeting with Dr J.

Finally Tod made a small offering. 'It's our second chance,' he said, rolling over. An intricate web of stretchmarks spanned his gut.

Over the course of the next hour as we went back into the water and came out again, the three of them divulged a similar course of events: they too had been about to be delivered into custody and given a reprieve. Dr J had been in the courtroom every time. And they had all been offered a contract. Rachel's was three pages long, mine yet to be signed.

'So what is it?' I asked. 'What is this place even called?'

You couldn't google it, Rachel had tried; it wasn't in any directory of youth services or rehab programs.

'They say it's a school,' Alex said.

'That is such crap,' Rachel retorted, shaking her head. 'You call Helen a teacher? You think they've even heard of curriculum? It's not education, it's some kind of wacko therapy…You know what this place is? It's a home for mental kids,' she announced. 'What they call involuntary treatment.'

The mentals. I thought about it, working out if there was truth in it. I said we could leave whenever we wanted, and Tod backed me up. 'Right now. If we wanted.'

Rachel: 'Sure, we could walk out the front gate, and then where would we go?' She was standing at the edge of the water, her feet sinking in the mud. Her legs were skinny but looked strong, like the rest of her.

Alex chimed in: 'How long was your drive here? For the last two hours of it, did you see a single car on the road?'

'I saw train tracks.'

'But did you see a train?'

Tod said he didn't want to leave anyway. 'Why would you?' And so forth, around and around. Could we leave? Did we want to leave? How would we get out if we did? But all of us sidestepping Rachel's assessment of what this place was, and why we were here.

Walking back after that first field trip, as the school came into sight through the trees, Tod led us into a joint roasting of Dr J, 'our great guru', and I remember the creeping feeling that this was a piece of a story with a traditional narrative and proper characters. I think for a moment I even dared think it was solid, real. If we could just reach the school, eat a meal, sleep and turn up to our class with Helen K in the morning…If we took small steps, the ground wouldn't begin to crack under our feet. If I was careful, this could be my plan.

A diptych: on the left it is a picture-book scene, a fine oil landscape—four teenagers in various stages of undress wading in a waterhole against a backdrop of bushland and white sky. Somewhere at a distance, but in the frame, is a goat.

The panel on the right side is a darker image of the twenty-four hours that followed. We are back at the school. Rachel's words keep replaying, resonating, as each abnormal hour passes, as each abnormal episode unfurls.

Back in the confines of the building, we are not students but patients, and *this is what they call involuntary treatment*. We cannot navigate our way because we cannot see. The right-hand panel is a paper mache monster with eyes in the back of its head.

We didn't get back until after dark. Tod offered to make omelettes but it didn't go to plan. When he dropped an egg on the floor, he went back to the carton and picked up another and crushed it in his hand. He nodded as though it had been an experiment and the albumen leaking out of his closed fist was the outcome he had predicted, which he seemed satisfied with until he shook his head and dropped it in the sink, picked up another egg and did it again. (At this point I exited the kitchen.)

I was exhausted but couldn't sleep and the thrashing around was starting to make me sweat. The air was thick, humid. I got up and tried to open the window before I remembered it couldn't be done. I was never much of a sleeper. At home, I'd get a few hours then wake up and go outside, lie face up on the concrete walkway; I could breathe better then. The sky helps; there's always something to look at—look at, listen to…The flats were a twenty-four-hour reality show.

I got dressed and left the room, planning to find a way outside. I didn't make it all the way around the corridor before I came across Tod walking the opposite way and then Alex, leaning up against the glass staring into the lights at the base of the pear trees. It was 3 am.

'Welcome,' Alex said, not turning around.

By the time I did another round he was lying on his back. Tod was still walking at an even pace, expressionless, like someone pretending to be mad for a joke. It was the worst time, obviously: no drugs, no sleep, their rhythms all messed up. I got that, of course I did, but it still made Rachel's words echo louder in my head...When Alex got up again they were pacing one after the other, a couple of caged monkeys, *mental patients*. The light in the corridor blurred into a nightmarish amber haze.

I headed for the stairs. A shuttered screen had been pulled across and locked. It was on my way back that I heard her voice. Rachel. At first a distant muffled call. I followed it and found her door.

Tod was behind me. 'Last week too,' he said. 'Pretty much the same stuff.' He shrugged. 'Sleeptalking.'

The words were muffled, but I could make them out, sometimes a phrase repeated with different emphasis:

'if the wax melts,

'it's the sun...

'Trembling...'

I slid down to the floor and closed my eyes to pick up clues about where she was and what she meant—the wax melting under the sun, the trembling.

'Tremble under the sun...'

I did not move. Every tiny hair on my arm stood on end. Be still my racing pulse: listen and learn.

Finally then, the sound of a hiccup. And silence.

History: the Origins of Tyranny

When I came into class the next day Rachel was sitting in a seat close to the window, staring at something outside. I looked out but saw nothing that hadn't been there the day before.

Helen coughed. 'Rachel, could we begin?'

The words didn't appear to register, and Rachel showed no signs of coming back to us. Unfazed, Helen got the rest of us to put on the headsets.

The first image was an old painting of a very serious Asian guy in a red smock and a weird hat that looked a bit like a bike helmet. It was a cracker of a story: the man was Prince Sado, Korean, mid-eighteenth century. The upshot of his early years was that a mean bastard of father and a bad bout of measles sent him mad and he started acting out by beating up on his servants and raping his consorts. Over time he became increasingly deranged until he launched an all-out killing spree, most famously swinging around the severed head of one of his eunuchs. When it got really out of hand his father called time and ordered him into a rice chest. It took eight days for him to die which, even in the circumstances, I thought was harsh. As Helen K opened it up for an ethical discussion on the death penalty—'how many heads can you swing before it makes it okay?'—it became clearer to me why she might have struggled to find employment in mainstream education.

(My take: put a bullet between his eyes, but no rice chests.)

The second image was a painting of tiny blue and yellow dots and squares. It could have been a map of some sort, an aerial view: the blue was water and the yellow was land. Fergus thought it was about infection, and the yellow was pus, which gave him the segue he needed into gammy legs in the blood-soaked trenches, a thread which Alex used to carry us into the death toll from the most recent suicide bomb. Even after Sado, what I saw were yellow blossoms against a blue sky, and the blue sky out the window, at which Rachel continued to stare.

When Helen scrolled us into the next image, I started to suspect that for every lesson she had a gallery to choose from, depending on how we presented on any given day, and that this next image was tailored to fit *catatonic girl at window*.

It was a painting called *The Great Transparents*. In the lower left-hand corner there was a cliff edge; the rest of the painting was a grey-blue sky filled with twisted, tornadic objects drawn in white lines, camouflaged in the air.

'The idea is that there are invisible energies everywhere around us,' Helen explained. 'Our minds react to them—accept them or battle against them...' She wanted to know what we thought of that idea, that something external can control us.

Alex said he could relate, but left it at that.

'I suppose another way to put it,' Helen went on, 'is to ask not can we control them, but do we want to?' Echoes of the Doctor. After some group shrugs she espoused a bit of theory about the need to harness the power of the energies, how if we let them they can make us brutal. She was linking us back to Sado, then Stalin, Hitler, Mao…Then ultimately all the way back to us. 'The artist,' she said, 'did not see the energies as terrible, but primal.'

My sense here was that she may as well have pointed us in the direction of Rachel as exhibit marked A: Rachel, staring out to her own sky, filled with the same energies, terrible, primal, whispering into her ear and obliterating rational thought. I was trying to remember her script from the night before, imagining that was what was running through her mind now, the jumble of words. When I went back to my room later I would write them down and try to piece it all together.

At the end of the class, as everyone filed out, Helen looked over to Rachel (still motionless) and cocked her head briefly to one side, more out of curiosity, it appeared to me, than concern, before packing up her folder and following the others out of the room like it was any other day. For a few minutes I sat there and considered my options, wondering if Rachel even knew I was there. Eventually I stood up and walked over to the window and looked out again in the same direction.

'Nice day,' I said.

When there was no response, I turned a chair around to face her. A laser beam of sunlight streamed through the window and landed on her ripped grey jeans, illuminating patches of brown skin along her thigh. Still she stared out into a fixed space.

'Knock, knock.' I thought if anything would get a response

from her, that might. 'Sorry,' I said, 'bad joke. Just checking if you're in there.'

I thought I saw a double-blink. I waited. After a few very drawn-out seconds, she turned to face me, and when I say *face me*, I mean she was staring at me the same way she had stared out at the sky, as though to find an answer, or to convey it—only now she was watery-eyed, like the answer was sad and terrible. And then she closed her eyes and held them closed. I sat for a few seconds following the veins in her eye-lids, knowing I had to go but not moving. From the first class to the field trip and now this: like some kind of opioid, she was penetrating the tingly place in the right side of my brain. The brooding, backwater girl with loud dreams...

When I returned an hour later she was still sitting at the window, her eyes open now, staring out. I went in search of Helen but the only teacher I could find was wearing a headset in a music class. I banged on Dr J's door without an answer. Greg appeared behind me.

'He isn't here,' he said. 'Can I help?'

'You can help Rachel,' I replied. 'She needs help. She's been sitting like a fucking zombie for like an hour.'

He nodded. 'In her own time.' Then he almost smiled: 'That is the approach here.'

It irked me. But I'd dealt with worse at my old school. I knew it wasn't going to end well with Greg so I headed to the kitchen— not just to avert the risk, but because I hadn't eaten since breakfast. It was closed, out of lunch hours.

Somehow Greg was behind me again.

'Can you open it?' I asked.

He shrugged. 'If only I could.'

I suddenly realised how hungry I was. Since arriving at the School my appetite had exploded into something unpredictable and uncontrollable; eating a meal was like feeding the beast—the more I ate the more I wanted. Now the double whammy of no food and no help was starting to make for a very bad day.

I was more forceful in my second request.

Greg didn't flinch, just explained it was an automated system: 'We all have to live with it. It's my kitchen too.' (So he said. Apart from Magnolia, I never saw a staff member in the kitchen.)

'It is a retarded rule.'

'No argument there.'

'So why don't you do something about it?'

'That is a fair question, Daniel. The answer is that I don't have access to the decision-makers.'

'What about the Doctor?'

He shrugged. 'You'd have to ask him—when he's back. I'm not sure when that will be.'

On anyone's view, my interaction with Greg up to that time had been limited. It was safe to say he dyed his hair and had questionable people skills, and I didn't much like the sandals. He'd showed me where to get water on my first day and brought me sandwiches. And now he was politely declining to help me out. *That is the approach here.* Boy with purpose. Except not here. Here, I was part of something I didn't understand. The panic started rising. I could feel it creeping back.

I don't see red; I see yellow, and it is blinding. I stared at the blond hairline, my blood rushing and heart racing with rage because of everything Greg was and Greg wasn't and everything he'd said and hadn't said, because of everything he stood for and for all he had done and for all he couldn't do. The truth, of course, is that in asking the questions, my self-diagnosis was askew. Rushing, racing, raging, yes; but (as was so often the way) the anger was secondary to fear, and the object was not poor Greg, but the terrible fact that I had no choice but to accept the answers he was giving.

I am not sure how the next bit played out.

I know I headbutted the closed kitchen door hard enough for it to hurt significantly then slumped to the floor and made noise. I don't know how loud, or for how long. I never do. It is a process I hand myself over to. There isn't anything else but this, and there is only one way to be rid of it.

Afterwards I could hear the others banging things in music class and out of the corner of my eye, there was Greg, standing by. I thought I saw him check his watch.

There are different versions, dependent on the trigger. This one ended with me back in my room thinking I might be able to climb down from my window when I noticed that there was a large bowl of mandarins on my bed. I stared at them for a long time before eating all nine and deciding against the window. At dinner Magnolia made her first appearance in the kitchen. She was from Columbia, as Tod had said, and had shiny lips and enormous breasts and sang quietly in Portuguese while she stirred. I asked her to cook me up a second serve of her pork and veal meatballs, which I ate alone while the others curiously watched on.

We were still sitting at the kitchen table when Rachel walked in like nothing had happened. Fergus asked if she'd had a good nap and she looked at him like he was barely sapient. I started mumbling bullshit about what she hadn't missed then left her alone. Even the sisters looked relieved to have her back.

Alex wasn't there. Alex didn't much come to dinner. He said he didn't like to eat at night. (From what I could see he didn't like to eat full stop, and now I'd seen him in the flesh I thought there was something deliberate about it—the incredible disappearing

69

man.) After dinner I went to look for him; started the lonely circle of the ground floor to see if any doors were open. There was one, the movement room, slightly ajar with just a dim light on. And this was it, a rightful end to the twenty-four-hour loop: I peered through and there he was, engrossed in the strangest cacophony of movement, his arms out to one side then, in a sudden jolt, bending at the elbow and swinging at the joint. As though separated from the upper body, the legs were moving to their own music, bowlegged then rigid, moonwalking, star-jumping , sliding—fluid then jerky—from scarecrow to ragdoll to rubber man. The finale was with his back to me, arms outstretched above his head and leaning back, swivelling at the waist and arching into a backbend. That is when he saw me, upside down, eye to eye. He smiled and sat on the floor. I joined him.

'Some moves,' I said.

He just kept smiling.

'Rachel's back.'

He nodded. 'I wonder where she's been.'

Vulnerable children. That was the phrase most often used when describing us in the transcripts. Not inmates, not patients, not delinquents—not any of the ways we saw ourselves.

Helen K got a particular grilling one day in the inquiry. There was a pattern with the way they questioned her. They picked out one of her images, then opened the door for her to start on her theories, and to demonstrate that we had been put under the tutelage of a woman who for all intents and purposes was bonkers.

COUNSEL: Let's start with the second image, Ms K. It is a boy with a horrific growth out of his left cheek. It is grotesque, you'd agree with that?

HELEN K: Seeing it as grotesque is one reaction to it. That is

70

your reaction. We had other reactions that one might categorise as more empathetic.

COUNSEL: Very well, Ms K, but you would agree these were vulnerable children...

HELEN K: Most certainly I would. And as such, you must follow their lead, explore the subjects to which they connect. This is adolescence we are talking about. It is precious and fragile, a time of rebirth.

COUNSEL: Ah, yes. Rebirth.

When he asked if she could explain that, she replied that just as a newborn opens his eyes to the world and screams with all the power his tiny lungs can muster, so the adolescent howls at the assault of adulthood.

As I read this piece of transcript my feeling was that she knew what she was walking into. But her pact with herself, with the world, with all of this, was to be who she was and to tell it like it is—the world through the eyes of Helen K.

For a page or so she explained that adolescence is a time of subconscious connection to the very essence of the universe—dark matter—leading into this final part of the explanation and the end of this particular exchange.

HELEN K: It is this realisation, at a subconscious level, that confronts the adolescent. They want to kick out, or shut down—or just not get out of bed. You know how teenagers are.

COUNSEL: Others might posit that it is hormones, as opposed to some sort of cosmic interconnection.

HELEN K: They might. And I would say hormones are a function of our brain, and the brain is the operational arm of our being—our soul, if you like—and the adolescent soul, these young people, in those key moments they see more, they feel more and they understand more. Listen to them. Listen, nurture, and let them be. It is the time we define ourselves, our instinctive responses: what will make us recoil and cringe and shudder, how we look into our own eyes...Look into your own eyes and in them, I dare say, you will see your adolescent self. You should try it some time.

COUNSEL: Thank you; I appreciate the tip.

The day I read this part of the transcript I did go home and look in the mirror and into my own eyes. Mine are a spotted hazel brown with a darker rim around the iris. Tiny red threads drift into the white. It took me immediately back to my second-year visual system classes, shifting restlessly in my seat and staring up at the diagram of the cortical pathways. And then the task at hand: what of myself did I see in them? I couldn't look at both eyes at once without the reflection becoming blurred. When I looked at the single eye, my focus was drawn to the imperfections, the irregularities, not just in the eye itself, but now around it, the space between the eyebrows, and then just the awkwardness of the components. There was a moment where that was uncomfortable, and there followed a sudden lack of recognition. What I was looking at was a strange animal. And finally, a funny thing happened. I remembered that first field trip. I remembered waking and looking into the eyes of the goat, and for a moment those eyes, the doey-brown eyes, were mine. I was looking out at myself, not at the man in the mirror, but at the boy beside the creek transfixed on the curious and gentle creature that did not run away.

I'm not sure that is what Helen K had in mind in her evidence, but there it was. A calm washed over me.

Legal Studies Core Part II:
Rights and Responsibilities

The Doctor had an end in mind, or a point to prove.

Much has been said about his tactics, about the lengths to which he was prepared to go and the risks he was prepared to take. Did he present me with versions of himself that were most likely to cut through? Probably. We all do that. Did he cultivate the sense we were on the same ride, that this was as hard for him as it was for me? It is possible; maybe he was that good—so convincingly imperfect, so perfectly fallible. But at the time, let me say, it never crossed my mind. I guess you had to be there.

What the transcripts told me was at age twenty-three, as a graduating medical student, the Doctor was presented with awards for both academic achievement and community service.

An outdated online bio revealed that over the course of three years he had volunteered in the medical corps, as a summer camp coun-sellor, at a mental health clinic, and at a homeless youth shelter. I found a photograph of him at that time wearing a baseball cap backwards and a blue T-shirt and surrounded by a group of black and Latino kids. Nine years later, he joined a Fortune 500 pharma-ceutical company and successfully launched the first outpatient clinical trials for a drug that was subsequently listicled as One of 10 Innovations that Will Change Your Tomorrow.

Like I said: versions, plural. Time gives us versions of ourselves. As we get older they can pile up a bit. By the time I met the Doctor he had plenty more. Every time I came to his door I was in the dark about which one would be waiting on the other side.

Our third session.

Even before the mandarin, he seemed to have a bitter taste in his mouth. As I went to knock on his door I heard him shouting: 'This was not part of the agreement!' The other voice was very quiet and I couldn't make out the words. The door then opened and Greg came out.

He saw me and smiled. 'I'd give it a sec.'

I waited five minutes before knocking. When I entered he was smoothing his hair and taking long breaths. He did a lap of the office and sat down in his usual seat. 'Are you hungry?' He was wearing the suit and tie again.

We both peeled a mandarin; he recoiled after biting into the first segment. 'It isn't good. Yours?'

It was a little dry, tasteless. 'Not great. It's okay.'

He insisted we bin them, dropping his from shoulder height to punish it for being bad fruit. When he sat down again he was distracted. He tilted his head from side to side as though to release a crimp in his neck, then straightened his spine and sat unnaturally tall in the chair. 'Would you like to try another?'

I said I wouldn't.

'Fair enough.' There were three left in the bowl. 'You don't want to take your chances.'

What I didn't want to do was talk about the mandarins anymore. I had been quietly looking forward to the session and was feeling let down—the way a small child feels when a parent spends their play-time cleaning the floor.

'I have an idea for the contract,' I said.

That seemed to bring him at least part-way back. 'Excellent,' he said. No real enthusiasm, but the sentiment was in the ballpark.

I explained that I wanted a way to open the kitchen, or I needed to keep food in my room. 'When I get hungry, this thing with the kitchen closing...'

'Ah yes, I heard that you had an issue with that. I heard it as it happened, as a matter of fact—I think our neighbours on the farm would have heard it too. Tell me then, your appetite. You're getting hungrier than you usually do?'

I said yes, glad someone had asked.

'I thought that must be the case. Let's take up your second suggestion: additional food to be provided in the student's room.' He made a note. 'Our intention isn't to starve anyone, that is what I said to them.' He smiled then, the first for the morning; an equilibrium returned, a focus.

Version two: he leaned forward in his chair in a *now I am all yours* kind of way. 'Could we change the subject?'

'Sure.'

'Fergus,' he said. 'How are you getting on with Fergus?'

I shrugged. 'Minimal contact.'

In all honesty, I didn't know where he was heading; he had

to direct me to the day of the field trip in the bush: 'Tell me about your conversation with him.'

'It was short,' I said. 'He's got a thing about his dreams.'

'Okay, and did that upset you somehow?'

'No, I just didn't want to listen to it.' I wasn't being evasive; I didn't have the sense I had anything to hide.

'And so you threatened him?'

I shook my head, a bit dumbfounded. I didn't remember it that way. It wasn't until he spelled it out that I remembered my threat to break his fingers, and even then my sense was still that it was a non-event. I remembered the phlegm and the war story. 'It would have just been a turn of phrase, you know, like an expression.'

'And what did you actually mean?'

'I meant: *I've got an idea—let's not talk anymore.*'

He smiled at that. 'I think he interpreted it differently.'

Through all this the Doctor didn't seem at all angry, and because of that I felt relaxed. 'How about this, Daniel,' he said. 'I'd like to get it into the contract that you don't do that again. Use whatever phrases you want with me, but not *them*. I don't want to make a big deal of it. I'll work on the food supply, if you agree to that.'

I agreed, but not with any confidence. It must have showed.

'I wouldn't ask if I didn't think you could do it. I know you can.' He left that hanging there. I didn't bite. 'Do you know why I know?'

I didn't. He couldn't know; no one could know.

'I know that you can do it,' he continued, 'because since our last meeting I've requested information about your school disciplinary record over the last two years. You know of course what the result of that enquiry would be...'

I shrugged. *Get to the point.*

'You would know that there isn't one. Over the last two years you never once came to notice. Zero incidents, zero threats, zero fights.'

I nodded. 'So?'

'So, that tells me you can do it. And it makes me wonder—the fact that you come here and within weeks have threatened a student and howled the place down—what is different now?' He didn't wait for an answer but instead suggested we go through my history at school, from kindergarten until the present. He talked about the importance of timelines 'so that we can view the whole and break it down into pieces, make sense of it. Because looking at yours', he said, 'it makes no sense at all. If we drill into it, you and I, we can find some, I'm sure'.

The timeline idea was familiar to me, courtesy of my Grade 6 teacher Mrs Pyke. This particular timeline, according to Dr J, kicked off the day I picked up Kevin Barnes and shoved him into a wheelie bin, the start of a spate of schoolyard infringements that had me siphoned into aggression replacement therapy midway through term four. Mary called it 'going berserko'.

'Could you tell me the reason behind that?'

Kevin Barnes. Little shit. 'He was small enough to pick up.'

Dr J nodded like he could see the sense in the reasoning. 'How old were you?'

'Ten, maybe.'

'And what do you think caused it to escalate from there?'

I started to ask myself why I had been looking forward to the session. But whatever the answer, I had committed to play ball, so that is what I did.

'Different things, stuff in my head.'

What I was trying to explain was that my behaviour was in part reactive to various external factors, but in larger part to the messed-up workings of my mind. Luckily for me, for us, he was an adept interpreter and had no need to prod where others would have done. He rewarded effort with restraint; he never picked at sores. That in turn kept me on the field.

'If it's a timeline,' I offered, 'the library was before Kevin.'

'Ah yes, apologies, the library. Do you want to tell me what happened there?'

I wasn't being difficult when I said, 'That's hard.'

Grade 5: the social sciences aisle of the school library. I knew where it ended up (books on floor, not on shelves) but I wasn't so clear about how it got there. There wasn't one single trigger. I went to the library because the playground was hot and loud and full of dickheads. I liked the library because I liked the world history section and the Dewey decimal system and the smell of the librarian, and on hot days it was cool, except for this day; the air conditioning was bung and the librarian wasn't there and there was a bunch of kids spitting at each other in world history so I ended up in social sciences. Not my usual section. I was surrounded by strange titles. One of the boys followed me and asked me, fairly insistently, what I was reading. He started dribbling and I was pretty sure he was about to spit at me. My reaction was to tear the books off the shelves (social sciences *and* world history). It probably wasn't the best call. Some of the kids laughed; one of the girls cried. A teacher came. They called Mary and there were some hushed conversations. Apart from a library ban, not much else came out of it. The same kids laughed; the crying girl and her friends steered clear. The year went on as usual until Kevin Barnes.

For Kevin and for those that followed, there was a simple and universal explanation for my going berserko: it felt good. I was made to delve into this more in post-Kevin therapy. My predisposition to aggression, it was explained to Mary and me, was due to a depletion in my serotonin level. They didn't measure it or anything; it was just a given. That meant my command-and-control centre wasn't sending the correct messages—less communication, less control. Communication is everything. Mary and I thought it was bullshit but we didn't argue because it seemed to be another way of saying it was not my fault. There was a culprit, and it was called intermittent explosive disorder and my triggers weren't triggers at all, they were 'cues of provocation'. What was happening outside of the crisis points—strange imaginings, a bad gut, stunted growth—those things didn't seem to factor in. The shrink had her boxes ticked. Mary and I nodded. Sure, miraculously it all now made sense.

Over the course of the following year, the cues kept coming and incorrect messages kept getting sent, culminating in a number of intermittent explosions with varying levels of fallout. The class thug: I was that kid. The word bully got thrown about. I didn't wear it like a badge of honour, but nor did I accept the stereotype. In the movies, you know him before he even opens his mouth: thick-set and plain, zero charisma, the character that never develops, the child actors who never make it as adults. The plot points require us to save our empathy for the rest of the cast. But pause on the thug. That's all I'm asking: drill down a bit. There are children who need to be contained—Kevin deserved a stint in the bin—and therein lies the role of the thug. I am not saying it is ideal; and, sure, it is a slippery slope: might is right, schoolyard cop, self-appointed disciplinarian, global warrior, the United States of America...

'There was this one kid,' I told Dr J.

Roger Bell. He fell at a bad angle and when I laid the boot in, my shoe made contact with his forearm right at the point of fracture, compounding said fracture and necessitating complex and worrying surgery. His parents wanted to call the police and Mary had to talk them out of it. I don't know what she said, but I got suspended instead of expelled or incarcerated. The condition was that I stay in therapy. My therapist talked about things I could do to express my feelings 'in a healthy way'. I told her I couldn't concentrate in class and that seemed to provide her with the missing piece: it was time for the pills—'Let's meet the happy chemicals.' (She drew smiley faces on a piece of paper.)

Here Dr J interjected. 'If we can stop there, I'll get to the pills in due course. But in terms of our timeline, I feel like this is a critical juncture. After the suspension, that was the end of it; the violent behaviour just stopped. From there the reports all talk about good behaviour, diligence in class...It wasn't the medication, we know that, because you never took it. So what was it?'

I shrugged. 'It just never happened.'

'You mean nothing provoked you?'

'I mean I just didn't look for it. I couldn't.'

'You couldn't?'

'I couldn't get called up for anything—you know, the pills, the sales...it'd bring attention.'

'Yes, I see, of course.' He was at it again, scratching his eyebrows, talking to himself more than to me, or to his imaginary sounding-board friend. 'You hear that? He couldn't!' He started mumbling something about a self-imposed regulatory system. 'I mean, there is an extraordinary degree of self-control in that.'

Bringing me back in as audience again, he leaned forward. 'At the centre of it all is this operation—this busines—of yours. So let's get to that.' The smile he threw me was like a wink. 'Let's talk about what got you here.'

This part of the story I was eager to tell. Time gives us different versions of ourselves. To date, this had been my best one.

The whole thing had been cast in such a negative light. In the courtroom, when they talked about the level of sophistication, the number of children on my books and the quantity of pills I'd sold, I found myself preening a little. I felt like getting up and saying: *Don't you realise what hard work it all was?* To ensure an adequate supply, to target the right market...*Don't I get any credit for that?* I was conscientious and responsive to my customers, I lived on four hours sleep a night and worked through most of my weekends—and I built a successful business. *Point me to another sixteen-year-old schoolboy who could claim that.* That is what I wanted to say.

And I built it in the ashes of a non-existence: Mary and me like cockroaches. Just us—Brian had gone—neither of us sleeping, me lying out on the walkway distracting myself with the night sky and the battles in the floors below while she scratched around inside. During the day she wouldn't even go down to the clothesline. Sometimes she'd stand on the walkway, but her world was pretty much confined to a living room, a four-metre square that fitted a stained two-seater couch and a TV, adjoining a kitchen with cracks in the swirly laminate and a sink that wouldn't drain. An inner-city Housing Commission block that developers circled like drooling wolves and no one wanted to live in but no one could leave. Our neighbour, Nina, had been there for forty-three years; she reckoned the kitchen drain had been blocked for the last twenty. The pipes in the place were universally stuffed. As for the tenants, there were the ones like Nina who called it home and grew herbs in planters, and there were the ones who pissed in the walkway and punched the walls. There was a central courtyard like at the School, but no pear trees; most days you'd put money on finding a syringe or a used rubber or an empty stolen bag under the bench. Sometimes the Ninas of the building cleaned it up or kicked up a stink; mostly it was just the way it was. And I couldn't see a clear way out of it. I didn't want to leave school but I didn't want to wait three years to make enough money to get us out of there.

That was when things started getting worse for me. The minute I stepped inside the flat my breath got short. We were rid of the tenants but I'd still come home to a red-eyed Mary sitting at the kitchen bench pretending she was straight, pretending she'd gone out, pestering me with questions about my day so she had something to fill hers. I avoided coming home in the afternoons because she'd be waiting; she sensed it, and stopped waiting in the kitchen—stayed in her bedroom to give me some space because at least that way I was home and she wasn't alone. I didn't want to feel this way; I didn't choose to, but you watch your mother on the slide and just her presence is enough, the sickly stench of air freshener and stale smoke…

The harm caused by drugs. As far as that bit of courtroom piety went, I got it. No argument. Mary was stoned most of the time and the users in the building were all scabby ghosts scavenging for their next hit. But their drugs were not my kind of drugs, and my trade was different. I was supplying a niche market. Ordinary kids just getting some help with their study or their ailments or having a bit of fun, and no damage done. Living their healthy lives unscathed. That was my personal stance and I was comfortable with it.

Dr J wanted to know how it began, so here's how: I told my GP the drugs were helping and she kept prescribing them and soon I had a Ritalin stash piling up at the back of a closet. Then came the light-bulb moment when a Year 12 boy got suspended for standing over the mentals for their pills; ADHD or not, they were a big brain booster, a steep improve in concentration. I got him on his own and said I'd make it easier for him. There were a bunch of kids pepping up around exam time, so I rationed out my stash, cheap at first. Then they hooked me into private school kids, more pressure to achieve, a more buoyant market. My supply ran out; I dived into the dark web, and there I found it all, a world of information and opportunity. Suddenly I knew what kids were taking in schools from Brussels to Boston. I made arrangements (free pills) with key people to keep me up on who wanted what and what they should want; I worked out ways to message and manage fluctuations in supply and demand. I was never late for a drop; I never accepted deferred payment or gave credit. Over five schools I serviced fifty-seven students.

Dr J listened. 'So I am assuming that what ended up before the court wasn't even the half of it.'

I shrugged. 'About half.'

'How much did you make?'

Seven envelopes stored in separate hidey-holes plus a bucket of gold coins (sometimes it was all they had, especially the younger ones). 'Twenty-three K.'

By the way he had been listening, I now expected a high-five at the final figure, and was perplexed when he reacted the way he did, which was to start laughing, not a pat-on-the-back sort of laugh, but more like a carnival clown, with a mouth stretched wide, his hands gripping the side of his shaking head. I didn't comprehend it, nor did I comprehend the words he spoke as he rose from his seat:

'And the animals escape from the zoo.'

Finally I said, 'Are we done?'

'There is another thing.' He poured me a lemon drink from the jug, the way we would usually have begun our session. Leaned forward so that if he chose he could have touched my knee. 'Your mother called.'

I don't know why I was surprised at the mention of Mary but I felt something shift, like an intruder had come into the room, and I was trying to work out if there was any way to eject her and everything that came with her. What had she told him?

'I can leave and let you call her if you like,' he said, but he didn't push it. He nodded through the silence, gesturing his agreement that it was a complex decision. 'She sounded quite well. And she was very pleased to hear about what is happening here.'

What had he said? How had he explained it? I wondered about that, but really what was at the front of my mind was the growing certainty that I could not speak to Mary.

Observing my reaction (I could the feel blotchy heat rising into my face), he held his hand in the air. A directive to the blood to stop in its tracks. 'Let's take that off the table. You will not telephone your mother.'

I'm not sure what he was seeing but he asked me if I'd heard that, and then told me to say it in my mind, repeat it if I needed to. 'I made no undertaking that you would call.' And more firmly this time: 'You will not telephone your mother.'

Feeling calmer, I nodded. He watched me, waited. When he asked me to clarify whether I was still concerned about her safety, I told him no.

'But you are concerned about her more generally?'

I spoke because I feared otherwise we would spend the remainder of the session on this, on her, on us. 'My mother doesn't leave the house. She is too scared. She is scared of lots of things, things that are not real.'

'And some that are,' he said.

I nodded.

'Are you scared too, Daniel?'

I didn't answer, but this time he got it, my need for it to stop. He told me I'd done well and went over to his desk, returned with the contract. He made an addition, and then passed it to me.

84

Here in my hands was my contract. There were the conditions as discussed in two parts: *The Student Agrees to…The School Agrees to…*I was surprised to find myself studying it carefully, considering the consequences of each of its terms. The requirement on me in terms of my sessions with Dr J was headed *Authentic Engagement* and went on: 'The student will to the best of his ability comply throughout the sessions with any reasonable request of the Director in regard to his education and *treatment*.' (My italics.)

What they call involuntary treatment. I shrugged it off. I can sign it or I can leave, I told myself. These were my negotiations. I am choosing this.

'So this bit about reasonable requests—like me not using my left hand…'

'Precisely.' And to my question who decides what's reasonable: 'You and I. The onus is on us to agree about that.'

'And if we can't?'

He was confident we'd manage it but offered to include a mediation clause; an independent third party could meet with us…I stopped him. No third party. I didn't want anyone else involved. 'We'll keep it between us, then.'

I flicked through the next conditions—weekly times of meetings, a handwritten proviso for food drops to my room—until I got to this one:

'There will be no intimate physical contact between the student and any other student at the School.'

It hadn't stuck out in the first session. Now I had no wish to give him any idea of my embryonic feelings for Rachel by objecting to it. I read it again, a couple of times over, thinking about the odds of her letting me come anywhere near her, and I moved on. My minimum hours in the sessions and on the video games, then next was the Fergus B clause: no threats of physical violence (or use of

85

words that could be construed to amount to a threat of physical violence) in the presence of any student of the school. I'd agreed to that: no going back. There wasn't much more to it. On the School's side, the Director agreed to provide his assessments upon request from the student along with copies of any and all written records and reports prepared by the Director during the Student's participation period.

'So I can get any notes or anything you've done so far?'

'Yes, but I haven't made any notes. I don't tend to. But if I do, you'll be the first to get a copy.'

'So how will I know what you think, then?'

'You'll ask. Oral assessments—let's change it to that. So now: "...the Director agrees to provide his open and frank oral assessments..." That better?'

There was a bit more fine-tuning along these lines. I thought I was pushing it, but I asked for and was granted a small fridge. I remember looking up at the clock and seeing the session had already gone two hours. The truth was that there was something very satisfying about the process: clarifying my entitlements and constraints, the extent of each of our commitments—the parameters of our relationship. With each new understanding, I felt on firmer ground, less at sea. I felt exactly the way he wanted me to feel—like I was part-owner of the process, a collaborator. It was Governance 101, of course. This was a contractual community and in our minds we were masters of our own destiny.

'And what happens if one of us doesn't comply?'

'In the event of breach,' he said, 'you are released from the contract.'

'And that means?'

'It means you are no longer a student here.'

'But what if *you* breach?'

'Same same, both ways. If you breach, if I breach, either way there will be no further requirement for you to stay. We will arrange transport for you to get home, of course.'

'And will I go back to court?'

'No. Your time here, however long it is, will conclude your legal matter. Consider yourself a free man.'

It was a bold move, I thought. At the first sign of bad times we could breach and be gone. Strangely, though, what was occupying my mind as we sat in our final negotiations was not the freedom to leave, but the threat of exclusion—the fact that a single breach could mean expulsion. I thought this through.

'This breach thing,' I said. 'Can we put in something in there about a second chance, like on both sides, so it isn't just one strike you're out?'

He hesitated. 'You mean like three strikes you're out?'

I nodded. 'Or just two...'

'Let's insert a warning clause. That'll give us both a bit of wriggle room.' He made the necessary change and looked back at me. 'Are we done?'

There was just one final thing, since I was on a roll: 'At night time, if we can't sleep, we need to be able to get down to the courtyard.'

His response to this was not immediate. When it came it was a shake of the head. 'That is a systems change.'

He could see the perplexed look on my face.

'No one can sleep,' I said. 'If we could go to the courtyard... Someone just needs to unlock the screen doors.'

Talking to himself again: 'This is precisely why I can't be constrained...'

'Sorry?

'It is a centralised, automated system.' He smiled. 'It is not my friend.' He seemed to think hard on that, eventually discarding the smile. 'It helps you, does it? You fall asleep when you're outside?'

'Most times I do. Or I just lie awake, but I don't mind then. There's stuff to look at; you're not inside your head.'

He looked at me for a while, his chin cupped in his hand. 'I can see the sense in it. Why not; let's put it in.' He read it out as he wrote: 'The Student will be able to access the courtyard twenty-four hours a day.' He gave me his warmest smile yet. 'To hell with them.'

As for Fergus B, I did manage to either avoid (preferable) or tolerate him. In classes he shifted into a seat with the boys in the back row, which I guess he felt was a safer bet, and within three weeks of that session with Dr J his six-month phase was complete. A second phase wasn't required; that's what he told us, sitting in the sun-filled courtyard with his bag all packed and waiting for his ride. We had a lot of questions for him in terms of how Dr J wrapped it up, but he had nothing remarkable to report, his answers atypically succinct.

The other reason I didn't find it so hard with Fergus (and this is one I've drawn on since) was something Dr J had hit on the head: when I needed to keep a lid on things at the old school, I did. I could. When framed as a matter of necessity, non-confrontation was easier. So that was where I placed Fergus. When he got me one-on-one and started on a new dream analysis (he moved on from his grandfather to a young woman working in a hospital in an unknown African country—and yes, her pus-filled dreams), I imagined him as a kid at school, a customer, and our interaction as one with an end-goal, a sale. I sat and thought about what I could give him that would mess with the dream-memory chemicals in his brain.

Fergus left us without further incident.

•

Sitting at the computers last week, I checked what happened to him. The first column, headed Criminal History, told me that Fergus's initial offence (none of us had asked him) was a botched armed robbery in which one of his co-offenders stabbed a pharmacist in the shoulder with a bottle opener. There were two further entries on his record after leaving us at the School, spanning a twelve-year period: both minor and non-violent. In the Education column, he received a short suspension from school (for reasons non-violent) prior to leaving altogether just before he was due to sit his final exams, after which he completed two out of the three years of a computer programming course. Apart from the words 'not a completer', that was it for Education. More broadly, he'd married, had two sons and started an extraordinarily successful online business that sold paranormal products around the globe. There was no notation under Personal regarding marital separation, so I felt I could assume that in Mrs B, Fergus had finally found someone prepared to listen to his dreams.

Applied Mathematics: an Introduction

By the time I'd been there a couple of weeks I had a better sense of how the place worked.

Apart from Helen K, the only other group lesson we had was Numbers with a baby-faced teacher who introduced himself as Mr PW. He didn't want us to use his first name, and he didn't like to call it maths. He said numbers 'had meaning beyond the mathematical' and my heart warmed to him. When he started on algebraic equations, he plunged into content usually reserved for extension classes. The two Bens rocketed through it so they could play their games. Grace sometimes lagged but got there in the end.

The only one to really struggle was Tod. 'You guys are freaks,' he said, third lesson in. 'I can't do this for shit.'

When Glen from the back row chimed in with 'Keep up, fat boy,' Rachel waved a small-dick pinky in his face and he threatened to crack her 'ugly dog head' open. The usual banter. I didn't normally partake but as I watched Rachel for a reaction—there wasn't one, she didn't flinch—I found myself willing her to turn my way.

'Or you could suck cum out of your own midget cock,' I said: my small gift to her.

She didn't turn, but she pressed her lips together to contain what I think would have turned into a smile.

Throughout all this, PW looked silently on. In an odd sleight of hand, nature had given him a face that invited people in—plump cheeks, a little ski-jump nose and perfect rosy lips—although he was not a warm person. Nor, I should say, was he cold, or even indifferent: he had a singular focus, as though the rest of his brain had been shut down. Like an attention overload disorder. He didn't laugh if someone made a joke but he didn't care either, making it impossible to offend him. After our usual attempt at crafting a name out of the teacher's initials—Piss Weak, Proper Wanker; none of them stuck—Rachel referred to him as Lobotoman outside of class. Inside class, they got on fine. PW didn't have to deal with her moods because in Numbers, Rachel attentively followed the screens without naps or argument.

PW still used the tablets and the headsets (we always did, whatever the class). A question appeared with an answer field and then we'd flick to the next. In some classes the program moved through the questions automatically, so you had to race the clock. We liked those because it was like a game, but whichever way, we didn't complain. Sometimes the teaching came through audio as well. He asked us to listen and then went into further explanation, which was, without fail, succinct and adequate and was only given once. If you missed it, any part of it, you just had to find your own way out of the dark. It meant that you didn't tend to miss it in the first place.

When Rachel first coined Lobotoman, Alex nodded his head and said it was like being taught by a machine, but I disagreed. To me there was something very human about the way he'd put the shutters up. It was honest, I guess that's what I mean.

This is what I can do for you. This is all I can do for you. After that you are on your own.

His approach, along with our aptitude, confirmed for me what I had already suspected, and nudged my narrative forward. With Tod as the possible exception, collected here at the School was a particular cohort of students. *A group of gifted delinquents, a boy and the chosen few—sent on a mystery mission to an outback facility with a chip implanted in their enormous brains. One of the chips is programmed to self-detonate at mission completion and blow the unlucky brain into a billion pieces…*A variation on the buddy movie: in order for the protagonist to grieve and redeem, one of them has to die. Or something along those lines.

So that was Numbers. There was Helen K and Numbers, and then there were the 'tutorials'. They were smaller sessions, usually one on one, and we all had different tutors for different things. In this, they seemed to play to our perceived strengths and/or needs. So Rachel had 'spaz English' (Imogen and Grace caught a glimpse of a whiteboard with a list of her spelling words and coughed them out all the way through a science session in the courtyard). Tod said he needed 'spaz Maths' but instead had Magnolia in the kitchen and a guy called Mr T in the movement room. I'm not exactly sure what the scope of Mr T's expertise was but it went beyond fat burning and muscle development, at least that's what Tod said one day when Rachel referred to him as a personal trainer.

'You learn how to breathe, you learn how to live,' he pronounced. None of us went near it.

Unsurprisingly, Imogen and Grace stayed together, splitting their time between business studies and music. The music room was soundproof so the only way we heard anything coming out of there was if the door was left open. From what I got, it wasn't strictly *music*. Bird tweets, bells, engines, whistles, thunder, all kinds of sounds, just snippets until the door closed. A couple of times there was a guitar, and once I heard singing. One of them sounded a lot better than the other. The first time I got a split response from them was when I asked, 'Who's got the voice?'

As for Alex, he had a tutorial with Helen K, and he had the dance man. I peeked in on a couple of sessions. In the first, Alex was sitting cross-legged on the floor as the dance man executed a slow hypnotic movement like a big black snake. The second time they were performing it in perfect unison and they looked like lovers.

The other regular fixture was the games room. To meet our quota Alex and I made a daily habit of meeting there before dinner. I was pretty crap. Alex was merciless. Sitting back on our beanbags and sipping sugar-free sodas from the stuffed mini-fridge, he opened up a bit about his seaside town, how his father moved them there because he didn't want them breathing poison air. In all Alex said, his father loomed large—a man of strange beliefs but, to his son, the embodiment of everything that was solid and strong. Five years after the move, Alex's father had a heart attack while bringing the shopping in from the car.

'I did CPR but I think I fucked it up. The ambulance took too long...'

When he got to that bit, Alex choked up, as he did pretty much any time the subject of his father came into conversation again.

I didn't start my tutorials until week four. That was because the school needed time to do an 'assessment', or so PW said when he informed me that mine would consist of extra time with him. I couldn't work out what sort of assessment had been done—no one asked me what I was interested in doing more of—but I thought they'd probably pegged it right, so I didn't complain. Being the only one to warm to him, I already felt a little proprietary towards PW.

I closed the door and we both sat on top of desks. He had a water bottle and an apple; throughout this and each of our sessions, he drank the water but never touched the apple.

'So, more Numbers?'

'Yes and no,' he said, and went on to explain that this was not Numbers or Maths or Science. We would be working by topic not subject, '...if you follow me. You and I will be looking at various phenomena in physical science, across key areas: energy, gravitation, magnetism. We'll begin with an observation, and work out what kind of physical laws apply. And then,' he actually rubbed his chubby hands together here, the closest thing to an expression of enthusiasm I'd ever get out of him, 'then we'll take it to the next level of mathematical abstraction.'

I was listening, but I wasn't convinced. And the thought I kept coming back to: this wasn't in my contract.

'You are shaking your head,' he said.

'I don't really have a clue what you're talking about.' I was being straight: I didn't want to set him up for disappointment. 'I don't think I'm your guy for this.' I liked the way things were with Mr PW and I was pretty sure that if I went along with this, it would shatter his belief in me.

But he wasn't having it. 'You understand it already,' he said. 'You just don't know it.'

I thought that sounded like a crock, but I liked that he thought it.

'Your answers, Daniel, in Numbers—you haven't made a single error, and in the timed questions, you're fast. A high-velocity brain with a basic understanding of the sort of equations we'll be getting into.'

It wasn't the first time I'd considered they were monitoring our responses on the tablets: of course, it made sense.

'The interesting part,' he went on, still monotone in spite of the stated claim, 'is that we don't just stop with the equations— we look at them as their own entity, with their own meaning and their relevance to other phenomena.' I was not looking interested, or convinced, but he didn't seem bothered. 'As long as you're prepared to try it, we can begin.'

I shrugged. 'What about chemistry?' I asked. 'I like chemistry.'

His response was definitive. 'Too easy.'

There is no need for me to craft any defence of PW. There has never been any cloud over his methods or his role at the school. You couldn't have said his approach was conventional, but in essence he taught in parallel, at least, with a curriculum: we moved through subjects and circled back on the knowledge I had gained. Later, at university, I looked back and pegged him as a cross between my lecturer in pharmacology (brilliant, methodical) and a laboratory guy called Mike who assisted in medicinal chemistry with the awe-struck wonder of a child.

My sense is that I owe PW a great deal. After I left, I arrived in time for the annual exams at a new school. There was a level of disbelief (on both sides) around my results, and at the beginning of my final year a man came from the other side of the country to offer me a scholarship at a university, where I somehow stumbled into an advanced stream. And still the influence of PW played on when I picked the wrong elective in a pot-induced haze (by now I had joined the merry throng), ticked bioinformatics rather than biology, and found myself back in the land of algorithms. I sat in the first lecture wondering what the fuck the list of linear models all meant, but when I went to the office to change to biology, something stopped me. A couple of whispered words: too easy.

I have not seen or heard anything of Mr PW. The only thing I've since learnt about him was a notation I found in my computer file last week with the name of the tutor—the answer to the name behind the initials. He was not Mr anything. P was for Professor, and W for Wise. His name was Professor Michael Wise.

At the end of week six, I'd spent my first sessions with PW rolling a bunch of different balls around the room and making observations. We even cleared the desks and played handball with them at one stage. When I needed a break we took turns in throwing up some numbers and seeing what the other came back with.

'Like what kind of thing?' Tod asked in the corridor one night when I attempted to explain what we were doing.

'Patterns, denominators, whatever—just anything that means something. Like word association, only numbers.'

Every night since the signing of my contract I had joined the sleepless wanderers and tried to open the screen doors at the top of the stairs: still locked. I returned to Dr J's office to complain about the withheld courtyard access but he wasn't there. Then that night the lock turned and the screen opened and in a smooth, sliding motion it disappeared into the wall.

I started down, then turned back. Alex was on the floor and Tod was shuffling towards him. 'I'm going downstairs,' I said. 'To the courtyard. He's unlocked the doors.'

Tod was hesitant, but Alex's eyes widened like he'd just woken up: 'Right behind you.'

Outside on the stone tiles, lined up side by side, were three mats and sleeping bags and pillows. The boys looked at each other as though they'd stumbled across a pot of cash. 'This is you?' Tod asked, and without waiting for a reply: 'This is good.'

And there was our sky. I climbed into a sleeping bag and stared up. It was different from the one I knew. There is a city sky and a country sky; I hadn't figured on that. It was as though until now I'd been seeing it through a cropped and foggy lens. There was no highrise to cut my view, no city lights, and tonight, no moon; it was a clear, blue-black panorama, bulging with clusters and constellations and shadowy faces forming in clouds of white dust. Tod asked me questions I couldn't answer, which star was which, where were the planets, what were the dark patches—how far away was it all? I shrugged them off; I'd looked at it enough but I'd never set out to become an expert.

'The dark patches are nebulae,' Alex eventually said. 'The dust of exploded stars—it blocks out the light from the stars behind it.' It turned out his dad used to point it all out to him from their front lawn. 'We didn't have a TV.'

As the night went on, it grew colder so we pulled the bags up over our noses and it muffled our voices. It was the first of our midnight sessions, the three of us out there, sometimes talking, sometimes quiet; sometimes we slept. I told them about lying out on the walkway at home, on the nights I couldn't sleep. I told them stories of what I heard on the floors above and below. They wanted to know more, about the drug deals and the screams—best of all when the two combined, the deal gone wrong; the best of those the one that ended in a body. I had to go through it twice, how I heard the rising voices down in the courtyard, what sounded like a single punch and the sounds of animal howling, then running footsteps. When I got down to look, there it was, the body. It wasn't a punch. It was a knife. The blood was still there the next morning, like paint on tiles. It was Rob, who was my friend Sam's dad. Sam didn't have a mum so he went to one of those homes, or maybe he found a nice family (that's what Mary said). As I got to the end of the story, I realised the whole childhood picture was starting to sound a bit grim, so I added stuff about the good bits, the other friends I made (there were a few; they'd just moved on) and the games we'd played (brandings from the walkways) and how sometimes old Nina made me baklava and it stuck to the roof of my mouth.

For a while then we were mainly just quiet. From time to time one of us would comment on celestial matters—the brightness, the haze, the distance, our minuteness—referring questions back to Alex. Tod raised the need for a midnight snack and I brought out oat cookies.

'Where did you get these?'

'In my room. I've got food. I've got a fridge. I put it in my contract.'

'You fucker!' It wasn't jovial; it was the first time I'd seen him genuinely pissed off. 'I never asked for any of that stuff.'

I told him I didn't think he really wanted food in his room, given the nature of his mission.

'Yeah, okay, but other stuff…'

'I was thinking about that,' I said. 'What you said the other day about getting more days outside. You need to sort that out.'

'He won't do it. He won't change the contract. I told you, I asked.'

'Yeah, yeah, but you just need to frame it differently. Make it one of your tutorials. You've done the stuff with Magnolia and Mr T, all good, but now you want to walk. Make it earnest—you feel the need to connect with nature, to get outside your head—that sort of bullshit. If he tells you that would mean a system change, tell him you want it anyway. He can sort them. Getting out here needed one, some crap about the locks being automated, but here we are…'

I stopped because I heard a rattle in Tod's breathing and turned to see that he was snoring. It was the sort of sound you'd expect from a baby animal and not a great lump of a boy. Either way, the night sky had done its job: he was asleep. Apart from the snoring, it was quiet—the hum of a generator, a cooing night bird, the intermittent bleat of an insomniac goat…the sound of our breathing. It was a strangely intimate scene, Alex and me, staring up at the stars. I wondered, now that he'd mentioned his dad, if he'd try to get personal. It even crossed my mind that his hand might creep across to cop a feel.

But that wasn't where he was headed.

'*Suck the cum out of your own midget cock*!' he said. 'What the fuck was that?'

'He's a dick.'

'Sure, but the only time you've bothered to say it is when he went for Rachel.'

'Whatever.'

'And the only time she's ever floated in the waterhole like *that*, by the way, was when she knew you were coming.'

'That's bullshit.'

'Hah. It's not.'

'What is happening with her, anyhow? That shit in class…'

'Yeah, I dunno.'

'…that's extreme. Like how many hours was that?'

'I know. Messed up.'

With not much more to say about that we changed subjects. He asked me about the drugs, what I sold.

I started listing them off: 'Ritalin, Adderall, Oxy, Valium, Klonopin, Xanax...'

'You tried all those?'

'Yeah. Well, I test them.'

'As any good dealer would.' With this he propped himself up on his elbow and looked down at me like I was the most interesting specimen in the world. 'It took a lot to do what you did—hats off. I mean it,' he said.

He seemed to want me to acknowledge that I understood what he was saying before he launched into more questions, all the details, where I sourced it all, how I delved into the dark net.

'There's no great trick to it,' I explained. 'You download a site, link into the right address and you're on: your very own crypto-market. I rented a PO box—that's where I fucked up; they got it through one of my vendors and I'd put it in my own name.' The questions kept coming and I happily gave it up. It was like anything online—you browse. Price, quality, origin: it's all laid out with user reviews, star ratings, online forums. 'It's another world; it doesn't matter who you are—you're just a username with a bitcoin wallet. It's all encrypted, then the police crack it and another site pops up, and you're on again.'

'So why not order some out here?'

I laughed, said I didn't even know where we were.

'Easy enough to find out.'

'And it will arrive in the mailbox and they'll just pass the envelope over.'

'Yes, okay. It needs some thought. But it'd be a nice time to have something to send us up into that cluster.' He pointed upward and stared for a while in what seemed like an effort to get there unassisted. 'Just saying...'

When he spoke again the tone had shifted. 'I'm not complaining.

This is good, Daniel, this is fine.' There was a warble in his voice. It sometimes happened when Alex was talking, mid-sentence, mid-thought, like something cracked and the ground dropped away, swallowing him up into the silence. Mary would have told him to stop being a sad sack, but I figured if I just left it for a while he'd come back.

'I don't think Rachel's right,' I eventually said. 'What this place is.'

He took so long to answer I was starting to give up, but in the end, he went on to give his version—more abstract than concrete: 'They bring us here and set it all up, the field trips, the sessions, the lessons and we're all sitting here asking: what is this all about? They're turning us in on ourselves...And now you get us this.' He raised his arms to the sky. 'I mean, this is everything that is beautiful. But I don't think it changes anything, if any of this does.' His voice started trailing off. 'Or it makes it worse. It doesn't matter, or it is worse...'

I took the bait. 'What is worse?'

'All of it,' he whispered. 'What happened, what is happening, what will happen.'

This was the thing with Alex: he kept moving the posts, but there was something so gentle in it—so thoughtful—that he brought you with him. He never offered it up, always waiting for me to ask, and then holding it back, until it felt like the most important thing in the world to know what was in his thoughts.

'What do you mean?' I asked.

'I mean the bad stuff—all of it, everywhere.'

What I learned that night as he continued to answer my questions was that so far he'd just been fiddling at the gate. On the other side of it—inside his mind—was the entire and endless gamut of human suffering. He began to step me through examples. Sexual

101

slavery across Europe, public stonings in the Middle East, the bombings of schools, of hospitals, mass abductions and gang rapes—sometimes with dates and places, sometimes just the abstract horror...bloody corpses and mutilated women, strewn limbs of children. When I say he stepped me through it, I mean slow steps. He spoke like someone trying to overcome a stutter, careful to convey the weight and meaning to be attached to each word. He moved from one to the next and then back again, to clarify and correct, like he was memorising facts for a test.

There were twelve on a bus
He was the last doctor in town
It was market day
There were four sisters...

I tried to bring us back. 'Okay,' I said. 'Enough of the heavy shit.'

But by then I don't think he even heard me. 'No, that's not right,' he said, frustrated at not remembering something, tapping the centre of his forehead with his fist. And then there was a break in his voice—the warble—and to close, a trickle: 'For every star...'

For every star.

Somehow above us now was not the most extraordinary night sky I'd ever witnessed, but a panoramic testament to the magnitude of human suffering, each cluster of stars a scatter of pain. Alex was sitting up now, in just his singlet top. It was cold, fucking cold; when I told him he was an idiot and to get back in the sleeping bag, he climbed up the rim of a planter pot and hiked himself onto the branch of a pear tree where he swayed side to side and let his head hang back, his mouth open wide like he was trying to catch invisible rain. I closed my eyes and tried to block it out. This part of it I was getting used to, ever since he licked his own bacterial growth off the agar plate, the jump into the waterhole (he'd started doing a balancing act on the higher branch), any chance to put himself at risk. Last week it had been fire—at breakfast he'd singed the hair off his right arm over the cooktop, then later worked on his eyebrows with the Bunsen burner. Sometimes it was sort of funny, like a kid's prank, sometimes irritating; more and more so, like now…When I looked up again he was lying back against the branch, perfectly still; I thought I could see a smile on his lips. And then suddenly his body was shaking. I watched him shaking on the branch, thinking he was a sick boy.

Sad sack, sick boy.

And I was heavy with the thought that I was losing something—a potential or a promise—and the longer he shook, the less likely it was ever to materialise.

Tod snapped me out of spectator role. He woke up and saw Alex and freaked. Reckoned he was having some kind of fit; I said he was just cold. Whichever way, we ended up taking him back inside. Alex had gone a bit pale but he was okay.

Tod put him to bed and told me to go too.

But I couldn't go to bed.

I started my rounds of the corridor.

Preliminary Physics: Magnetic Poles

It was not the stories of global horror that kept me from sleep. It was the two things Alex had said about Rachel.

The first—that my crack at Glen was in her defence—was only half-right. It was more just to go one up and get her to look my way. The second part—reading something into her way of floating—I felt certain was bullshit. But still, the licence it gave me to play it back a hundred different ways: the sight of her body at the centre of the waterhole as I came over the hill...

And as the reason for the contraction inside of my ribcage these last days began to sink in, for the first time I considered the question: *what does Rachel think of me?*

After a few slow rounds of the corridor, I stopped outside her door—not to answer that question, but to listen. I leaned back against the wall and waited. Silence. Still, I felt something, some connection here. I slid down to the floor. At this angle I could see just a fragment of night sky through the top branches of the pear tree. There was a hyperreal glow to it now that lit up the remaining leaves. It felt like there was some kind of meaning in that; I read it as a nod to stay: to wait, to listen.

In the quiet dark of the corridor, I felt alert. Nocturnal. Different from the day people. I imagined the leaves were not leaves but shadows of leaves and that I was sitting on the rim of a pretend world—a parallel narrative—and I was waiting for the word. The word would come from the other side of the door and it would make everything real again. I counted how long I could keep my eyes open without blinking. I counted how long I could hold my breath after the exhalation. I put my ear against the timber panel of the door. Still nothing, no whispers coming from inside. And here, outside, just me and the silence in the corridor with no beginning or end.

That went for quite some time.

Finally, it came. I heard it! Not a single word but a staccato whisper. I couldn't make it out... *What did she say?* Everything seemed to hinge on it. In a panic, I stood up. *Did I really hear it?*

I kept my ear to the door but there was nothing more.

What came to me then was not the image of Rachel in the waterhole, but Rachel in the classroom sitting alone at the window, staring at the sky and then at me. Her desperate eyes; pleading—was it a plea? Standing outside her door, it was only now I could interpret it: she knew something was wrong with her but she didn't know what it was. I could help her understand. I could take down all the words and decode the message and I could tell her what was

105

wrong and how to fix it (*in some sense, a predictable plot twist: boy on mission, boy saves girl*).

I can't remember making a decision to open Rachel's door that night. I could say it was in the delirium of sleeplessness; that of its own accord my hand rose to turn the handle of her door. But the truth was I had never felt more wide-awake, more alive with purpose. It wasn't that I was justified; I was compelled.

I open the door, and step inside.

In the misty darkness of her room, there is only the sound of my heartbeat. When it slows I am calm because it is right to be there; I am invited. That is what her whispers were. Still, only my eyes move. As they adjust to the darkness I see the room is larger than mine. I see the bed and I can see that it is empty—the bed is empty! White sheets strewn to one side and a cover on the floor. I scan the rest of the room, the outline of a bedside lamp, pale curtains along the opposite wall.

I gasp. There she is, standing in the furthest corner. The sleep-walker. She is not looking at me, but down at the bed.

She doesn't turn at the sound. Her hair is all to one side, partly covering her face. For a few minutes neither of us moves. Slowly, then, she raises an arm and walks towards the bed, and the whispering starts again.

I can hear the words now.

'Only the sun, trembling. The father, like him...'

Pieces of a sentence.

'...your father likes him...be there for the fire.'

When she stops I step closer, each small step a limbic cartwheel, and with each heartbeat, the liquid presses against the walls of my arteries, a contraction, paralysis. I stand at the other side of the bed as the volume increases, and she is spitting the words, commanding me. Her eyes are open, ablaze—the whites flashing blue against darkness; she is a zombie killer, but I am not scared. I am soaring through the air. I am falling.

I am in love.

Abstract Mathematics

When I stood face to face with a somnambulant Rachel and silently declared myself, I was going with my best guess. I felt it rising through my groin and my gut, into my chest and my throat (in that order) so that the words formed in my brain as a conceptualisation of the physical journey: *I am in love*...these exact words, despite the absence of any real illustration of the concept in my life to date.

Back to the timelines.

On the first day of Grade 6 Mrs Pyke put a timeline on the whiteboard of defining moments in the history of Australia in the decade from the First Fleet to Bass and Flinders' circumnavigation of Tasmania. 'We are talking, children, about what shaped our nation.' At the end of the class she said she wanted us to go home and make our own timeline of defining moments in our lives. Ours would be for eleven years as we were all eleven except James Mildren, who was twelve because he repeated kindergarten. She wanted us to bring our timeline back next week and share it with the class—a historiographical 'get to know your classmates' session. The handout with the blank timeline was headed: *What Shapes You?*

Mrs Pyke was a new teacher and I assume she had come up with the ingenious idea all by herself, not accounting for the fact that a third of the thirty-three kids in her class were from the Commission flats. It could have been worse. No one included the really bad bits—sudden disappearances of parents or dead junkies on doorsteps. Ben Jones didn't put the day his sister got raped. Basically, everyone lied. We all lied and we all knew we lied. We just served it up and played along when Mrs Pyke broke us into groups of five to share. It was mostly stuff about births of siblings or deaths of grandparents, broken limbs or operations, learning something or winning something.

Why I bring it up is that the day she assigned the task I did in fact go home and think about what I would have said if I were doing it for real. I didn't have to think long; it was just Dad moving out and then a series of names:

1. Josh
2. Gary
3. Brian

They were my events. What shaped me was who was living with me and Mary in the flat. It all depended on the tenants. (Not 'stepfathers' or 'boyfriends'—none of them was a father or friend to either of us. 'Tenants' was the best I could come up with.) Before they came, when it was just us, Mary and I had a level of control over our lives. We could plan a day, work out a budget, hang out, whatever; all of which was blasted away the moment a tenant bunked in. I kept trying to put my stamp on things but after so many obliterated plans I got used to not making them. Mary too. Brian had only just moved in when Mrs Pyke set the task. By the time Brian left, Mary had got used to not going out at all. At first she didn't; then she couldn't. Even when it was just us.

The word love didn't get thrown around a lot, or in fact used at all, not by Mary or the tenants. It was never put forward as a justification for their unwelcome and at times terrifying presence in the flat. Subsequently, my understanding was that in real life people coupled because that is just what they did, and if a coupling severed it was replaced by another coupling that was usually worse. (I didn't have any firm view on the universality of the pattern: Josh—Gary—Brian could as easily have been Gary—Brian—Josh, though my hunch was that the Brians usually come last.)

In any event, my perception of human connection was of a random set of energies moving people around, one to the next. The horseshit in the movies never even vaguely resonated with me, and when kids at school started holding hands and texting emojis I felt the same way about them as I felt about the kids that went to church: dupes, sucked into the orbit of the big lie.

What I shared with my Grade 6 group about my timeline:

1. The day I started school (I couldn't even remember it);
2. Falling off my bike and breaking my arm (that wasn't how I broke my arm);
3. Catching my first wave (that did happen, true story, and when I was in Grade 6 I still got tingly thinking about it).

•

I am in love.

Whatever they meant, the words imprinted that night. For the next four months the fact of them formed a significant part of my reason for being—I'd put it at about sixty per cent. There was a lot going on—appointments with Dr J, tutorials with PW, midnight sessions with the boys—so sixty constituted a sizeable chunk. I wasn't then, nor have I ever been, one to buy into the notion of a hundred per cent. Now that I have a lens on my overall pattern of proficiency, I can state that Rachel was (and is) my peak. I have been called many things—a narcissist, a liar, a solipsist, a loser—and I've never come back with a good retort. I am not a narcissist, but that occasion wasn't the right time to explain the difference between narcissism and nihilism. There was already broken shit all over the kitchen floor.

Tremble, bumble, tumble...

Rachel's words tapered off into a series of indecipherable sounds before she fell silent. For a few minutes she stared more closely at the bed as though she were reading a message printed on the sheets, then she climbed back in and pulled a pillow over her head. I wanted to stand and watch the clump of her but I retreated. I went back to my room and completed the task at hand by writing down all the words and the different orders in which they'd been spoken, the combinations coming together like a poem or a prayer.

The next morning I woke up to a wave of intense nausea. I assumed it was something I'd eaten until I saw Rachel in the kitchen at breakfast and my gut flipped into my throat. My symptom, it turned out, was the physical manifestation of our newfound connection; my heart was sending signals to the vomiting centre in my brain (there is one, seriously). Years later when I had developed a better understanding of physiological responses, I worked out it

111

was the same feeling I get with jet lag: as night flips to day, so too a hypodermic rush into a life with love. You are a million miles from take-off, upside down in the drop zone.

I walked into the kitchen. Tod was standing at the table, and Rachel sat opposite him. She looked at me like it was any other day: same place, my existence an ongoing irrelevance.

'You look like shit,' she said.

I must have stared at her for a while because she told me to fuck off and Tod flicked my cheek. I couldn't even eat his three-cheese omelette. I remember turning around and walking out of the kitchen with the thought: *This is not going to be good for me. Cease now.* The further I got away from her it seemed feasible— that I could back-step out of this hopeless, unrequited nausea. I passed Alex in the dance room on the way to class. He was alone, sitting on the floor with his arms wrapped around his knees and his eyes closed. When I tapped, he looked up.

'You coming?' I asked.

'You look terrible.'

'Yeah, I've been told,' I said. 'You coming?'

'Nah,' he replied. I was starting to work with his signals, when he needed to be left alone. It didn't mean I liked them, but I had other things on my mind. As soon as I got to the classroom, there was Rachel, two desks across and being stared down by Grace, and I was back in my own bilious fog. For relief, I tried to focus on Helen K's chest as she told one of her weird tales: Garuda, born to a mother who was a slave to a thousand snakes. The picture was some kind of humanoid bird; I just took a glance at it before turning my eyes back to Helen's wondrous freckly cleavage, but the sad fact was I couldn't smell her anymore. As though she'd caught on to that, what was happening with me, her eyes filled with a gentle pity.

As for the nausea, the fog, it settled over the next few days into something milder, like the feeling you get sliding down from an amphetamine high, about midway from the peak. On the next field trip I managed to stay a decent distance behind Rachel, and to wait at the rock where I met my goat while she got herself into the water. Mercifully she wasn't floating face up when I waded in; she was moving around with half her face under the water, her eyes unblinking, a crocodile.

I was so hard it hurt. That had never happened to me in cold water before.

Meanwhile, my sessions with PW continued.

We had started on magnetism—the observations: poles repelling and attracting. He was stepping through the physical laws when he saw that I was getting impatient. Even then I was always keen to skip through the laws to get to the abstraction. He understood that, of course, and empathised. PW liked to use the word 'beautiful' when it came to the numbers—the axioms, theories, algorithms—'beautiful' or 'very elegant' or 'grand' or, my favourite, 'the magnificent edifice of mathematics'. The reverence was just the fact of the matter, always delivered deadpan, no particular emphasis. In the same way he would occasionally slip in his spin on the meaning of everything. Intonation gave you no clue. All the while he would remain his seclusive self and yet some days, somehow, he'd climb inside my head and turn the light on.

Like this one day.

Reducing information on my tablet into whiteboard dot points, his heading was Magnetic Monopoles and the content was there are none. Next: the magnetic flux through a closed surface. Content: zero. I was trying to get my brain around it when he stopped.

'Before we complicate things too much,' he said, 'might we

backtrack...' There was no question mark but still he waited for my assent. 'What sits behind the physical laws,' he went on, 'are your own innate perceptions. The word is "primordial".' He lingered on this word as though someone had flicked his slow-motion switch; he did this sometimes—I assumed when he liked the sound of something. 'Do you know what that means?'

I did not.

'It is what is built into your brain: your instinctive sense of space, distance, motion...When you put your hand out to touch something, you know when to stop. When you bounce a rubber ball, you know the amount of force to exert. Since you entered the world, there has been a regularity of occurrence. You have interpreted it. You have innate cognitive mechanisms and over the course of your life they have developed a colossal internal data-base. As we learn, we are tapping into that, into our *primordial* knowledge. You know it, you just don't know you know it.'

He wanted me to nod along. 'But I am not a magnet,' I said.

He countered with the electromagnetic fields emanating from my brain. I never won with him.

There had been a regularity of occurrences over the course of my life, that was true. You only needed to look at the key events on my timeline, the tenants, all three: different versions of the same thing.

I don't remember a lot about Josh but my sense is he was the pick (if you had to pick). He took us to the beach once (first wave). I remember Mary walking on the sand with the grey ocean behind her; she was laughing because her curls kept blowing over her face. Some time after that the kitchen got smashed up and he gashed her arm with the scissors. Next came Gary. He asked to borrow ten bucks and she said she didn't have it which he said was a lie and he shoved her onto the floor. A shove, and I remember thinking it was better than Josh, better than a gash. But it got worse after that, banging and screaming and bruises, all outside my door. Then Mary laughed at him at breakfast because he liked Glenn Campbell and he punched her in the face and I charged him down and he fell and hit his head on the corner of the table and I tried to run but he grabbed my foot and dragged me back and Mary jumped on him and the blood from her nose dripped on my face and all over the muddy carpet, his blood, her blood...I copped a whack in the ear and my loose tooth got looser. It was him on top of Mary, holding her down with his fist up behind his head ready to swing, and I was pummelling him and he spun around and somehow had us both pinned, both of us crying and howling, and in the middle of all of it I heard the song. It was about the lineman searching for something in the sun.

Gary must have heard it too. He just stopped and let go. Sat back against the couch and said, 'Oh fuck this.'

I told him to 'fuck off out of here' and Mary didn't tell me not to swear. He said it was a perfect song. He didn't fuck off for a fair while. I should never have told him to go, because then there was Brian.

And now he is part of my database.

My *primordial* knowledge.

I remember later lying in the courtyard and thinking about what PW had said in the lesson that day, trying to work out what he was telling me, the phrases rolling around inside my head: *innate cognitive mechanisms, your internal database...our primordial knowledge*. In the end I concluded it was something simple. I think what he was trying to tell me is: 'Feel your way.'

Personal Health and Development 1.2

When I headed into my next session with Dr J, Greg was at the desk in the waiting room, ready to take my height and weight.

I had been at the School nine weeks 'to the day', he announced in a marvelling-at-time-passing way. In between measurements there was an awkward level of attempted eye contact, like he wanted to take a bite of me. I hadn't warmed to Greg; I didn't see much of him, but I still wanted to head-butt him when I did. It wasn't like a snapping thing, just an instant physical revulsion. I'm not suggesting I had some kind of crystal ball, but I sensed something. That's as high as I can put it.

I was glad to see Dr J signalling me at his door. Feeling pretty good about myself, I took my seat. I'd been here a couple of months.

I had made a friend. I was in love. The curved corridors and the courtyard had become my habitat; the stretch of land between us and the waterhole the accepted confines of my universe. True, I had the lingering sense that these people were strangers with candy (every day I wondered who was watching this play out and for what purpose) but this was candy none of us had ever tasted before or were likely to taste again. The confines of this place were what kept us from our former lives; the confines were our freedom.

Dr J didn't ask for any kind of progress report. Instead, he went straight ahead and tossed the bomb: 'Your mother has been in contact again; this time she has sent you an email.'

As he poured us both some water, I said I didn't really want to read it. He watched me, waited. Over the years I'd become good at not giving much away, but it was harder with the Doctor; his eyes circled my face, like he was taking a reading. When I didn't budge, he leaned forward and cupped his chin with his hand. 'Are you not curious to know what she said?'

I shook my head.

'Is that because you know what it is?'

I shrugged.

'How do you think she is feeling now?'

'She is alone,' I said, 'so it's better.'

'Tell me, if she doesn't leave the flat, how does she get by?'

'There's a neighbour, Nina. And some days she can get out.'

He nodded, refilled his glass. I hadn't taken a sip from mine. 'Very well, Daniel, I'll pass the message on to you as I undertook to do. You are under no obligation to read it.' He folded a piece of paper and I put it in my pocket. 'Let's move on, then. At our last meeting we left off talking about school and your business operation. I would like today to talk about what was happening at home.'

I'd assumed it was coming. 'Is that part of this whole thing?' I asked. 'Do I have to answer your questions?'

He shook his head. 'That is more specific than the condition we included. The requirement of you is to keep an open mind, to work with me.' He reached over and picked up the contract. It had its place there at the edge of the small table through all of our meetings: a third presence, an arbiter. He found the section and pointed me to it. 'The word we used was "cooperate". That is vague, deliberately so. If the condition was that you answer all my questions I dare say we'd just end up with a sack full of lies. There isn't much point in that. I thought we might come at it another way.'

He returned the contract to the table.

'Would you hear my idea?'

'Sure.' I'd heard plenty of ideas before; I wasn't worried about one more.

'There are a number of people involved in your story, none of whom I know anything about. To start, if we could just make a list.' He waited for my assent, content with my lack of objection. 'Number one is your mother, Mary, and then her various partners. There were three? After your father?'

'Yes.'

'And their names? Just for my list.' He was of course making no list.

'Josh, Gary, Brian.'

'In that order?'

'Yes.'

'So we have Mary, and then Josh, Gary and, finally, Brian. And then there is the boy at various ages, that is you. Five characters. You mentioned a neighbour, Nina; should we include her?'

I didn't think so.

'Anyone else?'

I shook my head.

'Then let's proceed. Have you ever seen a play, Daniel?'

'At school.'

'And there were actors playing characters on the stage?'

'Yep.'

'All right then. If you could go along with me for a minute: first, whatever was on the set of the stage at your school, take that away, so it is empty. You've got that?' He waited for my nod. 'And now, instead, use props to make it a replica of the living room of your flat. The windows and furniture, paint colours, the doors to different rooms.'

In spite of the fact that I had no intention of complying, the images flashed into my brain. I couldn't stop them.

'Second, I want you to do this: I want you to place your characters on the stage. The three men, yes? And Mary. Lastly, the boy.'

At this point he pulled some chess pieces out of his drawer and put them in the centre of the desk. When I looked closer at the carved wooden pieces, I saw there were no pawns or rooks but instead farm animal faces. Sheep, cow, rooster; you get the idea.

'If it helps, you can allocate a person to the pieces and move them around.'

This one I could stop. Fiddling with his rooster, I managed to keep my stage empty.

'Are you with me?'

'Sure.'

I had spent the better part of my childhood mastering ways not to get sucked into other kids' games. Kids use all sorts of tricks to lure you in. Adults too. It wasn't like adults before him hadn't tried—a whole gamut of tactics. I had a script in reply, depending on the angle they came at it, and dot points of details I'd share. I could list off the physical injuries, easy—hers and mine, from

119

the start, all the way up to the burns. Key milestones for Josh and Gary, down pat with pauses in the right places. For Brian I just said most of it took place on the other side of a door; I only heard it, and what I heard, I blocked. They backed away then, slowly-slowly. To questions on any of the more recent stuff I shot back with: 'I can't talk about it, *not yet*.' (I saw a note the last guy made on his page before court: *Persistent avoidance—explosive/ aggressive in response. Dosage?*)

Then came the Doctor's gambit—the 'work with me' proposal. What he asked me to do was to pick one of the characters to play—any one of them 'except the boy. You are not playing him. You have no control over what he does; things are just happening to him, around him'.

People had tried before, but no one had come up with something as stupid as this. It crossed my mind in a hypothetical way that he might be messing with me, like the left hand thing. But that wasn't the feeling I was getting. He was talking like someone giving directions on the street. I could feel pockets of cold fluid bulge behind my eyes.

'Open your eyes, Daniel.'

I think he had to repeat that, but eventually I did open them.

'What do you think of this idea?'

I am a truth-teller at heart. 'I think it is fucking retarded.'

He nodded. 'Thanks for your honesty.' And when I smirked: 'I mean it: thank you.'

'Okay,' I said. 'What's next?'

'I want to stick with it, in spite of your reservations. I know what you think—you have been clear on that—so there's no misunderstanding. Let's just give it a go.'

'Why?'

I look back on this part of the conversation now and wonder

why I didn't do a better job of shutting it down. As it was, the question opened the board right up.

'Why should you give it a go?' he said. 'My reason is that you received a diagnosis of post-traumatic stress disorder at the age of ten. We need to explore that. I think I'm right in saying that you haven't done that yet in any kind of meaningful way with the other people you've talked to.'

'I thought you didn't buy into the diagnosis stuff.'

'An open mind, remember?'

As he reached again for the contract, I stood up, walked to the door. Because I didn't know what would happen if I walked out, I went back again, and I sat down, spent a few minutes mentally rearranging books on the nearest shelf into reverse order by whatever numbers I could find on the spines. Long enough to make a plan.

'Okay, I'll tell you what happened,' I said, and I launched in (that was my plan): the first time, it was in the kitchen, he cut her with the scissors...

The doctor put up his hand, shaking his head. 'What we need, Daniel,' he explained, 'is some other perspectives in the room.'

I looked at him; he looked at me, and with a strange half-smile, he waved the contract, and repeated it, like a jingle, like a dare. *Give it a go...* 'We can just try it.'

My arms were folded, my fists clenched, and my fingernails were digging painfully into my palms. As I made no further effort to stop him, he continued. 'Let's say we start with the one who cut her arm. Is that Josh?'

I nodded. I could play along, until I couldn't.

'I'll ask him questions—'

'How many?' I said. 'How many questions?'

He smiled. 'Fair enough—no more than five.'

121

'Three, let's make it three.'

'Okay.'

'The answers can be as short as I want.'

He nodded. 'Let's begin then.' And when I didn't stop him: 'Okay, Josh—what are your favourite things?'

I laughed. *What sort of an idiot question...?* 'I dunno. The beach, he liked the beach.'

'You are him: *I like the beach.*'

And you are a mental case. 'I like the beach.' Josh, the flat...I put my mind back there to extract the next ones: 'I like TV, *The Simpsons*, and bacon and pineapple pizza. That's all I can remember.'

'Okay, thank you, that is good.'

'That's one.'

For the second question he wanted to know how I/Josh felt about Mary. I wanted to make this quick, but I needed the question clarified. 'When?'

'You've just moved into the flat.'

What I reported starts getting a bit foggy here, pieces of memory caught in the orbit of a non-fathomable nucleus. *I don't have a toothbrush.* Mary laughed and said she had a spare. *She's such a fucking nanna.* That's what he said when he saw the little china swans on the window ledge. 'I got her a rooster for Christmas and she put it in the middle of the swans.'

'And what about later, Josh, before you leave, how do you feel about Mary now?'

The words were the same but different. 'She is such a fucking nanna.'

His questions were up. Now it was Gary. He didn't ask about his favourite things. He asked how he felt about the boy.

'When?' I said.

'You have just moved into the flat.'

It took a while to extract this one. Mary told him what my teacher said; she shouldn't have told him. *He's a little smarty pants.* Then Mary, what he thinks of Mary, when he moved in (number two), and just before he left (three). *I'm going to get us into a house and buy a fridge with an ice-maker and get my kombi back and take us to Coffs.* And all the rest of it, like it was real, like she could make it real.

'And later?'

I shrugged. *A slut like the rest of them.* As short as I wanted.

I was hovering around all this like I was making it up, in and out of their heads, there but not there. It was easier than I thought. I found my focus falling on the doctor's hairline, in this light (a sliver of late-afternoon sun across his chair) it looked like it was painted on, like I could see all the carefully directed strokes. Even the markings on his face, the pigmentation and the scars, it all suddenly looked like part of a grand design.

Then it took a turn. He moved on to Brian. I tried my usual: *I was on the other side of a door; what I heard I blocked. I'm not really ready to talk about this yet.*

Dr J wanted me to try. An easy one. When he first moved in. 'How do you feel about Daniel?'

There wasn't an easy one for Brian, and no part of me wanted to even pretend to step inside his head. All I wanted was for the guy with the genius complex and the shiny hair to back off. When I got up again I knocked the table and the chess pieces fell onto the floor. Neither of us picked them up. I ended up over at the window watching the sky turn dark, the very same dark in a different form funnelling down my throat, the alien pressing against my ribs. My hand reached out to the shelf in a white-knuckled grip.

I got my balance. What I saw then was not the stage and the

bullshit players, but a photograph on the shelf. My vision was blurred but I forced myself to focus: it was the Doctor in a suit shaking hands with a silver-haired woman, a gold plaque in her other hand, and in his, the framed black-and-white photograph that was now on the wall, with the cliffs and the lake and the forest. In the photograph the Doctor looked to be mid-sentence and there was a row of people behind him, listening, leaning forward in their chairs. In these photos, there is less of him, less flesh, but more light.

I turned around and saw now sitting in the chair a man burdened by time, by events. *Have a break from yourself,* Mary used to say when I was little and she got sick of me complaining. *Focus on other people's problems for a while.* She had other tips too. *It isn't what happens, it's how you react*—that old chestnut. In times past they hadn't much resonated, but what was forming now was a morphing of messages, a different way of reacting. Looking back to the man in the frame, I found my own questions, my own game.

I pointed to the silver-haired woman. 'Who is she?'

For a moment he seemed to be considering whether to answer, his eyes dropping to the floor before rising again to meet mine. 'The director of a government department.'

I kept at it, a different focus, deflection: What department? When? His answers were vague. He was in the United States. It was a long time ago.

'Proud moment,' I said. Our eyes stayed fixed. 'And there is your photograph.' I pointed at the one on the wall. 'It was a prize?'

It took a while, but he responded. 'It was.'

'Did you make some kind of discovery or something?'

'You might say that.'

I did what he did, scoured his face for signs. 'So what happened?'

His mouth curved into a kind of smile, and I sensed there was something behind it, an answer to all this. Not that I expected to get it. Adults avoid, deflect, lie: I'd always known that. All I was trying to do was to blow up the session. I needed out. It made me nervous to see his mind starting to tick into the answer, and then: 'Come, sit.'

When I returned to my chair, he leaned in towards me and picked up the animals from the floor. 'What happened is that I was wrong. Why I am here…is because I was wrong.' There was such pain in his eyes as he repeated the words that I had to look away. I actually thought there was a chance he was going to cry. Then he caught himself. 'Enough,' he said gently. 'We are straying.' He picked up the contract. 'Let's be more careful.'

He was good with his words. It was a warning: we were stepping outside the agreed parameters, in breach, at risk, and a reminder—*let's* be more careful—that we both had skin in the game.

Still, I left his office feeling utterly victorious. I had a leverage point, a way to push back, deflect. And something more. Extracting his admission had given me a taste, a desire to know him better than the others did, to create our own special link—to see if I could get closer to a man without the world exploding into blood-stained pieces.

To characterise events now—a courtyard and the night sky, standing in a bedroom staring at a sleepwalker, the ninety-minute sessions with a doctor and a contract: if I have intimate memories, they are these. Within them, within the edging forward and back, within the questions and the answers, within the silence, our grip weakens, and in the next moment we are defined by a changed set of objectives. If I have intimate memories, if that is love…

I left the Doctor's room that afternoon with an answer that would inevitably raise more questions, questions that would slow burn over years to come, about how to unravel a story, the life and work of a man once lauded, now in retreat.

What I had started to learn is that the award in the photograph and the print on the wall were not a source of pride but of shame; and that his 'outback' existence was a form of penance, a last-ditch and desperate effort to reverse the damage he had done. What I started to understand that day was what we had in common.

It took me a couple of days to unfold the printed message.

Beyond full stops, Mary wasn't a punctuater. She always got it wrong, she said, so she just left it out.

> hi how are you doing. you know me im no good at writing but he says its better than calling. i am glad youre there. he sounds nice strange but nice. i dont expect you to write back but would be good if you did just to say youre ok. im thinking about you a lot and what must be in your head but I want you to let that go. that is what im doing. you wont believe that but its true. i love you

I got one a week like that for the next three weeks. It wasn't until the fourth one that I felt in the right state to reply. I kept it on point, and at the time of writing, accurate.

I am OK.

HSIE (Human Studies and its Environment)

When we look up at a night sky we see different things, different patterns. I liked to stare long enough at a cluster for a face to form and then wait for it disappear. That was my thing. I saw what I saw. For Tod, on the other hand, it was important that we had a shared experience, so we could be part of a joint enterprise in tasks like, for example, ranking brightness and taking potshots on distance. 'Do you see that?' It was a constant. Sharing for Tod was a process of validation; if it wasn't shared, it didn't happen. Tod liked to bring us in on how he was feeling in both mind and body. His diet was an example. Within the first ten minutes of every midnight session, he asked the same question: 'Do you know what I've eaten today?'

Sometimes we indulged him: a third of a cup of unstabilised oats and a hundred mils of almond milk, a slice of kamut sourdough, half an avocado. And sometimes we didn't: 'We don't give a fuck what you've eaten today, Tod.'

When he talked about the combination of amino acids that make eggs the perfect protein source, he was demonstrably frustrated that we showed zero interest, and again when he tried to tackle Alex on his food intake, or lack thereof. He had tracked it the previous day to a handful of grapes and a ginger snap. Alex was gracious about it, refraining from telling him to mind his own intake. In response to an inventory of all the reasons this kind of diet could lead to organ failure in the long term, Alex thanked him and said he'd take it on board.

'You don't worry about it?'

'No, I don't.'

'Well I don't understand that. You have to explain that to me, Alex, you really do.'

I was taken aback at the honesty of the reply: 'I guess it's because I'm not expecting my organs to be around in the long term.'

Tod threw his arms up and mumbled about bullshit talk. When Alex didn't show in the courtyard the next night, Tod thought it was his fault and vowed to limit the food reports (to items and not quantities) and the lectures (total ban).

'I am boring him.'

I said I doubted that was the problem.

'I'm not boring him?'

'I didn't say that; I just said it wasn't the reason.'

The second time Alex didn't show, I went to investigate. It was a bit before midnight. I knocked on his door and entered. There was light from a large computer screen on a desk in the corner of the room. The room was the same size and configuration as mine, only there were shelves and a second desk, all stacked with books. He was sitting in his day clothes facing the screensaver; the image was a tranquil ocean beneath a setting sky.

'You have a computer?' I asked, surprised to see it.

'Part of my contract,' he said, without turning his head. His tone was flat.

'Are you coming down?'

'I won't tonight,' was his answer. I left it at that until later in the week when I knocked on his door again and we had another version of our conversation: *I won't tonight*—Alex seated at his desk, this time with a different screensaver: a waterfall against a backdrop of dense jungle. (I later learned he changed it every morning, first thing, until he didn't.)

During the day he seemed solid enough. He was a fan of the way Helen's lessons were panning out: in place of the images we were now given pieces of music. She called them listening lessons. 'The way you listen affects what you hear.' No one argued. The first one was *Bitches Brew* by Miles Davis. As a start, she suggested we follow different instruments. The sisters rapidly (and somewhat freakishly, I thought) identified them all: three keyboards, an electric guitar, two basses, four drummers and a bass clarinet.

'You hear that? The conga coming in there...'

Grace said it, but Imogen was the one to start banging her desk. And off we went...The intensity of their connection to the music was infectious, and they actively brought us along—all of us, Rachel included. (My sense was that the sisters had come out of a very tough playground themselves and were only now getting accustomed to the relative ease of this one.) During an explosion of trumpet around the thirteen-minute mark, Imogen took a hold of big Ben's forearm and told him under her breath it was 'fucking insane'. I think she was grabbing for the nearest thing to hold on for the ride, but Ben didn't pull away and no one could disagree with the assessment. There was a lot to listen to, and a lot of ways to listen. In the last few minutes my heart was racing and I actually started to sweat. As for Alex, he sat back in his seat with arms folded behind his head. No one was required to speak and at no time did Helen state a purpose for what we were doing. I'd surmise now that if there was an underlying intention, it was to demonstrate that the cacophony in our sometimes-wondrous and often-scrambled brains was reflected nowhere better than in the greatest examples of the musical art form. We were being asked to find our rhythm.

Not long after that, Alex stopped coming to the games room for our sessions, so I stopped too, surprised at the hole that left in my day. And then there was the courtyard: a week or so of just me and Tod and it was losing its sheen.

I cut Tod off in the middle of his journey through the galactic clouds at the edge of the Milky Way (*yes, I could see them, sort of*), wriggled out of my sleeping bag, and went back to tap on Alex's door.

Again, he was dressed and seated at his computer, only this time he hadn't gone to the screensaver. He was watching a video. There was no sound, but when I went to speak his hand shot into the air to silence me and, without looking up, he gave me a simple directive: 'Don't come in here.'

It wasn't just the message that was different; the voice was not recognisable to me. I don't know how to explain that, only to say it was hollow, like an echo. Thinking *Fuck this, I've had enough,* I went to oblige by leaving, but reconsidered. *If I leave, I won't be back; he won't be back*—my thoughts went something like that, enough to flag to me how much I wanted him back and to make me turn around.

I wanted to see if he would look at me, so I edged nearer to the desk. His eyes were still glued to the video, the light flashing across his profile as it came into view. He made no effort to stop me. When I got close enough, I had to look twice at the footage to make out what it was. Low quality, black and white. A head...the head of a woman buried to her neck in sand, surrounded by men in flowing robes throwing rocks. It was a stoning. The woman wasn't conscious, her head rolling back and forward as it was pummeled by the rocks. She wore a dark headscarf so it was only when the head rolled back that you caught a glimpse of the mash of blood that was her face.

The video ended. Alex looked up. His eyes were not hollow like the voice, but filled with pain. He had the look of someone in acute physical pain, as though his own head was in an invisible vice and if I spoke even a single word, the screws would turn, making it tighter, more unbearable.

Some part of that constituted the trigger for what happened next. In hindsight, of course, I do not put it forward as a proportionate response. Survivors have a very singular perspective, that is what I can say. The mire in Alex's head was messing with everything, not the least of which was my first big win in this place (aside from the shower): our friendship. On a kill-or-be-killed level, the pain in his eyes and his apparent penchant for blood were a threat to me, and it was on that basis that I proceeded.

I know this ended up in the transcripts as confirmation of a previous diagnosis, but to me terms like 'explosive' and 'uncontrollable' miss a critical step, which is that there is a moment you re-enter, a familiarity in the surrounds—an acceptance that this is you and a rejection of the rest of it, the sham. You are back; all of you is back. Welcome back. *Welcome.* When you say it out loud it sounds textbook, trite, but here it is: it is a good place. There is a reason to return. We don't *snap* or *explode*; we choose. We develop intentions.

What I did was this: I took hold of Alex's chair and with all of my strength I threw him out of it onto the floor. When the chair landed between us, I kicked the backrest as hard as I could so that the whole thing lifted slightly, one of the legs catching the top of Alex's ear as it torpedoed over him. The odd part, and what I remember most clearly, was that when he looked up at me again, there was something different in his eyes. Not the pain, not horror or rage, but something gentler. What was in his eyes as he lay there, head on the floor with a ripped and bleeding ear, was gratitude. I know that is what I saw because it fed me, bolstered me.

The demon that Dr J had talked about? I didn't visualise it. I didn't really know how big or how old it was. But I knew what charged through its veins, after the violence and before the self-loathing. Righteousness. People say they wonder how men can justify the horrors they do. Not me. It is a switch that some of us have: flick it and, for a brief and shining moment, we are soldiers in a holy war.

I left Alex and went to Rachel's door. I stared at it for a moment before giving it a moderately hard kick and walked on. Next, I proceeded downstairs and looked through the glass at the fat kid talking to himself in the courtyard, and then made my way through the waiting room to the office of Dr J.

It felt bigger in the dark, cold. I walked to the computer at his desk, mainly because it was the single light source in the room. When I looked down at the screen I think I was half-expecting to see Alex's video replaying, but that is not what I saw. Instead, shining out of the dark, the screen was split into twelve frames, twelve camera feeds.

Video surveillance, but not of us and not of this place. I scanned from frame to frame and saw no one and nowhere I knew: a group of boys playing handball in a fluoro-lit corridor, others lying on a concrete floor—it was daytime there, a white sky—and then there were classrooms, more kids in a kitchen, and on they went, each image numbered.

I clicked on a white arrow on the right of the screen and another twelve appeared, and again, until I got to number twenty-six. In the last frame two boys sat at a table painting a picture and ignoring a third boy standing in the corner behind them. He wore a yellow beanie that was too big for his head and he looked somehow misplaced, unreal, almost like a projection. He appeared younger than the other boys, not more than twelve or thirteen, and after a few seconds of me watching, he looked from the floor directly up at the camera, as though our eyes had locked. I had a weird sense there was a moment of mutual recognition, compounded when he stepped forward, raised his middle finger and mouthed a remarkably intelligible *fuck you*. After that he said something to the boys at the table and they flicked blue paint at his face.

Boy in corner: I later found the face etched in my memory. At the time, I didn't pause to think any more about him, about any of them. Instead I stepped back into the centre of the room and I imagined my headphones were back on. I picked my track and followed the instruments every which way. And I did what I did; I did what I'd come to do.

Starting with the bookshelf and finishing with the computer that screened the boy in the beanie, I tore up the room.

When I was eleven, just before I finished primary school, we received an eviction notice due to damage to property. I was the one who opened the envelope. The public housing people always took a lot more interest in what was happening in our flat than the police did. That was in the equation for me early on, in terms of measuring impact: what gets a reaction—harm to property or harm to person? That was my takeaway.

Dr J had his own peculiar slant on the whole incident.

It got its share of pages in the transcripts. *In the early hours of May 9, a student broke into the office...* The inventory of damage: shelves of books destroyed, curtains shredded with scissors, the upholstery of two chairs slashed, water glasses smashed against the wall, a desk upturned, drawers turned out. A computer destroyed. They focused on the fact that even though they had CCTV footage of the perpetrator of the crime, the Doctor did not notify the police or the courts, and in fact appeared to have taken no action at all. From his perspective as my therapist, what were the Doctor's thoughts on what I had done?

> DR J: I had a number of thoughts, but if I were to pick one, in terms of my immediate reaction at the time, I would have to say that I found it helpful.
> COUNSEL: Helpful? As in, time for a spring clean?
> HIS HONOUR: If we could skip the sarcasm, Mr Byrne.
> DR J: I meant it was helpful in that Daniel was being up-front with me.
> COUNSEL: Up-front?
> DR J: Yes, clear in his message.
> COUNSEL: I see, and what was that message?
> DR J: This is me: that is what he was saying. Do we end it now, or do we continue?
> COUNSEL: I can think of other interpretations, along the lines of 'Take your school and your therapy and shove it'. How can you be sure that wasn't his message to you?

DR J: The landscape. He didn't touch it. There was a landscape photograph on the wall in between the paintings. The paintings were destroyed but the photograph was untouched...The reason I am sure is because I knew him. I knew what he was telling me. I couldn't have been surer had he taken me by the throat and shouted the words into my face.

The fallout was not what I had expected.

At breakfast it was business as usual. Tod made buckwheat crepes with blueberries, and he'd started a green juice thing; it tasted like vomit but I drank it. Alex had a bandage on his ear, clocked up by everyone as a day in the life of a teenage self-mutilator. We headed to class, passing Greg in the corridor. Greg was rarely seen in the corridor, but there he was, his eyes locking onto mine for just a second before I looked away. I didn't try to read it. I went to class, sat at my desk and waited.

Helen started as soon as Alex and I sat down—the rest of them already seated with their headsets, Rachel's the only seat empty. We were about to embark on Mass in B Minor but first we needed to get through a couple of Latin phrases and some basics on tempo and metrics. The sisters' know-it-all eyes glazed over, but the rest of us were working from a zero baseline, swiping through the screens, nodding our heads, taking in what we could. The last picture was an image of the man himself, Johann Sebastian. Helen talked about him for a bit, how he composed the mass over a lifetime until he started going blind.

That was where she was up to when Rachel appeared. She didn't sit down but stood feet apart at the front of the room next to Helen and cast her raging amber eyes over each of our faces, her lips arched into a snarl. She was incandescent: magnificent.

To start, the voice and the language were strangely contained. 'Who kicked my door?'

No one spoke. She gave us a full ten seconds. I looked to Helen K, expecting her to step in and override the interruption. She didn't.

'There is a dent,' Rachel went on, less contained, then totally unleashed: 'in my fucking door!' The crescendo came in the echo of the initial question: 'Who the F-U-C-K. Kicked. My. Door?' The power of it wasn't in the volume, it was in the sharpness of the consonants and the length of the pauses. The stringing out of each of the six words, so the rest of us were leaning forward in anticipation by the time she got to the end of it.

When she did, Helen K gave it a few moments and then, finally, stepped in. 'Good morning, Rachel.'

Rachel didn't respond; it was like she didn't even hear it. My sense was that she'd be suspecting it was a sister, but her eyes glanced over both of them and settled on my face, the same eyes that had stared straight through me in her room, now fixed on mine, a tractor beam of truth.

I stood up.

She stepped forward. Between us there was just a few inches, and a heat like I had never felt before. Helen—bravely I thought—put a hand on Rachel's shoulder. 'Can I suggest you two take this to the courtyard?'

And out Rachel spun in a reverse storm, me in train, my heart liquefying, pouring out through my ears and dribbling down the side of my head...As if I could have loved her any more.

The surrounds of the courtyard were on my side, her anger immediately diluted in the translucence of the amber autumn leaves, their dappled shadows on the mossy concrete, the soft chorus of bugs and birds. She sat down on the bench between the trees. When I sat next to her, she swung her legs over so that we were facing opposite directions. I stole a glance at her profile, and saw there was a tear on her cheek, a perfect single teardrop like it had been drawn onto the skin.

'Oh fuck, don't cry. I'm sorry...'

'I am not crying you fuck-knuckle,' she said, flicking the tear away. She did call me a fuck-knuckle. I am not making that up. 'Stop staring at me...Why do you stare at me all the time?'

There was my opening. I wanted to tell her the truth and I wanted her to tell me about the wax and the sun and where the fire came from and why the father liked him, *liked who*? I wanted to be her cure, and I wanted her to be mine. That is why I kicked her door. Instead, I was staring at the formwork of the building and doing my numbers. (Between storeys there were 3 rows divided into sections, each with a varying number of plugged holes, like domino pieces but without obvious pattern: 4, 7, 9, 3...)

'I don't,' I eventually said. And when she turned to face me, and cocked her head: 'Okay, I do. But I...'

Her eyes softened. 'It's a bit psycho, that's all. You're dealing with real people here. Do you even get that?'

The question stopped me. There was a familiarity in it, a knowledge of me she didn't have; only somehow she did, and somehow I knew that already.

'Yep, sure,' I said, 'yeah, sorry. I'll stop.' Or at least I meant to say something to that effect; I'm not sure if it came out as actual words. The fact she was still there beside me had triggered an acute stress response that seemed to momentarily suction the saliva to the back of my throat and paralyse the base of my tongue. Unable to keep looking at her, I could see in the corner of my eye that she was nodding. Overwhelmed by the kindness of that simple move-ment, I felt I owed her the truth, or at least a subsection of it.

I regathered. 'I sat outside your door one night when I couldn't sleep, and I heard you talking...'

She stiffened, said nothing. When I turned to her she had screwed up her eyes; now she dropped her face into both hands. After a minute or so she raised it up again. 'Why did you kick my door?'

'Dunno. It was there.' That is what I came up with. It made her laugh, more than was probably warranted but I laughed too and it felt like the right response. I was back staring at the formwork. Getting the holes to a total and section average gave me a place to look other than her face, and made me brave enough to get to the next bit.

'We come out here at night. They give us sleeping bags,' I said. 'I might get kicked out of here,' (it was about fifty-fifty, I thought) 'but if I don't, if I stay, one night you could come out too.'

You could come out too. There, I'd done it; I'd asked her.

That was when I noticed Greg standing in the corridor, again, watching me. I thought that meant curtains: he was taking me to pack my bag. Suddenly it felt like the final, precious minutes, so I launched ahead.

'I kicked your door because I want to know what happened to you.'

What I saw in her eyes in that moment was first a flash of terror and then something hard-shelled and slow-moving. I felt it, our connected inner demon. Or so I thought.

'You have your own shit, Daniel,' she said. 'You keep yours; I'll keep mine.'

I took it as a no. But even in that, I misread her.

Dr J wasn't wrong in what he told the inquiry, but nor was it the whole story. In tearing up his office I was laying down the gauntlet, no question, but there was despair in it, too. That I had been duped into thinking a connection could count for something, that this was a place that could hold us, that we could be transported by a night sky: Alex's face as he watched that scene in the dark had made a mockery of all that. The act of vandalism was my ejector-seat button, knowing he could either watch me hurtle out of the cockpit or override the controls: take me as I was. I expected that I'd get at least an indication over the next few days, but there was nothing. It wasn't until the time of my weekly appointment that Greg came into class and handed me a note. He didn't make much of an effort to disguise his disdain for me these days. The skulking in the corridors had continued, every morning between the kitchen and class. Tod never passed him without a greeting.

'Looking good, Greg,' 'You take it easy, Greg,' 'Top of the morning to you, Greg.' To which Greg gave a move-on head-flick. I wasn't that bothered. I never figured Greg to matter much.

The note said:

Notice of Rescheduling/Cancellation
On behalf of: Dr J
Re: today's session.
Reason: minor repair works in progress.

On the next outing, each of us wandered at our own pace into the bush. I didn't want to be at the waterhole so I walked past it, further up the creek to a part where I'd never been. I could see the fence where the neighbouring property started. It was a way off, on the other side of a rough paddock full of dips and boulders, the ground a blanket of woody weeds and thistles. I thought I saw the goat on the other side of a blackberry bush so I continued on, the swards of thistles piercing through my socks. When I reached the bush the goat wasn't there, but I heard a dog barking. I could see a shed on the property now, still in the distance, and then I saw the dog, and all of a sudden I became aware of all the space around me and I felt small like the dog in the distance but as light as air. The ground was uneven but it didn't seem to matter how I walked; I didn't stumble or trip. As I neared the fence I could see a quad bike at the shed door and, sitting on the bike, a small boy with a helmet that looked way too big compared with his body. I heard the bike start and watched him ride away, the dog chasing the bike. There were trees behind the shed so I couldn't see where they went—a house somewhere, I guessed, or to feed the goats.

As the thistles began to dig into my ankles I thought of Mary and her messages, and I felt in my pocket for the Doctor's note, the paper wearing thin in my fingers, the reason for our cancelled meeting: *minor repair works in progress*. The words imprinted the way some words do, so that they come back later at unexpected moments. (In this case many years later, after my first and worst marital screw-up: I ventured into therapy in search of an explanation for my unexplained behaviour and some reassuring words about rock-bottom and redemption. When nothing hit the mark and I cancelled all further appointments, the only real salve I came up with was that phrase: *minor repair works in progress*.)

There was the dent in his wall and his torn curtains—and then there was me, DG, school student, peddler of prescribed and illicit substances. Maybe he just meant the curtains were being replaced, but that isn't how I read it. *Minor repairs*. The Doctor was a man playing a strange game, I don't argue that, but still: there was his ability to pull us back when we tottered on the brink, to intuit what each of us needed to hear, even if just a few words.

Our session, when it finally came, was a bit all over the place.

The office smelled of fresh paint; the furniture had been repaired or replaced, the computer upgraded. I was braced for him to lay into me, ready to counterattack with a demand for answers on the twenty-six videos and whatever the fuck was going on with the boy in the yellow beanie, but there was no reference to my solo visit. He said there was something he'd missed on my school records about my being absent from my last exams. 'For medical reasons.'

I nodded. 'My hand.'

Four months before coming to the School, I punched a wall and fractured the fourth metacarpus in my right hand. The incident didn't happen at school, I told him; it was on my record only because I couldn't sit the tests.

'You were at home?'

'Yep.'

'Which wall?'

'Bathroom.'

It was a repeat break. A few months earlier, same wall, same bone. I didn't tell him that, and he didn't press for details. Instead he asked me about my classes and the outing. He wasn't troubled that I'd walked beyond the waterhole and was pleased with the reports from PW about our tutorials.

'Do you know what he told me last week? He told me that his university students would struggle with concepts that you are picking up in a single class.'

He could see my surprise and seemed to be pondering that when he spoke again: 'I wish we could show you.'

'Show me what?'

He smiled. 'Make you understand.'

Quite suddenly then he got up out of his seat and walked over to the undamaged photograph clinging to the otherwise empty wall. He pointed at the signature in the bottom left-hand corner of the print.

'Let me tell you something about him, this photographer,' he said. 'He was a very successful and famous man. As a child, he had no time for lessons or for schoolyard games. His only interest was nature.' He stared for a while at the photograph, as did I, the strange bracken in the water like a dark portal to what lay beneath the quiet surface. 'Do you know what his teachers said about him? They said he was hyperactive, that he couldn't pay attention. He was expelled from seven schools. And then one day his father gave him a camera, and that was that. The pursuit of beauty, the love of stones and water. And some of the greatest photographs ever taken...' His voice trickled off as he turned back to me and said he thought that was enough for today.

At the door I stopped. It felt like the right time to raise something that would fall outside the bounds of a normal session, outside the terms of our contract. I had just demolished his office without any apparent repercussion. I felt I was on safe ground.

'You need to help Alex,' I said.

'I hope I *am* helping Alex.'

'Well, you're not. He's worse.'

'He is suffering, it is clear.'

'There must be some kind of medication...'

'Really? What would you advise?'

He was making light of it. I tried to remain calm. To demonstrate the seriousness, I told him about the video I'd found Alex watching, sitting in the dark of his room. He looked at me and poured himself more water.

'Alex is saddened by the state of things,' he said.

It was just a tiny opening but it seemed to me a significant one, forming a precedent to talk about the other students. He wasn't meant to; we weren't meant to—even then I knew that—and for that reason it felt to me like a glittering prize.

'He is saddened by the state of things,' he repeated. 'Others turn away, or just don't look. He looks. It isn't an illness, Daniel. There are no pills for it.'

I thought about what he was saying, the sense in it, and then the nonsense. 'So you just do nothing?'

Again, he hesitated. 'Why don't you ask him?' he eventually said. 'You ask him what we are doing—what *he* is doing—and if he tells you, come back then and we'll talk about what help he needs.'

I didn't see Alex again that day. He wasn't at dinner or in the court-yard for the midnight session. I was late, and when I crawled into my sleeping bag Tod's 'hi' was more a sigh of relief than a spoken word. He didn't ask if I wanted to know what he'd eaten today. Instead, in a more tentative voice he said he'd been reading about black holes.

'There's millions of them and some are a billion times bigger than the sun,' he said, 'but you can't see them.'

And that was all, the immensity of his effort to contain further commentary weighing in the air between us with the smell of his sweat and the screeching of distant bats. Later he told me he'd been doing work on his lunar breath—old air out, released, whatever—but the silence was accepted. I was a solo viewer, eyes pinned open to form a screen, a frame for a sky full of everything I could not see.

It took just a few seconds for the outer rim to blur and send my jumbled mind flicking between images—*As between the School and DG:* from the back seat of the van all the way to the building at the top of the driveway, the curved glass and the pear trees and the shower and the first haze of steam; Tod on his good egg days and his bad egg days, Helen K and her freckled hollow...the boy with the bulbous growth, and the shape-changing man...*If he suffered as much as he did, should he die? Should Sado have been let to live?* All the clues made up of cosmic dust: Rachel (*hallelujah*) in the waterhole—the halo of hair, and the rest of her…Alex and his bird-covered chest—out on his limb and gorging on his own bacteria, PW bouncing a handball, the Doctor leaning in to tell me he was wrong, the dog and the boy in the distance. And right now, whatever the scenes playing out upstairs in the bedrooms of Alex and Rachel, a corpse in the stony earth, wax melting in the fire of the sun, his gratitude, her blazing eyes and her beautiful rage.

For a boy whose survival had been dependent on his separateness, after a period of just twelve weeks I was now in their grip, treading the same biosphere, the same battleground. Coded into my brain was a different set of messages and key responses. *There is a regularity of occurrence that forms our primordial perceptions*; as I stared up I was suddenly conscious that the regularity had been disrupted, my perceptions altered. Alex and Rachel had each in their own way entered my inner orbit and yet remained profoundly out of reach. And even further still, there at the edge of the dimmest region, lay a speck of antimatter—a third character at the edge of the stage, the opposite of everything, wearing a mask with eyes like mine, like a goat…

I wish we could show you, the Doctor had said.

I wish you could too.

And then they did.

Introduction to Computational Neurobiology

It sounded simple when the Doctor said it: *You ask him what we are doing.*

Over the next few days I started framing the question, but every time I got near Alex, it jumbled with a bunch of reasons not to ask. His eyes were gooey, and not just in a sad way. We thought it was conjunctivitis but turned out it was an infected tear duct. He tried to clean it up but at breakfast there was still a pearly film over the bottom half of his pupil and yellow gunk caked in his eyelashes. Rachel said it was disgusting and could be contagious and he should go back to his room. For me, it just heightened his weakness rating, and my aversion to hard questions in case they made him cry.

And: who was I to ask?

And: maybe I didn't want to know.

And (of course): I got distracted by other things.

When I came in for my next lesson, PW was sitting straight-backed at one of the desks. In spite of his colourless demeanour, he affected a series of well-worn retro tie-dye T-shirts featuring designs and decals ranging from iconic to kitsch—Michael Jackson, Darth Vader, Malibu sunsets, an acid house smiley face that I thought was a Pac-Man. For a minute, in the beginning, I thought he was gay, but he didn't feel gay, and I didn't dwell on it. Today it was a V-neck Snoopy in shades of purple and fluoro blue. Wearing a headset plugged into my tablet, he continued to tap and swipe as I sat down next to him, and then cleared the screen and removed the headset.

'Something different today,' he said. 'You ever meditate?'

Do I look like someone who meditates?

He saw my lip curl but was undeterred, tilting his head and staring at me too long like he was processing a new data entry. I knew what the others meant about PW, but I saw something like the way a dog stares when it wants to be part of the human race. 'Or not,' he said, 'not yet...I'll lead in.'

I shrugged.

'Let's make the links.'

Whatever.

'A couple of weeks ago we were talking about magnetism and electrical currents, and we got on to the electromagnetic activity in the brain. You remember that?'

'Sure.'

He did the recap thing at the beginning of every lesson, reeled off a set of facts and paused when he wanted me to fill in the word:

'So, the human brain contains about a billion...'

'Neurons.'

'And the neurons are electrically charged by...'

'Ions.'

Sometimes he threw in an oddball like: 'Last Monday I was wearing a T-shirt with a picture of...' 'Wonder Woman.' I had a jackpot memory, he said (deadpan; the same way he'd break the news if I had an inoperable tumour).

'What it means for us is that we can record activity, neural oscillations, better known as...'

'Brainwaves,' I interjected. He hadn't even told me that.

'That's right...Through a technique called EEG. Heard of it?'

'Yeah, I think so.'

His tone changed at that point. He paused, weighing up what should come next, then when he spoke it was tentative, like he was trying to sell me something without being exactly sure of the product. 'It is limited, what we can do. We can observe different levels of activity, create cluster maps; but we need to know the source. We have only really just started to do that, develop the algorithms. We've come a fair way with sleep stages...' He tilted his head again, gauging my reaction. 'You with me?'

I nodded. 'Sort of.'

He nodded back. 'You can imagine the complexity,' he said. 'The last algorithm to determine the signal location of a brain-wave was half a million lines long—' He broke off into some of the mathematical concepts for a while, then stopped himself mid-sentence and picked up the headset. 'May I?'

I assumed he was going to put it on, but instead he reached over to me (he had a lemony smell) and placed them on my head, pressing gently on the forehead and behind my ears. Nothing went inside my ears; there was just the headband.

'Where are the earpieces?'

'You don't need them.'

'So how will I listen?'

'You're not listening. Watch.' He plugged it into the laptop. And then tentative again: 'Its function's not audio. It's biofeedback.'

He was observing me to see if I understood, as he would have if he'd been explaining trigonometry. When my face remained blank he turned his attention back to the computer, pushed a few keys. After a minute or two he said, 'Not quite,' and then: 'Yes, there you are!' It was language I'd heard before, from Helen. *Hold off, not quite there yet, okay, there you are...*

On the black screen there appeared a series of animated data visualisations. The first was a bar graph, separated into different bands of fluoro colours labelled theta, alpha, beta, delta and gamma, each bar in constant flux. He pointed his marker to it, and he tapped his hands on the desk as though mimicking a drum roll.

'Meet your brainwaves.'

When I say drum roll I mean just tap-tap-tap. This was all very calm and careful and normal. If they were after someone to deliver this new information without causing alarm, PW was their guy.

I was only now starting to twig. Stage one in the penny dropping: there *you* are. The headset—*this is me, my brain*—the different bands rising and falling, and the larger graph—a circular shape with ten axis points representing the same bands, from high to low, the chart constantly morphing in colour and shape.

This thing on my head is monitoring my brainwaves.

'It measures the voltage intensity and fluctuations. The software is breaking down the millions of neural signals according to their cycles per second.'

He gave me a minute to take it in, looking relieved when eventually I came up with a question. 'So what does it mean?'

'They represent the levels of activity, the different frequencies. Twenty words or less: beta has the fastest frequency, delta is your deep sleep; alpha and theta are somewhere in between.'

'They're all going at the same time.'

'That's right. There are several patterns interacting. The predominance of one pretty much determines your state of mind.'

It took a while, and even then there wasn't a lot to my response: 'Out of control…' I said.

He took it literally. 'Not really.' And he dived into an explanation of how different areas of the brain emit different signals. 'That's where the algorithms come in, trying to locate the source. Once we know that, we can find ways to better interpret the meaning. There are certain structures, in the subcortical region—' He pulled up the brain map and circled a section with his finger. 'There are well-known patterns we can detect here. But, like I said, it is limited, what we understand about the neural sources. We know beta is left hemisphere and theta is right, but it is as broad as that.' He shrugged and smiled. 'There are people working on it.'

By now his voice had faded into a background noise. I didn't really understand what any of it meant, but already I was somewhere else, mesmerised by the dancing rainbow on the screen.

PW had to tap my arm to snap me out of it. 'So try doing something,' he said. 'See what happens.'

'Like what?'

Returning to his opening play: 'Meditating is a good one.'

I thought about it for a moment. 'I don't know how to do that. Can we do something else?'

'Sure. Focus on something, an object…' He put his water bottle in front of the computer.

'You want me to think about the bottle?'

He shrugged. I didn't get the sense he had any real plan. 'As best you can.'

I stared at the bottle trying to keep one eye on the screen. On the bar graph my beta shot up and the circular shape pulled to one side and flatlined.

'Is that bad?'

'No, it means you're focused.'

'So that's good? That's what you wanted me to do.'

'Well, you are hi-beta.'

'So that's...not good.'

'It indicates a state of agitation. If it is persistent, it isn't good. It is a stress response. A stress hormone is flooding your brain.'

'So that's bad.'

He shrugged. 'It is notable, that thinking about a water bottle brought it on. The theory of brain plasticity is that there are things they can do, to tune, reset....' He saw me stiffen. The shape blew out into a sort of starfish. 'That's not what this is about. This is about you being able to observe it and get a better understanding. That is all.'

To prove it he moved back to the maths. 'Let's talk about the algorithm. If we go back to the ionic currents,' he minimised the screen and turned to the brain map on the whiteboard, 'here, in the frontal lobe...'

And there was the shift: *just like that*, I thought, *from lab rat back to student*. I started taking off the headset. He stopped me.

'You can leave them on, if that's okay.'

I obliged, wearing my headset as we worked on the whiteboard. It was only then that the realisation came. Stage two, the bigger picture, our story here at the School: we weren't watching my brainwaves anymore, but this thing was still on my head and someone else was watching, or recording. Someone sitting at a different interface, in a different room. I thought back to the day I first put the headset on. *Noise-blocking, surround sound,* Tod had whispered. And then just the pretty noises that switched off once the images started. Later there were the video games and the music, so it seemed to come with a legitimate purpose. But that was not the purpose, not the music or the games. *The function isn't audio. It is biofeedback.* And I was the *bio;* we all were. We were dutifully putting on our hi-tech headsets, because what teenager wouldn't, and—

I started to put it into words. 'Whenever we wore them, whenever we wear them…' He waited for me to finish my thought, a glimmer in his eyes urging me on. (I am not really sure why, but through all this, there was never a minute I didn't feel that that PW was on my side.) 'Whenever we wear them,' I repeated, as it sank in, 'we are being tracked.'

He nodded. 'OMR,' he said. 'Observe, monitor, record.'

Thinking on this now, I will generalise and say that adolescents have very particular concerns with privacy: lay a finger on their phone and they'll rip your head off; covertly track the inner machinations of their mind, and they're cool with it. In questioning PW as the plot revealed itself (or as he revealed it to me), the feeling was more excitement than anger—excitement that I was the one uncovering a hidden truth. We all knew there was one; but I was getting the scoop. And it fitted with my narrative, or at least I could work it in: *handpicked youth, handpicked brains*…I accepted it all without prodding for purpose—that wasn't my priority. This was: 'Are you showing the others?'

'No.'

And the big question: 'Why me?'

He took a while on this one. 'He asked me to.'

I don't have to tell you how good this made me feel. Me.

Handpicked out of the handpicked. My next question was more just to test the boundaries. 'What if I tell them?'

'You mean what would happen to you?' He looked away; the sense I got at this point was that this was very much someone else's game and someone else's rules. 'You'd have to look at your contract.'

And of course, there lay the answer. I couldn't discuss my treatment: as between the School and DG, and as such it must remain. I'd had my warning, so it would mean I was out, once and for all. I had a flash of home, and then I looked around the room, envisioned beyond the door and through the curved corridors: all this for my silence. And what I thought was, open and shut case. Fair trade.

I wish we could show you.

For the weeks that followed I met with PW and put on my headset and watched as the software broke down the millions of neural signals according to their cycles per second. He took me through the basic science of wave propagation and psycho-acoustics and I got to know my patterns—when I blinked, when I focused on a thought or tried to clear my mind of them, and finally I agreed to give it a go: to meditate myself out of hi-beta. PW knew more than he'd let on, guiding me with chakra points 'like mental stepping stones'.

'Chakra points. You buy that shit?'

He shrugged. 'I think it's useful for things like this. You see that?' he said, pointing to the alpha jumping up and down. 'That is spontaneous wandering.'

'That's bad...'

'No, it is a default activity. It is good. It processes your experience. You need to do that.'

152

My issue was when I had too much beta. I went beyond hi-beta, PW said, into hyper-beta (the resting state of paranoid schizophrenics, I later learned).

'You should see what happened when you got to the end of Miles Davis.' The others went into low alpha, but me, I surged into hyper-beta. He almost smiled then. 'It's like you were wrestling every bar of it to the ground.' (I remembered finding the last part a struggle.)

That brought me to the question: 'So...when I lose it? I mean like *lose* it...'

He nodded. 'Any kind of explosive behaviour, sure, we'd see a beta spike. Any kind of over-arousal, hyper-alertness...But remember we see the same kind of spike with complex thinking. It isn't all negative. If we could track the brains of the dead geniuses we'd see a trail of hi-beta. Isaac Newton, massive rage issues.'

'Kurt Cobain,' I added.

He nodded. 'Kurt too.'

'What about this here?' I asked. It was the last of the band frequencies, a lime green that barely registered.

'Gamma.'

He explained the deal with gamma: it is so high we can barely detect it and we don't know what part of the brain it is from or how it's generated. Some even question its existence. 'It is a bit of a Mecca of brainwaves.'

I had no ambitions of Mecca. I was just happy to have my own label. I was a beta-boy. That gave me plenty to focus on, playing through the events of the last few weeks and pinpointing my beta bursts—the obvious ones: in the corridor with Greg, my midnight session in the Doctor's office. But others too. Bush-bashing on the first field trip, sitting outside Rachel's door, moving wooden animals around an imaginary stage, and yeah, Miles Davis...

All those times the heart started beating faster and I could feel it moving, gravitating, some kind of energy, good or bad, good *and* bad...the buzz in the brain, the electric charge. Every adrenaline rush, every shower session, the beginning of a berserko: hi-beta, hyper-beta—whichever way, I had too much. In hindsight, of course, it raises more questions than it answers. But give me a sixteen-year-old who delves deeper into their motivations than the pattern of their brainwaves and I'll eat my laptop.

The short of it was there was a profound and liberating simplicity to it. Beta was the reason I did what I did—beta was the reason I was me.

For the next few weeks, a load was lifted. That was my initial takeaway from the meet and greet with my brainwaves: I was off the hook. It was hands down the best tick-a-box diagnosis I'd ever had, because this one I had seen for myself. There was the odd day when I didn't have enough of it, when I dipped into the mental fog (Ritalin is all about the beta boost). But whichever direction I moved—morphing according to voltage—I noted it and brought it back to my sessions with PW.

I jumped in too deep. When I should have been in the now of alpha, I was assessing oscillations. It was all *I am experiencing the release of neurotransmitters. I am in the drop zone.* Never just *I am.*

And then it started slipping out in conversation.

In the courtyard: 'Way too much talk, Tod—hi-beta...'

'What the fuck?'

I didn't realise I'd said it. 'Nothing.'

My new world started leaking through into my old one. Even without the headset, I started visualising the activity, estimating the amplitude. Like the separation between church and state, there is a sound structural reason to let the executive centre do its thing. Observe, record, interpret and decode, all that, but do it at a distance. The self-monitoring started to swallow me up. When I put the headset on, it was like I could hear it, the infrasound.

Looking back on it now, I see it was an early warning sign of what happens when a guy like me messes with different levels of consciousness. The end of my first year of university, in a cannabis-induced rut, I met a woman called Fiona who suggested that I keep a notebook by my bed and write down my dreams every morning. Because I very much wanted to get into Fiona's pants, I dutifully did that, my regular reports back to her providing a justification for ongoing contact. Day by day I remembered my dreams with increasing clarity, able to scribe page after page of stuff and nonsense from the garbage pit of my subconscious. Then a strange thing happened. The dreams started to appear throughout the day—like visions, mundane and outlandish—as though a portal had been opened and a black, viscous substance was seeping through into my only sunlit place. In a perplexing blurring, I began to question whether memories were dreams or dreams were memories, until day seven when I started babbling like a garbled mess and Fiona stopped taking my calls. I never even copped a feel. (I probably don't need to paint a picture of my psychedelic bender with a bucket of magic mushrooms in the summer of that same year.)

Anyhow, it was something akin to what happened with me and my brainwaves. A portal leakage. I got too close. Staring up at the night sky I felt myself putting beta to bed, slipping into the hypnagogic drumbeat of delta, queasy on the crest of a slow-motion undulation...My chakra points vaporised in the border zone, leaving just the echo of a mantra:

I am an ocean...I am an ocean...I am an ocean.

Out of the corner of my eye I could see Tod staring. I'd done it again.

He reached over to pat my hand. 'Sure, why not?' Even on the question of sanity, he was prepared to give me the benefit of the doubt. 'I am an ocean too.'

Suffice to say, by the end of a six-week intensive with my brainwaves—in spite of the answers they offered—I was feeling a bit suffocated. They were the invisible new friend sitting on my shoulder; or, in this case, a group of semi-clad back-up singers lounging against the cushion of my meninges. Like any relationship, things had been great in the beginning, fresh and new, but it turned out there was no off button. First with Tod, then with Alex and even Rachel, for a couple of weeks I was just watching people's lips move while the nag in my brain jumped up and down: 'Look at me, look at me...' I even gave up a shower session to sit cross-legged on my mat and try to find a way to get past my root chakra, the pelvic plexus.

I needed space. PW picked up on it. We stopped looking at the charts and graphs, and moved away from anything to do with oscillations and waves.

'I think we need to put it in perspective.'

It was a sound strategy: pick a subject to show me and my brainwaves up for what we really amounted to: an infinitesimal speck in the universe. Physical cosmology. He launched straight into it, pulling up an image of the farthest galaxies, each dot of light an individual galaxy some ten billion years old. He grounded us down in particle physics and the Big Bang and the mystery of dark energy and we went gangbusters, safely fumbling from the basic ratios through to equations denoting the cosmological constant and the expansion of the universe...It wasn't a great leap to get back to where we started (from the vibrations in the fabric of space-time to my own mind-body vibrations) but it was the circuit-breaker I needed. Me and my brainwaves back on level ground.

There was just one thing that kept niggling, whenever I put the headphones on: the fact that someone, somewhere, was watching, recording, making judgment.

For that I came up with my own solution.

Up until this point, Dr J and I had largely stepped around the subject of my brainwaves. When I brought it up after PW's big reveal, he had been interested in my reaction and said we could incorporate it into our 'work'. When I then resisted coming back to the 'work', i.e. the task of recreating my fucked-up childhood on the imaginary stage, he asked me to consider my reaction: 'Imagine the headset is on. What would the graph tell you?'

'You watch it?' I asked. 'The graph?'

He shook his head. 'I get reports.'

He talked about my 'range', and my 'little peaks of theta'. During video games there was a distinct levelling out in fluctuations and when I listened to the Beach Boys I sat on the alpha-delta cusp for eleven seconds. But he didn't want to dwell on my brainwaves. He didn't want us to go too far 'off course'. The course for him was still the same. We were up to Brian.

He held firm.

'What happened, what he did...I want to bring it a bit closer to the surface.'

I thought of the old western movies, a knife plunged into the gut of a staggering cowboy, and I remembered watching them and thinking—*just pull it out*. But you can't. You can't just pull it out, because it might well kill you. And I wondered now if it was worth the risk, and I felt that longing that I felt all my life: you would do it if someone could just tell you it will be all right.

I was trying to read that into his words when he suggested a way forward. 'Let's come at it another way: you be Mary.'

157

More out of exhaustion than anything I sat back down. I hadn't been Mary before. I let him go. He asked her the same questions and I gave him answers or I just thought them to myself:

Horoscopes. David Attenborough. Madonna. Yum cha.

Just meet him, baby. He's different. He was; Brian was different. He looked better, sounded better. He bought her a necklace and took us to laser skirmish. He didn't use; he didn't even drink. His dad had overdosed in prison. He told the story and Mary cried. *That poor little guy...*He started staying over that night, then he brought his things. I asked him where he lived and he said he was between places. There was a bend in his smile but she didn't see it. She wanted to believe; so did I. It didn't start with a push or a cut and there was never any sorry or any crawling back. He made her crawl. And I watched on. He lived with us for eleven days.

And the third question. The day he left. 'You're in the flat... Where is he? How do you feel about him now?'

'That's two questions,' I said. 'He's in the kitchen.' And we left it at that.

It was my turn.

'The brainwaves: why did you tell me?' Everything seemed suddenly to hinge on it. My place, my existence here, my survival... *Why me?*

'You look concerned,' he said gently. 'Don't be. Trial and test, that's all.' Then came a broad smile. 'Here's something: your measurements. I have an explanation for that appetite of yours. In just over two months you have grown 3.6 centimetres.'

He could see he had my interest, and he could see that I was pleased. But it wasn't just measurements I needed.

'I want a report,' I said. 'Like you get. I don't want to watch the graphs anymore. But I want the report. I want to see what you all see.' When he hesitated, I pointed to the contract on the table.

'It's in there: *School to provide student with copies of written records and reports…*'

He nodded, impressed. 'So it is. Fair request.'

We sat for a bit, mulling over where we had landed.

Finally: 'I'd like to keep this up,' he said. 'Any other questions you have…Turn this more into an open book, so to speak—a sort of conversation among equals. How does that sound, Daniel?'

It sounded fine. And I had a question ready.

'You told me you were wrong—when I asked why you're here. What were you wrong about?'

The answer was that he thought he could find a cure for something, but it was not a cure at all.

'Was it a drug?'

'It was a new way to name things, a new way to use old drugs.'

I shrugged. 'So now you find the right way.' I could tell there was more to it, but there was another question I wanted to ask. 'You say I can ask anything?' I said.

He smiled. 'Within reason.'

The boy is untied and taken to a room. A man in a suit enters. He asks him to think about the purpose of his existence, and offers him just one wish. It takes the boy only six seconds to decide what it will be.

It wasn't just a wish. It was an acceptance of his offer. Basic bargain theory, quid pro quo…

'I want to know what happened to Rachel.'

Social Demography and Global Citizenship

At this point everything opened up in a way that had me searching for an underlying logic, some kind of universal algorithm around human connectivity, the domino effect of open doors.

While around us the evergreen bushland was unchanging, in the courtyard the pear trees were bare, leaving a last layer of crimson red leaves scattered on the pavers. In the morning when it was quiet the currawongs flew down to forage in the leaf litter and the benches got splattered in bird shit.

As for Rachel, my focus had been on making good on my undertaking to stop staring and to mind my own crap. My recent plunge into the world of brainwaves had made that a lot easier than I'd anticipated. Whenever she appeared in class or in the kitchen, even at the waterhole, I managed to hold my gaze steady and estimate the impact of her presence on my oscillations. The brain varied day to day; the heart was constant. All that was left was to wait, as I did each night, for her to take up my invitation and come to the courtyard.

Greg hand-delivered the first of my weekly reports.

'As per your request,' he said in a tone I disliked.

I thanked him (*fuck you*), closed the door and sat down on my bed with the orange envelope addressed to me, c/o the School. The document inside had a cover sheet with my name and date and a small image like a company logo: the bottom half of three blue capsules sprouting green leaves. The second page was a series of sketched headshots—aerial view—colour-coded and set out in table form, five by five, with horizontal and vertical descriptions cryptic enough for me to scan them and turn over into the explanatory text. In just over three pages, it addressed two things: my areas of high-level under-arousal, and my areas of high-level over-arousal. The fact that the lingo sounded more sexual than neural made me suspicious. Without reading on, I jumped up and performed my umpteenth search for hidden cameras in the area of the shower recess.

When I resumed my reading, my concerns were dispelled. This was strictly about my brain—and, more particularly, what personality traits my brainwaves were producing, or not producing. Nothing came as a surprise: in the domains of fogginess (their word), easily hurt feelings and low self-esteem, I barely rated; at the other end, I was pretty much off the scale in impatience, agitation, and holding of resentments (again, their term; I liked that one). By the final paragraph it was starting to read to me like one of Mary's weekly horoscopes. And there was definitely an unfair focus on the surplus and deficits—too much, too little—but I wasn't bothered, and Greg could go to hell. It was mine, my brain dysfunction, in my hands. I wouldn't have let go of it for the world.

Outside of the report there was more. My growth spurt continued (another 4 mm over two weeks), and Rachel actively sought out my help with a calculus question after PW refused her any. ('He is a complete cock,' she said, loud and powerfully alliterated.) Tod had started making gnocchi with burnt butter and crispy sage—I'd never eaten anything like it, nor do I think I have since. And on top of that, Alex was making signs of re-entering the biosphere. He still spent most of his spare time in his lesson room with the door closed, but in class or in the kitchen he was a living, breathing presence again (as against the rotting amoeba cluster he had become). And most importantly, he returned to the midnight sessions. One night he just showed up, commented on the almost-full moon and crawled into his sleeping bag.

'You know, Alex,' Tod said after only a few seconds of silence. 'You can talk to us about things you might think we don't want to hear.'

'Thanks Tod,' he replied. 'That is good to know.'

In an effort to avoid boring anyone, Tod stuck to questions. His persistence eventually bore fruit, Alex telling us stories about his father and their hinterland house.

'He reckoned we should live at one with nature,' he said. 'We had this big old macadamia tree outside the kitchen. It was too close to the house and the roots messed with the plumbing but Dad wouldn't touch it, said it'd been there longer than we had…And he had a thing with birds. He filled the balcony with grevilleas and then left the doors open so the birds could come right inside. We got a nest of blue wrens in a wall vent once. Even when it brought rats, Dad said they had a right to be there.'

162

Tod sought clarification. 'You mean the birds?'

'Birds, rats…whatever. I guess it sounds pretty weird.'

As I'd been listening I couldn't help but compare it to the flats. 'Sounds exceptionally cool to me,' I said.

'You're right, Dan,' Alex replied. 'It was. *He* was.'

A couple of weeks after his comeback, Alex flagged me in the corridor and said he was behind on his video game hours. I was too. Off we went like a pair of old chums, settling in for a session of Dark Souls Rising. It was Alex's favourite. You are a bank teller in a shopping mall that is infested with chainsaw-wielding zombie killers. Pretty soon the place is plastered with decapitated heads and nude body parts. Alex was right: the graphics were 'out of the park', the howls of the injured so real you wanted to go back and put the poor bastards out of their misery.

Sitting back in defeat, the blood-smattered screens seemed an obvious segue into the as-yet-untouched subject of the time I busted him on blood porn. But where to start?

'That night on the computer, the video,' I said. 'What the hell's that all about?'

During the silence that followed our eyes remained fixed on our scores. I sensed that he went to speak a couple of times, then finally: 'You think I'm fucked up.'

'I guess it depends on why you watch it. Like, yeah—if you're getting off on it, I think it's fucked up.'

He laughed, then stood up. 'It might be better if I just show you.'

My first thought was that he had a little library of videos and he was planning to share, but when I started to decline he told me to get up and I dutifully pushed myself out of my beanbag and followed him. We walked around the low-lit corridor, the courtyard still dipped in the orange glow of twilight. When we stopped at the door to his lesson room, he turned around and bit his bottom lip. I felt a nervous, almost erotic excitement. His head cocked at an awkward angle, his pupils just a pinprick in his blood-rimmed eyes.

'I'm not sure if this is a good idea, showing you this...I mean, like you might just think I'm fucking crazy.'

He was looking at me for an assurance, and I was drawing a blank. I wasn't sure it was a good idea either. But when he started stepping back I realised I wanted very much for him to open the door. The words of Dr J came into my head: *You ask him what we are doing. And then come back and we'll talk.*

When I spoke, my voice was surprisingly firm. 'You are showing me this because I want to see it,' I said.

He looked relieved, grateful. 'Okay,' he said. 'Well that's that then.'

The room was dark. When the light came on, I just stood where I was and took it in: a series of large whiteboards, some handwritten or hand-drawn, others with printed maps and diagrams, each of them dotted with hundreds of coloured magnets and post-it notes filled with unreadably small text. It seemed I wasn't the only one spending my days charting new worlds. This is what he had been doing, day after day, all those hours.

I stepped closer, moving from board to board, Alex by my side all the while, watching me, waiting for a cue. I could hear his tentative breaths, feel his eyes following mine.

'The thing on the computer,' he said. 'This is why.'

On the biggest board was a series of colour-coded world maps, each with the same legend at the bottom of the map with a range from Data not Available (pale green) to Extreme (blood red).

There was no explanation of subject matter, so I pointed to the one closest to me.

'Child slavery,' he offered.

In the bottom right there was a bar graph of the corporate perpetrators. He tapped a red country with a black spot. 'Cocoa farming—to make the chocolate bars for the kids in the yellow countries.'

Something about what I was seeing brought to mind the children in the videos on the Doctor's computer—the boys playing handball and the girls at the art table; the different classrooms. But Alex had already moved to the next board.

'Landmine fatalities.'

Then malaria, then drought, then school shootings…

He is saddened by the state of things.

On the second board was an index of countries—Zimbabwe sitting at extreme, all the way up to Denmark. On the third were two more maps: the percentage and growth rate of the world's evangelical population (North America out in front on percentage; fastest growth: North Korea), and last, a whole map and index just for Yemen.

'The woman you saw the other night,' his voice wobbled. 'That was Yemen.'

Others turn away, or just don't look. He looks.

Alex shook his head. 'Yemen,' he repeated, like it was enough just to say the word.

I nodded to confirm that it was, suspecting he might offer more of the detail or pull up another video. Sparing me that, he braced himself and stepped over to the last whiteboard. This one offered a closer analysis. There were labels, so I had a go at inter-preting it myself.

It was brain-bending stuff. From a single dot point in the

165

bottom right-hand corner labelled *A Guide to Human Suffering*, faint lines reached out to other nodes, each with a theme and a subset of branching lines: a spider diagram. There were twenty or more on the board, like the map of a starry sky, the themes ranging from social disorder, infertility and ignorance through to war, injustice and the absence of God. The graphics were a dog's breakfast, the tiny text decipherable only at close range, but the content was strangely compelling. The subsets drilled into the primary theme. From human death, for instance, sprang not just starvation, cannibalism and urban fires, but also inadequate riot control, child martyrdom, unnecessary gynaecological procedures and dangerous toys. There was a messy crossover into human disease and disability, which extended itself to include desynchronisation of bodily rhythm by international travel. (*Who knew?*) Crime encompassed erosion of moral values, addiction, urban slums, antisocial behaviour and late-night entertainment and finally, in the case of mental pollution—the least populated of the themes—it confined itself to individualism and ugliness. *Ugliness?*

'Where did you get this stuff from?'

'Websites. And some of it she gets in for me.'

'Helen?'

'Yep.'

Me and my beta waves, Alex and the human misery project.

I remembered one night in the courtyard he talked about when he was a little boy and he had 'bad thoughts', how he wrote them down on scraps of paper and folded them up and stashed them around his bedroom. A decade later, and this: what was real instead of what was imagined, whiteboards in place of folded notes.

After a pause, I said, 'Awesome,' because it was. He peered back at me as if to gauge that I was genuine before allowing himself to smile, proud of his work.

'It is good, I think,' he said, 'to set it out like this—to get a handle on it.'

Again he was seeking confirmation from me, which I gladly gave. I sat down and listened to him flesh it out: how many people in how many countries suffering in how many ways. He was doing that thing where he slowed it down, slow enough for someone to take notes: 'They haven't done the estimates in a while, so with the conflicts and refugees and the sea levels, it would be higher again.'

Next he turned to a laptop on the desk and scrolled through another set of tables (human trafficking, vitamin A deficiency, malaria, teen suicide) to a page where the numbers were constantly ticking over.

'And this one,' he said in a tone of wonder, the crimson rising into his cheeks, 'this is real-time, per second—see here, these two: as of this morning there are 670 million obese people in the world, while just today, twenty-five thousand have died from hunger. And it's only 5.48 pm.' Tick tock.

Alex wasn't finished, rolling us now into the fastest-growing causes of death. There was more; there was always going to be more. As his audience, it started to feel to me like gluttony. As his friend, I began to see the shape of the beast that he was feeding. Placing my hand on his shoulder, I looked around at the hundreds of scribbled thoughts, and back to the blazing eyes of their brilliant creator. *It isn't an illness, Daniel. There are no pills for it.* The question I'd had in my mind—*and we need to know all this because?*—was answered. Same reason I'd got swallowed up in my brainwaves—same reason, same strategy:

Know your enemy.

Know all there is to know.

The same strategy, I thought, just a different target. His enemy was the world around him; mine was within. When it was time to go he found me staring into one of the spider diagrams in the *Guide to Human Suffering*.

I pointed at a spot: at the centre was 'behavioural deterioration' and around it the branches of traumatisation, conflict and malevolence.

'I guess we work out where we fit,' I said.

He narrowed his eyes. 'I never thought of that...'

With a tilt of the head, he looked on me gently, if briefly, and then ran his finger across the board, pausing midway. 'I think where you fit would depend.'

'Depend on what?'

He squinted, hesitant. 'On whether you're talking about what you've done, or what's been done to you?'

I don't think Alex would have put the question directly to me. Alex felt no need to unpeel other people's problems. He was more high-level than that. What he was framing now was an empathetic response to my query within the scope of the broader project. He must have felt me stiffen.

'I mean, where you fit depends on that...I imagine there is a bit of overlapping.'

If anyone cares to ask me these days about my thoughts on human connectivity, the first thing I'd say is that I don't think we really see each other. I don't mean that necessarily as a criticism. My sense of it is that most of the time we are pretty happy with that—sneaking around in the shadows, until we are not happy at all, alone, misunderstood, invisible. (Some of us seesaw more rapidly between the two extremes.)

By and large a shadows man, it wasn't until I got to the School that I considered the value of transparency. Through Dr J and then Alex—the way he was looking at me now in front of his whiteboard—the School was my introduction to the fact of the matter: sometimes we need to be seen.

Through his lens—from his angle—as the seconds passed, a perspective emerged. Alex didn't just see the problems of the world; he saw mine too, more clearly than I had ever suspected.

What you've done or what's been done to you.

The overlapping...

For the first time, it entered my mind that they were one and the same thing.

Microeconomics

As we fell into our formations over the next weeks, there was an unexpected development.

Ever since Miles Davis, big Ben had gone quiet in class. It seemed to me more respectful than disengaged. When the sisters came out for a courtyard science session one day, he ditched the video games and came too. Taking his place next to Imogen, he complied with Helen's directions even before they were out of her mouth. It was interesting to watch. Ben and Imogen edged closer to the foaming beaker and closer to each other, the experiment quickly becoming an all-engrossing joint enterprise which blossomed into something bigger, and for a week or so Grace could be found in the back row with Glen and the other boys. Then one sun-filled day they all came together—the sisters and the boys—into a single contented cluster: one big happy gang. Thus embraced, Grace and Imogen seemed to let go of their gripe with the world and their inhibitions more generally. As I watched them hooking up with the boys between the pear pots, a few things became evident: they were not lesbians; Ben and Imogen were not possessive people, and when it came to physical contact, none of them were constrained by contractual conditions.

That left Rachel and Alex and Tod and me: as the other group came together, it seemed to firmly ground our own. Outside of class the two groups did not commingle. We ate in the kitchen and they took their meals to the courtyard. We claimed the waterhole; they stopped coming out on field trips altogether. There was a background and a foreground: them and us.

A Tuesday morning class. The theme, Helen announced, was phosphorus.

The intro was not her usual. No gods, no paintings; instead of an image, Helen played a segment from Special Ops, a third-person shooter video game. The narrative is the elite Delta Force wiping out enemy forces with zero regard for military conventions. In our short grab, the lads were making some morally ambiguous decisions about the use of white phosphorus munitions. The mission was to take out a Middle-Eastern stronghold, but it turned out the site was in sad fact a makeshift hospital. All round, a very bad error. There was a lot of screaming as defenceless civilians including a number of young children either burned to death or choked in toxic smoke.

The game was in Alex's top five, the narrative right up his alley (I was already envisaging a new asterisk on the whiteboard), but his focus wasn't on the screens. It was on the set-up for the

171

experiment on the bench—specifically, on the contents of the first glass beaker. Helen had outdone herself today. She had the real deal right there: tiny pieces of precious phosphorus. Wearing her white rubber gloves (I loved it when she wore those gloves), she called us to attention, tweezered out a piece and placed it in the second empty beaker, then asked Rachel to measure out a hundred mils of carbon disulfide. The phosphorus dissolved in the liquid and she used a dropper to release it onto a piece of filter paper. We watched as it evaporated, then *kaboom*, a burst of flames, the moment of spectacular spontaneous combustion. Our eyes lit up. I heard Alex swallow. It was as Helen turned to the board to represent the process as a mathematical equation ($P_4 + 5O_2 = P_4O_{10}$), that he leaned in and swiped a bit of phosphorus from the first beaker (no gloves, no tweezers), and shoved it into his pocket. Rachel elbowed him but he didn't wince. We waited for the last slides, for the one with something cryptic and sad and beautiful, but it never came. It ended on the maths, and Alex made his getaway.

Later in the day when I saw blisters on his palm he said his pocket caught fire. I could see it really hurt and he confirmed: 'like nothing else'. I also said it would be worse if it got infected and he said, 'Let's see what happens.' It was irritating but I shrugged it off as a case of Alex being Alex. The next day the blisters had spread up his forearm and they had to get a nurse out from the nearest town.

(The transcripts were abuzz with all this of course—an incident of self-harm put forward as evidence of a tendency, as part of a series of events during which an intention was formed. It was characterised in different ways by the various witnesses. In hindsight, Rachel summed it up best when she first caught sight of the pustules in the kitchen the next morning: 'You and your retard brain are going to get you killed.')

Rachel got seriously pissed off with Alex when he did this kind of stuff. *Boys will be boys?* She never copped that.

'You think it's a bit of fun? You're a fucking moron.' She said it with such force he almost looked apologetic.

When it came to Alex, I was focused on the whiteboards. In showing them to me he had opened things right up: a shared secret, and a connection I nurtured as a prized asset. We never referred to it in the presence of the others, even in the midnight sessions. But when it was just the two of us it was our default. He'd launch into the daily stats, recent massacres, earthquakes, anything else playing on his mind—more a flow now, less a lecture, his disembodied voice soft and silvery under the night sky.

He moved his focus into projections: how bad things will get in a decade, in a century; venting frustration on the limitation of current calculations, the neglect of so many subsets of misery. No one was making predictions about child martyrdom, youth suicide, school shootings—at least not in any systematic way that he could find. I started thinking about how we might be able to do that. PW was happy to bring it into our lessons and we started mapping trends and identifying variables to develop predictor algorithms. Waist-deep in the top ten ways children across the globe were taking their own lives, I started to feel the black hole in my chest fill with what I needed most: the putty of fresh purpose.

On that firmer footing and with my acceptance of Dr J's offer to share, I could step into my next and most challenging project.

The first thing I noticed when I entered Dr J's office was the fruit bowl. It was filled this time with a darker, larger, more spherical citrus. He had not, it seemed, forgiven the mandarins. He saw that I noticed.

'Would you like one?'
'Maybe later.'

'I'm sure you'll find them quite delicious.'

Not wanting to get into a compare and contrast between mandarins and tangelos, I said I'd look forward to that. I had an end in mind. To ease into it, I told the Doctor that Alex had shown me his whiteboards. I thought he would be pleased, but instead he nodded like he already knew and got up and sat behind his desk, resting his chin in his cupped hands, his thick fingers cradling his face. I waited for a prompt.

After a while, he shrugged. 'You are so keen to ask the questions. Go ahead.'

I walked over and sat opposite him in a chair at the desk. It was wooden, the back sloping awkwardly, giving me only an option to sit forward. His eyes were fixed on mine, the dark circles beneath them more apparent in the lamplight. When I asked if he was all right, he began to nod, or at least I thought that was what he was doing when in fact he let the full weight of his head drop forward and arched it all the way back, then side to side. 'Did you hear that?'

'What?'

'My neck. If you listen…'

I didn't want to listen. Today of all days, when my focus was laser sharp, his seemed to have been hijacked by an invisible third presence. As he began to ruminate on the reasons for his restricted movement, I could feel the hi-beta band getting back together— palpitations in my chest, the seed of frustration, the precursor of rage…

I took a breath. Pulled back. *Not today.*

Between the last session and now, I had reinvigorated my risk-aversion strategy—the one from my days of dealing at school. It was a three-step process, simple but effective: define risk (explosive reaction to disengaged Doctor), box risk, move on. The process had been enabled by an emerging purpose. The Doctor and I had been through it before: at school, I had stayed out of trouble because I'd been consumed with the business of selling drugs. It wasn't just the money, the profit; it was the enterprise and all its parts. Securing product, tapping into demand, managing risk. It was a start-up, every bit of it a struggle, every bit of it my creation. There was no external approbation: a satisfied customer was one who came back; a good day was more dollars in the drawer. Apart from intermittent explosions outside of work hours, I was a highly functional mini-mogul, and that was everything. That was (and is) the nature of my personality.

Arriving at the School—understanding where I was and what I was doing in the place—that had taken me so far, but even with PW and the brainwaves it was no substitute. It was only in these last weeks that I felt myself climbing back to peak levels. The driver was not commercial but sociological. It was something akin to a new market: my tribe.

Sitting across the desk from the Doctor, I didn't want to talk about his neck any more than I wanted to talk about his fruit. I wanted to talk about Rachel. Something about my demeanour must have suddenly reminded him of his promise, but initially he seemed to want to burst my bubble.

'The thing about Rachel,' he leaned forward, 'is that Rachel doesn't talk about what happened to her. She doesn't tell anyone. No one knows but Rachel, and whoever else was present.'

I pushed on, undeterred. 'But you said—'

'I said I'd tell you what I know. The backstory.'

'So tell me.' I waited.

He mumbled something to himself. All I could really make out were the words 'utterly unethical'. When he got to the end of it, he paused, went to speak again and then stopped himself. He was looking at me now as if for some kind of silent assurance.

I nodded: encouraging.

He seemed to consider that for a moment, then finally he sat back and shrugged.

'She lived on the outskirts of a small town,' he began. 'The father was a miner—disappeared—and her mother was in and out of prison so she was raised by an aunty and ended up in foster homes, a succession of different families. She ran away from the last one and went back to her home town. When DOCS found her, there was evidence of self-harm and other injuries—superficial cuts on her forearm, as well as rope marks on her wrists. She wouldn't say how she got the injuries, or where—whether it was with the foster family or back in her home town. She was seen twice by a child psychologist but told him nothing. They questioned her foster parents, who appeared to be good church-going people. They couldn't shed any light, or refused to; nor did they put up a fight to keep her, accepting that whatever happened, it was, as they put it, the Lord's will. Rachel consented to a physical examination and there were no other signs of interference or injury, so they abandoned their inquiries. She was almost sixteen by then. They couldn't find other foster parents—it isn't uncommon when children get to that age—so she ended up in a girls home. She broke into seven houses in three months. And now she is here. That is what we know.'

I listened, shook my head. 'So it was the last family. Where something happened.'

'That would be my guess. Or there were a series of incidents.'

'And she won't tell you?'

'I haven't asked.'

For a minute I sat processing my dead end, my disappointment. 'She talks in her sleep,' I finally said. 'In the corridor we can hear her.'

'Yes, I know. She appears to be reliving some part of an event.'

'Don't you need to know what happened, to help her?'

He paused then, the first of his answers that required some thought, and across the space he looked back at me with gentler eyes. 'Is that why you want to know? Is it the same thing as Alex, you think we are not doing enough for her?'

I said yes, in part.

'What is the other part?' And when I hesitated: 'Do you think it would bring you closer? Is that the aim?'

This wasn't what I'd had in mind for the session, but it felt like it was the agreement I had entered into: open dialogue. And I was relieved he was warming to it, that the conversation had at least been kept alive. So I answered him the best I could: 'It would make me feel good.'

He got up from behind the desk, picked up his chair with one hand like it was a paperweight and placed it next to mine. 'But would it?' he asked, his jugular vein bulging. 'Without knowing what it is you will learn, how you can you be sure?'

It wasn't a warning; he looked genuinely perplexed by the question. As it happened, the answer rolled off my tongue, as though to speak of such matters was the most natural thing. 'Because I will know her. That is what I want.'

He seemed to linger on that piece of information, like he was placing it somewhere or using it to construct a path forward.

*Because I will know her…*To state it so simply, so directly: *That is what I want.*

It was a statement that would replay in my mind over and over in the years to come. My feelings for Rachel over the past weeks— this intangible sense of connection—was driven by the mystery of her, the lure of the infinite and unknown. Love is a desire to infiltrate. If you are strong enough to resist, you have me for life. Rachel: my case in point.

(Out of pity, she will occasionally throw me a bone. I bury it in a safe place so once in a while, when I am down and out, I can dig it up, retreat into a corner, and chew on whatever is left.)

During the inquiry, the lawyer pursued a similar vein of questioning.

Referring to the fact that the Doctor at no stage identified the source of Rachel's trauma, he stated that he struggled to find the logic in that. To process her experience, surely she needed at some point to confront it?

> DR J: She was confronting it every night; I thought it wise to focus on safer memories...If I might suggest, I think it would be useful if you come at this another way.
> COUNSEL: If you could just answer my questions, please.
> HIS HONOUR: I would like to hear what he has to say. Go on, Doctor. What other way might that be?
> DR J: If we were to focus on the strengths, rather than the deficits...Rachel V was not your average girl. I am not just referring to her academic abilities. In spite of what had happened to her—or perhaps in part because of it—when this girl looked you in the eyes, she emitted a kind of energy. A...presence, that is what I am talking about. The only way to put it is that it was humbling. Look at her progress since leaving us at the School— you'll see her potential is playing out, and the world will be better for it. So we can talk about all that was wrong with her, the somnambulism, the catatonia and so forth. We can do that, or we can turn it on its head. My approach, the underlying logic, as you put it, is simple—it is to tread with the lightest touch. My rationale—and I am not speaking in hyperbole—is that these minds are as valuable as any resource on the planet.

In the courtyard that night, it was cloudy and starless and all I could think of was Rachel and the fuckhead families who passed her one to the next, and most of all, the one that made her run. When the wind picked up and the sky cracked open with thunder and then rain, it felt made to order.

Back inside, I stopped outside Rachel's door.

With the sound of the storm killing any chance of hearing her coded invitation, I opened it, telling myself it was just to check, to listen, to help, but even when I heard nothing, still I entered Rachel's bedroom for a second time and closed the door behind me. Looking back now, I could try to explain my perverse and moronic logic, but it is best summed up by saying that in the tangled web of the adolescent pre-frontal cortex, I resided in a universe of one. And at the time it seemed like a good idea.

As my eyes adjusted, I scanned the room. She was not standing in the corner but lying in bed, peaceful, asleep, her limbs splayed against the white sheets. Outside, the storm had picked up and gusts of wind rattled the windowpane. I stood at the foot of the bed and stared down at her, feeling now for the first time like a predator. I imagined the scenario, a stranger crawling on top of her. I imagined her broad-shouldered silhouette emerging from the struggle and rising up...

And then I tried to imagine her version, the real version—what it was that she saw when she stood night after night and stared down at the empty bed: who occupied it, what was happening to them? *What happened to her?* I started running the script through my head.

I watched. Waited.

After minutes of near-perfect stillness, she rolled onto her right side. There was a brief lightbulb moment when I thought it might be time to get the hell out of her bedroom, but the very next instant Rachel opened her eyes.

She opened her eyes.

It isn't easy to explain where I went with this. It just seemed that, while for the rest of the day Rachel was a minefield, a deadly obstacle course, this was the time when she let me come close. Unconsciously, but still. This was *our* time. So I repeat: with me on the verge of retreat, she opened her eyes. I could find only one way to read it—the first pass in a wordless dialogue:

Don't go.

Motionless, she stared up at the ceiling. There was a long minute of that before she pushed herself up and rose from the bed. Her brown skin disappeared in the dark, leaving just the pale grey singlet, a floating torso, and the whites of her eyes. Now that I look back on it, it was fantastically creepy. In anyone else's imagination it could have been a quest-line in Dark Souls Rising, the girl as something other, *a thing that feeds on souls.*

But like I said, my younger self had a particular take on it. When you want something bad, the brain is a beast of its own—a primitive neural network deactivating critical pathways in search of reward—so this was my parallel imaginary vision: *The girl stands in the middle of the room, and things are different between them. Her ferocity has ebbed into something softer, more accepting of the visitor in the room. In a silent acknowledgment of his presence, she flicks a strand of hair from her face and stares down at the pillow. Her singlet is hitched up on one shoulder, the neckline plunged more on one side into the crevice of her cleavage. The whisper when it comes is barely audible, but she is trying to tell him something.*

'*...the wax melts in the fire,*

'*the blood and the only sun.*'

The details the Doctor had shared with me were scant, but they formed a link between us, a connection across different states of consciousness. When a branch thrashed the window, I didn't flinch

180

in case she woke and found me there. We were ready to move ahead, to move together. I willed it. And as though to script, she looked up, away from the bed. *At me!* Anything was possible. She took a step forward, her first step, the beginning…A drop of sweat rolled slowly down the curve of my spine, the chamber of air between us too thick to breathe. She spoke again, still no more than a whisper.

'Your father like him.'

Hallelujah.

In the perfect silence of the room I replayed the highlights of everything she had ever said to me, every story, every put-down, every question.

I don't mean like the ones they chew. I mean dead dogs. Their bones.

I am not crying you fuck-knuckle…Why do you stare at me all the time?

You swimming?

When I stepped closer, it was no longer a conscious decision. I was encoded to her. She wanted to bring me in; she wanted me to understand. I stepped closer again, the blood rushing inside my head and a torrent raging in the narrow space between us. And Rachel, the glisten of her skin against the ribbed cotton. Again, she began to whisper. This time so close, so slow, I could make it out, every word. I was wrong. It was not 'the sun'. Rachel stood inches from me and put it all together:

'As wax melts before the fire,

'May the soul be redeemed by the blood of the lamb.

'By the God who gave up his only Son and created man in the Father's likeness.'

His only Son.

The Father's likeness.

The blood of the lamb.

All that was left was the final command: 'May you tremble and flee.' And then she started again at the beginning.

I remembered what the Doctor had said—her last foster family were church-going people—but my focus was not on her words, it was on the energy humming now between us. *It isn't possible to feel more than this,* I thought, and yet I wasn't going to explode or melt or turn to water. I was solid, and I knew why. It was a brain state beyond anything I had experienced. It was gamma. From the thalamus through to the hippocampus, gamma waves were sweeping my brain, neural clusters firing in a progressive rhythm— and beyond the brain, signals shooting, surging into every part of my body. I was here and I was everything, and Rachel and I and the rest of humanity had connected in a unity of consciousness. When she looked up, our eyes locked and burned. It was now.

It is now.

I reached my hand up to her face, and with the lightest touch, I brushed her cheek.

In a surprise to me, her skin was cold. Her skin was cold and mine was burning. It was the first clue: the disparity in our temperatures. As it happened, I had no time to interpret it and respond. I don't have much of a memory of what happened next— just the widening whites of her eyes as her head flung back, and the cracking pain as her forehead slammed into mine, sending my gamma crashing against the orbital ridge of my skull, and my world temporarily into darkness.

Ancient History

The morning after my tête-à-tête with Rachel, I slumped in my chair, more than happy to go with the flow.

Classes continued to consist of guessing games about cryptically related images followed by seemingly random discussions. But the subject of history was not altogether ignored; it was designated to that part of our curriculum known as E-learning, consisting of tutorial sessions on our tablets, through our headsets, in the comfort of our own rooms. The topics included Japanese isolationism, the unification of Italy, the causes of World War II, and the Arab-Israeli conflict. We were to complete two of the four topics, and for each topic there were three two-hour sessions. By 'complete', I mean put on the headset and push play.

Nothing was said about the order in which we listened to them, and no questions were asked about any of it. It didn't seem to be a problem if we slept through the lot. All we were really told was if we had something to raise we could bring it to class. No one did. Except this one time.

In front of us today was a black and white drawing of a glorious, round-bellied woman with hair spinning down all the way to her milky thighs, naked but for three crescent moons positioned over box and breasts. She was superimposed over a mandala wheel with her feet planted in the centre ring, where a series of detailed images depicted life on earth: mountains, vines, people pushing barrows. Springing from her hand was some kind of rod that shot up into the outer ring of stars and clouds and cherubs.

After giving everyone a crack at it, Helen K revealed that the woman was called Sophia. I was disappointed to learn that she was more concept than flesh and blood—a feminine entity that gave birth to the material world, a power surge from the galactic core. Lately, Helen had been getting pretty loose with this stuff, and never more so than now as she explained the theory behind Sophia, the way in which the currents of living luminosity burst forth the origination of the human genome, 'her spiral arms enfolding opalescent shafts of light...'

Tod drew a doodle of the divine vulva. (It wasn't bad.) Rachel side-eyed it and groaned.

The second image was similar to one we'd seen before, the blue and yellow dots (in which I'd read yellow blossoms and blue sky and Fergus had seen pus), only these were encased in the shape of an oval against a black background.

'It is a map of light,' Helen explained, 'a photograph taken by a space telescope of a glow of radiation: a fourteen-billion-year-old echo of the big bang.'

The bubbles and dots were micro-radiation, the different colours determining which parts of the cosmic pool would form our universe. We settled here for a while. Continuing in the same effusive manner, she took us through the timeline of a single point: explosion, cooling, cosmic evolution, 'all from a ten-million-degree sea of neutrons and protons, giant clouds forming the stars and the galaxies.'

While I flicked back to Sophia and mentally removed the little crescents (wondering what it would take to stir her currents), Alex fixated on sterner things post-big bang, the impact of dark energy on the expansion of the universe. Unsurprisingly, he had his teenage brain around the theory of it, positing his personal slant on the inevitable annihilation of the planet as a merciful end to millennia of human suffering.

Slumped in her seat behind me, Rachel's deep, extended breaths were getting louder and longer. Finally:

'This is all really interesting, Helen,' she ground out. 'But why can't we just focus on what actually happened? I'm listening to the tapes; I'm just coming through the Weimar Republic and the bad shit is starting to happen. Why are we looking at the naked chick instead of talking about the SS?'

'Good question,' Helen said, in a tone that imbued the comments with more respect than they in fact contained. 'What does everyone think?'

'I'm not asking everyone,' Rachel interjected. 'I'm asking you. *You* decide what we do in this class, so you tell me why we spend all our freakin time learning about stories that never happened.'

'Maybe she doesn't decide,' I said. 'Maybe someone else does.'

'Whoever determines our syllabus—' Helen came in, only to be cut off.

'*Syllabus!* You cannot be fucking serious!'

I was beginning to wonder if Rachel hadn't taken the better part of the knock last night; if it hadn't unleashed some kind of reaction in her brain. Helen made a valiant effort, sidestepping the swipes and entering into an earnest spiel about why we retell stories, how we use them for different ends, what they mean to us, 'What they tell us about what it feels like to be a human being living in the world.'

What it feels like to be a human being living in the world. Through it Rachel sat staring ahead and I braced for her to blow. I was even tempted to try to head her off, but I didn't, and I'm glad I didn't. I think I was right about the knock: she was opening up like a flower. I wish I had her actual words in transcript form—like the evidence in the proceedings—so I could read and re-read rather than recollect and piece together. It started as a ramble; she flicked between images without telling us which one she was talking about. In no particular order they were each dismissed with the same kind of brush—'the vagina goddess', 'nonsense stories', 'bullshit science'. And though none of the images from other lessons were there, it was as though she had them right in front of her, flicking though them all and playing back our discussions—discussions for which she had appeared to be present only in body. Her tirade indicated that not only had she taken them in, but she could now recount them in extraordinary detail. In a hushed silence, we listened. All of us: the sisters, the boys, the teacher.

'The stories just mean what you want them to mean, what you tell us they mean…You package them up as survival tips.'

She reeled them off in dot points, talking way too fast, the story and the message, counting on her fingers like she'd been learning them for a test. 'The psycho prince who got locked up in the rice chest: control your bad energies. But use your good power: the bird that saves his mother from the snakes. Mutation is survival, change is growth: that disgusting thing on the poor guy's head; the god who turned to water when the sailors pinned him down...you hold on and don't let go. If you use enough force for enough time and cling together and form your swarmer cells—only then will you be saved.' And a last line that was all her own: 'And so the wicked perish.'

Rachel had not simply zoned out, slept, entered a catatonic state. She had taken in every word. And somewhere in there I suspected were coded clues to her own untold story. To finish, she banged the table a couple of times with a flat hand. 'You want to know what I think, what I think about your stories?'

Helen: 'I want you to feel free to talk about anything you want.'

'*Feel free?*' Finally her voice was rising. 'I don't feel free. We are not free. We are *here*. Your stories are group therapy for the mental kids and that's all they are. You pick and choose and add bits or take them away depending on who's spinning out. There is nothing very subtle about it. And the music? Follow the instrument, listen in closely...It's not music, it's sedation. Helen, I like you all right but you are no teacher.'

You might have thought the teacher would be offended by some of this. Not Helen. At this point she started clapping, as though her pupil had just answered the million-dollar question.

Rachel dismissed this and turned to the rest of us: 'I told you before, this isn't class. We're not students. She wants to know what it feels like to be us—how *this* feels?'

I didn't see it coming. Just as I was starting to get comfortable with the 'us and them', lining myself up with the sniggers from the back row, she spun around to me, just me, and pointed her finger right into my face. 'You. You want to know so much? You want me to tell you what happened?'

When I didn't answer she held her hand up. I could see that it was shaking.

'I can tell you all of it if you like. Is that what you want?'

She was looking not into my eyes but at the bruise on my forehead. When she spoke again it was (fractionally) gentler.

'You can't just sneak into someone's room and steal it.'

I nodded like a puppet—*I know. I know*—I didn't say anything; I couldn't.

She stood up and walked out of the class.

The night before, when I climbed back to my feet, I found Rachel lying in her bed again, just as she was when I'd first entered, splayed into a shape not unlike a swastika. Had it not been for the bulging pain in my head, I might have wondered if what had happened— her ghostly rise and approach, my advance, the terrible cracking of skulls—had happened at all; if it hadn't been some strange hallucination brought on by an explosion of neurotransmitters. As it was, the pain was front and centre, or rather off-centre. By the morning it had formed into a deep blue half-moon above my left eyebrow, as clear as a crayon drawing.

'That's quite a bruise,' Dr J commented as I entered his office. He leaned forward to take a closer look and, without enquiring about the cause of the injury or the identity of the assailant, he played the physician and satisfied himself I was not concussed. 'Brave man,' was all he said. Of course, he knew where I had been. Later I'd go hunting again for hidden cameras, but for now I welcomed the introduction of the subject of Rachel.

What preoccupied me was that he had never asked her what happened to her. No questions for Rachel, while he'd spent session after session getting me to move farm animal chess pieces around an imaginary fucking stage. I didn't feel like he was living up to his side of the bargain. All morning I had been framing a way to mount a challenge, reminding myself we were playing to different rules. Open dialogue. *Ask away...*

I pulled the chess pieces from the shelf and stood them up on his desk. 'Did you try it with her?'

He looked at the pieces and back at me.

'Here is Foster Mum,' I went on, 'here is Foster Dad. And here is Rachel...Did you try that?'

'No, I didn't.'

'Aren't you people meant to have a method?'

He shook his head, clenched and unclenched his jaw. 'I don't know even what that question means.'

'That is bullshit. And what the fuck is it with the videos on your computer? I saw them that night...the sites...'

'Do you want to talk about that? Or do you want to talk about the difference between you and Rachel? Isn't that what you want to know?'

I hesitated. He was getting the better of me, I could feel it, but I wanted to hear what he had to say. I waited.

'The difference between you is that she won't let anyone near it, whereas you, Daniel, you came in here and tore the place apart; you took me there yourself. There is a reason for that. There is something you want me to know. I don't know what it is yet, but I am starting to see the shape of it. I think I am.' He did that thing where his eyes drilled in and I did mine and blanked him out. 'I am piecing it together. Your numbers, your faces...you are looking for patterns, Daniel. You are trying to make sense.'

Here he stopped and picked up the pieces and set them down side by side. 'I want you to see your part in it,' he moved the centre piece forward, and spoke softly: 'And their part, her part. I want you to see it for what it was: a group of people making terrible

189

mistakes, and a boy in the middle of it.'

He paused, holding his hands in front of him like he was cradling a ball, keeping it steady. The stretched brown skin, the broad span of his hands. He was seeking my permission, giving me the chance to leave.

I didn't. I waited to see if he was getting close.

'When the tenants have come and gone, Daniel,' he finally said, 'when it is just the boy and his mother. What happens then?'

That night a quarter moon sat low in the sky. It was warm under the stars and we unzipped our sleeping bags to form one big blanket that reached all the way to the planter boxes, giving us space to spread out. Tod wondered what a sight it would have been to witness Sophia's primordial explosion and I set us the challenge of constructing her body parts out of the shadows of the nebulae cloud in the top right of our screen; for tonight's viewing pleasure...I had just begun the commentary of my first efforts when we heard the steps behind us. Each of us turned.

Standing there, with wild bed hair haloed in the Milky Way, was Rachel.

Without a word, we shuffled around to clear a space and, in between Alex and me, she lay down on the ground. For the first hour she asked questions about the night sky, wanting us to share with her everything we knew, and when we ran out of things to tell, she took over.

Starting at a place she called the beginning, she told us her story.

Colonisation

In the navigation menu there is a section headed: Student Overview, Female.

The sisters appear first, Grace above Imogen. I click into Life Course, Key Events. Theirs are busy timelines. Between them I count four marriages, nine children, eleven career changes. Nil nervous breakdowns. They were just girls who got bored easily.

Next is Rachel V. In her thumbnail photo, she looks younger than the girl I remember, but it makes me stop to think of the child she was. Still, all these years later, I see the same look in her eyes, the look of a captured animal. Still, now, it is a face that means everything.

I scroll through the metrics and the indicators: maternal health, education, out-of-home care placements, marital (single), children (none).

By now there are a number of biographical sources, starting back with what she told us at the first of her midnight sessions through to the transcripts, and then of course all this, the notations and reports. There is the list of her causes and committees and commendations. As a friend and supporter, I stand in awe and say she spreads herself too thin; that no one can sustain this level of output.

I am dismissed. The Doctor was right in the proceedings, of course, about all of it. For every rung she climbs, the world is a better place. Those that speak of anger as a deficit have never seen Rachel at the helm.

The event itself appears in none of the written material. Nor is it my story to tell. But it appears now with the consent—or rather, at the insistence—of its subject.

'You leave it out and what have you got? A story about a bunch of white kids.'

What I already knew at the time of the telling was that Rachel had moved from the edge of a small town to live in houses filled with strangers, then for a brief time back to the town again. Somewhere along the way she got hurt.

'On my fifteenth birthday I was placed with a new family.' Their name was Boland, and they were the last family she would ever be placed with. 'If you can call them a family.'

To flesh out the details I found in the transcripts and the database: early testing indicated that while her reading level was below average, Rachel's numeracy skills were off the scale—which was considered something of a miracle given her poor attendance at primary school. There was quite a bit about this in both her school and social-service records, notations of which ended up as footnotes in the digital files. It was this that landed her a scholarship at a selective high school and attracted the attention of the Bolands. Rachel summed it up nicely, describing herself as 'show-and-tell for their church group—the hard-up black with a brain'. (Out-of-home-care placements was a hyperlink in her computer file. When you clicked it a cohort of 180 names appeared, each in their own row with columns of coded numbers.)

The Boland family were a white couple in their early fifties, Eileen and Joe, with an adult son called Leon. They lived on a small dairy farm on the outskirts of Sydney and had horses and chooks. Rachel missed her home town but liked the horses, and there was better food than the other places. 'They didn't keep a count of things.'

For the first few months, she adapted well and excelled in school. A report tendered to the inquiry included effusive quotes from both her teacher and form supervisor. She developed a good relationship with Eileen Boland and helped her with the horses. She told us a story about when Joe was away one time and a horse got caught up so bad on a barbed wire fence Eileen had to sedate the animal to get him free; it took three hours and the horse fell down and rolled right on top of Eileen, his whole leaden weight— nothing moving except his eyes spinning in their sockets, and his heart, Rachel could feel his heart pounding, racing, and finally she got him to budge enough to get Eileen free. If it wasn't for Rachel, she would have been 'cactus'—that is what Eileen said when she hugged her and for a full minute wouldn't let go.

Eileen was supportive with Rachel's schoolwork; she read the books on the English syllabus so that she could help with her essays. 'No one had ever done anything like that for me before.'

The school was secular, non-denominational, and Joe and

Eileen insisted she attend their local church each Sunday. 'My aunty liked church too, but it was a different kind of church. This was one of those joints where the people in the pews get up out the front and talk shit.' It was called the Ministry of Mercy. When Rachel started to arc up about going, Eileen and Joe relented, but the adult son, who was a senior member of the church, 'kept pestering'. Leon was the one who attended her parent-teacher evening. There was no explanation for this.

During her brief evidence to the inquiry, counsel assisting referred to the reason she left the Bolands as the 'catalyst' for her offending and tried to draw her out on it.

COUNSEL: Could you tell us about that?
RACHEL V: No, I could not.

They went around in circles. The judge agreed she was an unhelpful witness but was reluctant to press any of it. It 'seemed sensible' to him that she was making every effort not to dredge up the past and to find a way to move on. 'Let's not hamper that process any more than we need to.'

One day six months into her stay with the Bolands, Rachel was helping Eileen hang out the washing. A magpie landed on the fence.

'I told her that where I came from that meant something bad was coming, and she said that was rubbish talk and got all riled up. I said, "Calm your farm"; didn't have to mean the same thing here, just where I came from. But she couldn't see it that way. For Eileen, there was one truth in every place.'

In telling her story, Rachel kept stopping and starting, like she'd gone far enough, or she shouldn't be telling it in the first place. While I was in two minds about her going on (I wanted to hear it, of course, but I had reservations about it being shared), Alex and Tod filled the silences with different ends in mind: Alex to assure her we could talk about something else (offering up segues

194

into the impact of religious fanaticism in Latin America if she needed an out), and Tod to keep her to purpose, bringing her back with questions on benign detail (how many horses, how old was Leon).

When she sat up, we all sat up and that is how we stayed for the rest of it, cross-legged in a semi-circle.

Leon was single and childless and balding, 'even his eyebrows. Like he'd been zapped'. He was Eileen's child but it felt like he was in charge. He told her when the path needed sweeping and he went through her mail and decided what bills should be paid first. He was the one to bring it up again, the thing about the meaning of the magpie. More interested in it than he had reason to be, he started asking Rachel questions about her family, how she grew up, what they believed.

'I told him some things. I told him my aunty said there were people who can be in two places at once, for real, and that she got pinned down by spirits in her sleep, like a jolt of cold air through her bones. I told Leon I got that too. I shouldn't have told him that; he twisted it all up.'

She went quiet, and Alex stepped in with a story about a thing called the Fundamentalism Index. It was pretty convoluted; suffice to say there was a hierarchy, with God (whichever one) on top and women and children at the bottom.

Tod chimed in to bring Rachel back. What did she mean—how did Leon twist it up?

'You know what he asked?' she said. 'He asked if they were assaulting me. The spirits. I said, "How do you mean?" He said, "I mean sexually." That is what he said he meant and I said *of course bloody not, that is sicko stuff*. That was Leon—his mind went to sick places. I should've got out of there then.'

When she told Eileen she had a bad feeling about Leon, Eileen said she would be okay, but Rachel could sense that even Eileen started to worry. She heard them fighting sometimes, Leon and his mother. He said Rachel should be home-schooled. He'd shout over Eileen, but she stayed in it.

'That all changed with the sleepwalking.'

As her voice trailed off we could hear a dog barking in the distance and, closer to us, the goat was bleating again. A layer of cloud dimmed the sky. I couldn't tell you what time it was. I'd lost any sense of it. I couldn't tell you if I wanted her to go on or to stop. Somehow fear had crept into it as she edged forward, as the story started to reshape her and leave something permanent, unchangeable, and render my part irrelevant. Suddenly I was saying goodbye to the girl in the room with a secret history, unsure of who would be standing there in her place.

When Rachel was little she got out of bed and walked straight out the front door and all the way to the river.

'I've always walked in my sleep,' she said. 'My aunty worried I'd end up drowning myself, but no one ever tried to put a meaning on it. Leon did. Leon put a meaning on everything. *His* meaning. Same as Eileen, same meaning for everyone in every place.'

She didn't say yet what the meaning was, just that an old man started coming to the house 'who was always smiling but never really was'. He was from the church and they called him Father; she'd hear them in the kitchen whispering. 'One day they asked me to sit down with them and Father said if I came back to church, God would help me there. I said I didn't need help from God and he asked me why I thought that. I said I deal with my own God just fine. There were looks between them like I'd just fessed up to some bad thing.'

One night, Rachel was passing the kitchen and she saw Leon showing the old man a video on his phone. She could hear her own voice, but it was nothing she'd ever heard herself say.

'Turned out he'd been waiting up at night to video me. I didn't just walk, I talked as well. I didn't know that until then…I tried to grab the phone out of his hand and he palmed me off and I lost my shit.' She looked at me. 'A bit like you do. I guess that was like a justification for them; gave them a reason. Leon said Father was going to start home-schooling me, and I refused, and then a week later…

'I'd known a few people who'd done bad things, but I hadn't really known a lot of bad people. That all changed when I stayed with the Bolands.'

No one spoke into the silence. There was no place for us in it. We waited. It was getting colder now but we copped it, stayed sitting up out of our sleeping bags.

'I haven't talked about it to anyone,' she finally said. The clouds drifted across the sky now and gathered in affinity around the moon. 'Something that no one knows—I thought I'd have a better chance of it not mattering at all.' And to none of us in particular: 'You ever think that?'

I answered. I said I had. I did. It was the first time I said anything since she'd sat down with us.

'Yeah, well. Here is me trying it the other way, I guess. Here's what happened.'

It was a Sunday, after breakfast. Rachel started feeling drowsy, nauseous. She went to lie down. Eileen came in and sat on her bed, looking like she had some bad news to tell her.

'How do you feel?' she asked.

'I just want to sleep,' Rachel said, and Eileen nodded; took hold of her hand. Joe came in behind her and when Eileen turned back to him he said, 'It was for the best.' He looked at Rachel and

197

repeated the words. 'It is for the best.' His face was harder set than Eileen's. Rachel assumed they were delivering the news that she couldn't stay there anymore, and she felt some relief in that—in the idea that this chapter would be over; she'd leave Eileen and the horses and find herself another place. But that wasn't it.

Joe sat down on the bed too. He didn't take her hand, just nodded and said, 'Father knows.' He appeared then, at the door, Father; Leon behind him. Eileen and Joe got up like they were following orders, and it was the four of them standing around her bed, Leon in a white, collared shirt and Father with his cross around his neck. Before she tried to move, in that first moment, it just felt ridiculous, almost funny. *I won't go to their church so they are bringing the church to me.* That is what she thought. But when she tried to tell them to go away her words were slurred; she tried to get up but she strained to lift her arms and legs. And it dawned on her that she wasn't sick; she had been tranquilised, like the horse stuck on the fence. Inside the leaden body, her heart was leaping and pounding, louder, faster.

Joe tied her wrists, Leon the legs. To the bedposts.

Eileen cried.

Father laid his hands on her shoulders and her arms, then her stomach. He said she had been invaded by the enemy. He was not there to harm her, but to save her.

She found it within herself to release a sound, more counter-attack than scream—more brain stem than limbic—low pitched and garbling, the reverberations sending her body into convulsion and expelling any last doubts in the room. *Father knows.* When he started up again, it was with Eileen standing right beside him, and he spoke not to Rachel, but to the demon inside her.

The three of us listened, as it dawned on us what we were listening to—offering up a chorus of whispered support, condemning the perpetrators—'maniacs…top-of-the-range fucking lunatics…' As the new Rachel took shape, growing bigger, and slowed it down. Careful and steady. Telling it like a story that needed to be told.

To commence the ritual of casting out, Joe passed Father a large silver bowl filled with water. Father dipped his fingers in the bowl and flicked her face with the water.

'Tell us your name. Who are you?'

'I'm Rachel.'

'Tell us your name.'

'Rachel.'

And so it went. The more she answered 'Rachel' the more he flicked water in her face and then down the entirety of her body until the sheets were drenched. When the bowl was empty he ordered Eileen to refill it.

'I saw her at the door and I shouted out to her: "Don't leave me." They thought I meant the demon and it ignited this mad frenzy, all of 'em shouting: "He is lying to you. He is tricking you, that is what He does…"

'I got my strength back around then and I remember hearing the horses arcing up and I was thrashing around and making sounds I'd never heard myself make before, from some place I didn't know was in me.'

Leon was like an echo of Father, no matter how loud she got their voices flooded over hers; the more she thrashed the more water came, into her eyes and mouth.

'There was long enough like that that I started to wonder if they weren't right, if there wasn't something in me, because I could feel my skin crawling and a weight in my chest—this hard thing rising up, with its own eyes, like everything I'd ever done and thought was inside it. That's when I first had the thought, the thought they wanted me to have: it isn't Rachel. That is what they'd been saying all along: they weren't speaking to Rachel. *Tell us your name*—all their hate wasn't for me, it was separate to me. Now I was willing it to be true. The only way I could stay alive was to be separate from it, and to help them drive it out. I don't know what I said, but they thought it was another voice. They thought they were talking to it. There was this terror and joy in the room, clapping and crying, and they kept telling me to cough and spit. Spit him out...I did what they said and coughed and spat.

'Leon kept shaking his head. "It is here. It is still here."

'Father nodded and cradled my head, a gentler voice: "We will release you."

'Joe passed him the knife, a little kitchen knife with a green handle that we used to peel carrots.

'"We need everyone," Father said, stern again.

'Eileen came to the other hand—Leon and Joe took my legs. They all had their job, their part, and Father cut, three times on each side, I counted them but I didn't feel much, just the blood trickle down my arms as he repeated the same lines over.

'*As wax melts before the fire, may you be driven from the living soul.*

'*May the soul be redeemed by the blood of the lamb.*

'*By the God who gave up his only Son and created man in the Father's likeness.*

'*May you tremble and flee...*'

Rachel was bound in the room for seven hours. They threw water in her face but gave her nothing to drink. She blacked out several times. They had to retie her hands twice. Once when she came to she found they'd pulled up her shirt and Leon was standing with his hands over her stomach. She threw up.

'All the way through I kept looking out to find Eileen, to make sure she was there. Near the end, she was standing behind them again. Her face white, her eyes closed. It was hard to make it out at first, what she was saying. "I am speaking to Rachel," she whispered. "I love you, my girl."

'And the saddest thing—the saddest thing of all—was I think she was telling the truth.'

With the end of her story—the chorus silenced, speechless, just the fog of our breath in the cold night air—she put her hands over her face, and cried.

The rest I've put together later. Bits and pieces over the years she has told me; details from the transcripts and digital files.

She couldn't report it because she couldn't speak of it. She left the house and never set foot in it again. She once wrote Eileen a letter, then burned it.

When they untied her she walked out the front door and kept walking. 'I think they thought I'd come back.' She had only the wet clothes she was wearing. It took her three days to get herself back to her home town. She slept on couches. A cousin said she'd keep her but the department wouldn't approve the house because a window was broken and there were no locks on the doors. Another cousin stepped in but her criminal record didn't pass the check.

'They just kept coming back with reasons to refuse till everyone felt it. Everyone felt the shame. That is what they do. The cut marks on my arm, they assumed I'd done it to myself. I don't know how they figured the rope marks got there.'

They put her in a home, and one of the other girls showed her how to break into people's houses.

QUESTION 2

In answer to the second of their questions,
it is a longer one (requiring an assessment of
our management and treatment), with a longer
answer, but I guess what it boils down to is:

1. Yes and No

Camp

The night walks. There were pages of transcript on the night walks: how did a set of conditions exist such that *vulnerable children* were permitted to roam free through the bushland in the dark of night? (The adjective always pointing where they want to go: damaged, vulnerable, delinquent, dangerous.)

In permitting a question over objection, the judge determined that it 'sat behind the broader question to be decided in the proceedings: whether the overall management and treatment of these children was appropriate and reasonable in the circumstances of their confinement'.

What struck me as I read this part of the transcript was not the question, but the last word. *Confinement.* The word was used intermittently throughout the proceedings and never corrected; but in many ways, I had never felt a greater sense of freedom. Nor have I since.

After she shared her story, we didn't see Rachel again for three days. Helen K said she was 'taking time out'. When I sat outside her door I didn't hear a peep.

'Don't even think about it,' Alex said; my nocturnal visits were by now common knowledge. 'Go to bed, Dan.'

Forty-nine hours later, on the third night, she appeared in the courtyard. A fourth sleeping bag was ready for her, but after a few cursory answers to our questions ('I slept', 'I feel good', 'Fine') she was up and pacing, then stepping sideways with her back to the glass and angling her head up to the outer rim of the building.

'If we can get out here,' she said, then pointed up and over towards the bush, 'why can't we get out *there*?'

When she looked at me for the answer, my mind spun into action, and landed pretty quickly on a possible solution: the doors might already be unlocked. It was a *system thing*, the Doctor had said about access to the courtyard. If he had unlocked one door...

I left to investigate, strolled through to the external door in the waiting room, turned the handle, and opened it. (Dr J, in a series of answers on the point: it was his decision to open the courtyard but no, he had no hand in directing the system to work this way, nor could he explain the reason for it. He suspected there was someone who could, but it was not him.)

The next night we ventured out.

There was a thrill in it, the risk of detection, sneaking our way around the side of the building, out of the light into the safety of darkness. There was a thrill, and then terror. I hadn't thought it through any further than getting out; I hadn't prepared myself for the bush at night.

We stopped at the edge. A throaty rustling was coming from beyond. I stared into the maze of tunnels, dark between the trees, and felt something staring back.

Following the others, I stepped in and looked up in search of sky, a glimpse of yellow moon, only to see a canopy of dancing shadows. During the day was one thing, but now the darkness was an inky vortex of old fears that threatened to swallow me whole.

Unperturbed, Rachel moved forward. 'Keep a skip in your step,' she called back as she took off.

'Fuck,' Tod said. 'We'll lose her.'

He was the only one with a torch. ('How did you get that?' 'I asked for it.') He waved the beam all over the place but there was only the sound of her footsteps—fast, like an animal being pursued. When Alex and Tod took off too I tried to keep up, tripped over a tree root and reeled forward like a drunk, a sequence that repeated itself in a number of variations every time I heard a sound I didn't like. When I reached the other side of the bush I fell to the ground, flat on my back—alone and in pain and adrift from my frontal lobe, hallucinogenic hormones taking hold as I imagined my goat nearby, morphing—more woolly ghoul than doe-eyed friend. It took everything in me to regather and get to my feet and push on to the waterhole, letting it rip as I hobbled over the rise: *You didn't think of fucking waiting. You had the only fucking torch. You left me in the fucking dark, you fucking pieces of shit.*

Their collective response moved from a quizzical interest in the wound on my leg to a brisk no harm done, keep up next time—and Rachel: 'You gotta learn to pick up your feet.'

At some point the anger ebbed enough for me to step back and take in the scene. Where among the trees there had been no moon to see, here it hovered centre stage, casting a golden light through the leaves of the willow tree and a tinge of moss green across the surface of the water. To the side of it, where on other days we had left our gear and gone our separate ways, the three of them now sat together, perched on rocks; giving me stick for having taken so long.

'Come on, we waited,' Rachel said, stripping down to her singlet and underwear and disappearing into the water.

One by one we followed, breaking into frantic strokes to beat the cold and wading in close together, a defensive line against whatever lurked below. Legs brushed against legs until someone kicked out, and then we all did, a medley of splashing, a free for all with mass dunking, more kicks and spitting water like kids in a backyard pool. Exhausted, we crawled up onto the bank and lay flat on the cold, muddy earth, panting to catch our breath, numb to the bone.

'We should keep doing this,' Alex said. 'Coming back here.'

And we did. Every few nights we came back. We packed our bath towels and sleeping bags and trekked through the bush back to the waterhole; I went behind Rachel and got better at keeping up. Once we were dry we climbed into our sleeping bags at the water's edge and gazed up at the stars or lay flat on our stomachs and fixed our eyes on the surface of the water to watch the world of insects—dragonflies dipping in and out, and water striders, hundreds of them, sculling across the surface like it was skin. If we kept quiet and still for long enough, once in a while we were visited—a wombat clambered around the trunk of the tree, a fox darted in and out of the bush. There were big ants and spiders and strange sounds but we weren't bothered by any of it. When it rained we sat under the overhanging rock or beneath the branches of the willow; we knew the curves of each rock, which ones to sit on or lean against and which to avoid. We knew where to find the wombat hole and the spider webs. We were protected by this place. We were part of it. It was a sanctum, and it was ours.

On our third night-time visit Rachel talked about the feeling she had that she'd lived through everything before, as though what was happening now was a memory. Tod offered déjà vu as an explanation.

'Yeah,' she said, 'but like all the time.'

I said it sounded as though something weird was going on in her brain, 'like some kind of rejigging in your space-time continuum'.

She propped up on her elbow and stared down at me as if it was just me and her.

'I had it at *their place*,' she said—I knew she meant the Bolands—'the feeling that what was happening was a picture that had always been in my head—that everything was leading up to it. And then afterwards I had this sense I'd been right all along: this was it, this was my fight. I know, it sounds weird.'

I shook my head. 'Not weird.' At least not in the way she thought. What was weird, what was *confounding* to me, was that she was confronting what had happened to her (as she had been confronting it night after night in her room), assessing it from every angle—as a projection and as a memory—and wrestling it to the ground.

I didn't know where to take it. She lay back down. I think she fell asleep. And then it came to me—my role, my purpose. This was Rachel, I reminded myself. She wants to bring me in. She wants my help.

I thought of my sessions with the Doctor, the stage. Doing what he asked, week to week, it was like drip torture for me, imagining my players and moving them around. But lying beside Rachel now, listening to her breathing, I found myself picturing the room, the four fuck-ups around her—two sitting on the bed, two standing back, and I placed them on the stage, how I imagined them (pasty, bland, ugly). The scene was malleable and I was forming it, positioning the players and directing the action. It was my version. The story was this: *The girl is strong and the ropes loosen as she struggles. They are not quick enough to hold her down. She kicks out and Father is toppled to the floor. The others freeze. The woman begs forgiveness. It is not granted. The end.*

Then, just briefly, there was my room, the flat—just a flash of it. There was a moment when I looked back at where I was, where they were, and for the first time, didn't feel the need to scramble to the surface, to hold my breath and run.

It was Tod who started us talking about our tutorials. He asked me what I did in mine.

I told them how PW and I had worked our way from electrical currents to brainwaves, and more specifically *mine*. (As per contract, I omitted any reference to headsets and covert monitoring.)

'Alpha is when you chill,' I explained. 'Beta is alert, and hi-beta is when you're wired, like hyper-focused, but you don't want to go too high...'

'And you watch yours go up and down?' Rachel asked.

'Well yeah, and I get reports.'

Their reactions ranged from impressed to envious. 'You lucky mug.' (Alex.)

'There are ways to reset how you react,' I said.

'Is that what you do?'

'No. We do OMR. Observe, monitor, record.' They thought that was funny. 'And we work on algorithms to determine the source of electromagnetic activity.' I concede this was an effort to impress.

'You understand all that?' Rachel asked.

I nodded. 'Most of it, yeah.'

Next was Alex and the Human Suffering Project. This took longer to explain. 'Data and maps and stuff' didn't really do the job.

Rachel: 'You mean like how many people are starving?'

'Yeah, that.' He took a breath. 'That and more, other things.' He sounded like the kid in the playground trying to be like the rest of the kids. This wasn't easy for him.

She cocked her head. 'Why? I mean what's the point?'

His voice, thin at the best of times, was getting drowned out now by the cacophony of cicadas. 'So I can get a better understanding of what is happening.'

'Okay I get that, but...' Rachel gave no sign of relenting. It started to rain, big random drops on our faces. When Alex put his hand up it wasn't to stop the drops but to stop her questions. Easier for him would be to show, not tell. As he had done with me, he invited her in.

When it came time, Tod was in the middle of making spanakopita triangles with Magnolia and was loath to walk away from the pastry, so it was just me and Rachel tapping at the door to Alex's tutorial room. He was head down, superimposing a graph on a map of Nigeria—a breakdown of child labour and hazardous practices, child kidnappings, child sexual slavery.

We stood in silence and watched, Rachel scanning the whiteboards. When Alex was done, he smiled and said 'welcome' in a way that made me picture the old man he would never become: slow-moving, squinting, softly spoken. (Rachel and I would argue in later years about whether he was an old soul, or so, so young.) He took her through the whiteboards and the maps, the trajectory and index. He talked too fast and sometimes mumbled when explaining things, but Rachel appeared to take it all in, nodding along. Then she turned around and went back to Nigeria.

'…three hundred million in child labour? Worldwide?'

'Yep.'

'I'm guessing a big chunk of them work with Mum and Dad on the farm.'

He agreed there were different categories, but waited to hear her out.

'There are worse things, aren't there?' Rachel went on. 'I mean I get that it might not be ideal, but like, define suffering.'

Stepping through the long-term implications of child-supported families, the intergenerational production of poverty, Alex mumbled less and began to point fingers in the air as he spoke. I realised this was Alex in his happy place. Every now and then he'd stop and say, 'With me?' and sometimes when she questioned him he repeated a set of words like a refrain—'disease, injury, illiteracy', or 'discrimination, unemployment, exploitation'. When he started in on percentages, he paused and took her over to the trajectory.

'Yeah, okay,' she conceded. 'I think this is good, really good…I'm just trying to work it out: is the idea that you want to do something about it?'

He nodded. 'Define the size and scope.'

'But then what?'

'Then I'll know.'

She wondered what good that was and when he mumbled something about certainty, she was unrelenting. 'So you have certainty; that's nice for you.' She pointed to the maps. 'What about *them*?'

A chasm appeared down the centre of his face as he took in her question, a chasm between where his mind needed to go and where it couldn't—the hopelessness, the evil that men do…To her credit, Rachel handled him. 'You need this, size and scope. Feed it in is all I'm saying.' And when he looked blank: 'I don't know how. Just somehow…There must be a million ways to come at it. I mean, who is dealing with this stuff out there?'

'You could be one of those journos that do horror stories—famines and all that,' I offered.

She looked at me like it was a bad example but then launched deeper into the realm of the ridiculous. 'Or get out and do a talk that goes viral and get a million shares…' And on she went: aid agencies, academic posts, 'Go on *Australia's Got Talent* and start reeling it off. I once saw this twelve-year-old do the history of the world—the sixteen-year-old human suffering guru.'

Alex laughed. I chimed in, 'We should let him get the data right first.'

That was enough for now. It felt good. Among this talk of all that was wrong with the world, somehow something was more right than it had been before. We all felt it. We went to dinner. We slept in our beds. By morning, around the kitchen table, we listened to the sisters complaining about a joint project they hadn't finished for their music tutorial and we all had the same idea.

Alex said it first. 'Let's do the tutorials as a group, the three of us together. Tod too, if he wants.' There was a brief discussion about the inclusion of Tod (even in the morning these days he was MIA). Rachel wasn't in favour (too many stupid questions); neither Alex or I really went into bat for him. He'd keep coming to the midnight sessions if he wanted to show. That was enough Tod.

I was nominated to take the proposal to Dr J. He listened as I went through it: 'We alternate between human suffering and brain-waves Tuesday to Thursday, and we keep them separate Monday and Friday.' (At her direction, we left Rachel to her solo sessions in remedial English—'I suck. You don't want any part of it.') Dr J agreed to it before I'd even finished. I was so upbeat about that, I wasn't bothered that he showed no surprise at anything I went on to say—just nodding when I told him that after all this time Rachel had come out with her story. I felt that in this I had trumped him somehow, her choice to tell us and not him; we knew and he didn't. I almost expected a pat on the back.

I didn't get it. 'How did you react to it?'

'What do you mean?'

'Well, how did it make you feel, hearing about what happened to her?'

I hadn't thought about it. 'I don't know. Angry, I guess.'

'Did it make you feel closer to her? Knowing?' And when I hesitated: 'I recall that was a motivating factor for you.'

I question now if it was a typical therapist's question, or a case of emotionally inept foraging. At the time, I took it as par for the course. 'Sure, in a way.'

'Your instinct was right, then. That's something to remember next time.'

I wasn't sure if he meant for me or him. I was thinking back to what Rachel had said at the waterhole, the picture of the room, and how I'd reconfigured it in my head. I told him how my version ended, in her escape.

'I did it like the stage, like you said.' My question now was: 'Then I changed it. Why haven't we done that?'

'Changed it?'

'Yeah—instead of just moving them around, the people, the pieces, the stuff you've told me to do, you know...'

'I'm not sure I've *told* you to do anything.'

'Exactly.'

214

'Sorry, I'm not following.'

'Okay, so you just said to put them in place and see what happens. So they stand in a room, sit on a couch—waste of time. I could have changed things.'

'Like you did with Rachel, you mean…'

Somehow, I persisted. I didn't name the player, just gave more generic examples. 'Like I get to the scissors first. Or I don't let him up again. Or I crack a chair over the back of his skull…You know, like change the ending. Why didn't we do that?'

He nodded, smiled. All the while he had been creeping up from behind.

'We can do that,' he said. 'I guess that's what you just did.'

It was his slam-dunk moment. I get it, the theory behind it. I got a sniff of it even back then (it isn't rocket science). How we deal with the past: it happened to us, and now we're fucked. Done and dusted. *Or* we have some control.

It allows you to go near something you have sealed tight and inject some oxygen around it; it lets you put out your hand and touch it. It isn't like you become friends or anything. It is just something you can coexist with. That's the theory anyway. I wasn't there yet, and I'm not saying I buy into it. It has the obvious flaw: every time I put myself into a hero act it just reminded me of the anti-hero I was, forever stuck with the fact of what I failed to do, and what I did.

'Try it with the next one,' he said.

I baulked.

'You don't have to tell me. I don't need to hear it. Just do it in your head. Go back to the worst of what happened, and change it. Get to the scissors first.'

'You mean do it now?'

'Now is good.'

I dropped my head, thought about the pattern of the carpet at my feet (mottled grey-green diamonds). 'Okay. I did it.'

'No, you didn't.'

'How do you know?'

'I don't. I just don't think you did.'

'Yeah, you're right. I might do it later.'

'Okay, let me know how that goes.'

'If I do it.'

'Yes, Daniel. If you do it.'

I had plenty of other things to occupy my time.

The group tutorials were up and running—one day comparing brainwaves (starting with the blink and the water bottle, moving through to meditation and algebra) and the next, wandering around in the multi-dimensional deprivation index of various third-world countries. Alternating between a kind of virtual exhibitionism (watch me, watch my brain!) and the scene-setting stage of a quest to save the world.

The three of us canvassed causal factors of white nationalism, globalism, big government, free markets, the alt-right. We dredged up some great stuff about organ harvesting in refugee camps and gang rapes in South Sudan—Rachel called them fun facts. For her benefit and his own piece of mind, Alex took it on himself to add a whole new category to the Trajectory of Human Suffering—there, in a space above the absence of God: the presence of God—as well as adding fundamentalism and fanaticism into the spidergrams of fragmentation, ignorance, war, injustice and mental pollution. Like little terrorists we started plotting cyber-action through dark web cartels. We were running out of blank space. Rachel asked Helen for new stock and we started whiteboarding problems into solutions. That was the only way she could ever come at it: *we are not talking about theory here.* I heard echoes in her later work: *This is not hypothetical—this is urgent and this is shameful.* Helen took it up in lessons, loading our screens with offensive political memes and the heads of global citizens good and bad and ugly; the slums of South Asia; cluster maps of social media activity.

Rachel gave us another reason for pause one day. 'Shouldn't we be looking at any positive stuff? There must be something good happening.' And when we sat dumbfounded: 'I mean like medical discoveries...Some of this must be getting better.'

Alex looked at her with an air of 'way to ruin a good time', but he was ready for it. When he went into the zone—as he did now—I wondered to myself if his diagnosis put him on the spectrum. 'Improving trends in HIV and child mortality, malaria...Schooling for girls in Sri Lanka. There's a machine that can convert sewer sludge to drinking water; that could be big—2.5 billion lack access to safe sanitation. There's a nanosheet that absorbs oil spills.'

It was his suggestion to put all that up onto a separate whiteboard.

Tod made a joke of missing his invitation to the 'new groups' but didn't seem to mind. He needed to 'stick to his own thing anyway', which we assumed was the diet and exercise routine; we assumed he'd been having trouble staying on the wagon. Then he stopped coming to the midnight sessions. He said it was because he was sleeping. I didn't really buy that; it looked like he was having some issues beyond weight gain—I saw him arguing with Greg outside the waiting-room window—but there wasn't any reason to dwell on it. Magnolia had taken over in the kitchen and embarked on a festival of curries. The midnight sessions were winding down, now by arrangement only. We had all started sleeping.

There was one night—just one—when it was only Rachel

and me. Straight up she placed a ban on any talk about brains and misery (*enough already...*) and asked instead about the kids at my school. I shrugged, said there were two camps: 'potential customer' or 'irrelevant to my existence'. She appeared appropriately impressed when I told her about my business profits, turning on her side to face me, but was equally firm that I needed now to cease all operations. I turned to face her too, immediately deeming our new positions as a natural and destined progression—not just side by side, but face to face, soon to be a single entity in a changed universe. The next move was mine; that is how I read it, wriggling closer in my sleeping bag so there were just inches between us. When she eyeballed me my entire chest cavity pulsated in a way I hadn't imagined it could, and as she reached over to put her hand on my bare arm, I remember wondering how more people didn't die doing this.

Seen in that context it's possible her next words saved my life: 'This—*us*—is never going to happen.'

Undeterred, undeflated (not even close): *It already is happening.* That was my thought. But I didn't use words to argue the point. Instead I hovered my hand over hers, so that she could feel it too, the voltage transmitting cell to cell...and in that electromagnetic moment, I became certain of two things, both of them pivotal in defining the shape of things to come.

It would happen (however, whenever). And I would never in my life deal drugs again.

Design and Technology

I see faces in things. We all do sometimes, but I see them several times in a day. In cloud patterns, agar plates; in the skin on the back of my hand. We were looking at the whiteboards this one time—the dot points of suffering—and even when I looked away and back again, I could see it: a charcoal profile with eyes cast down to the ground. A face that carried the despair of the world.

Soon after that it came up in one of our sessions. I was looking at the black lake in the photo (no end of faces in that pond), and he said I was finding meaning in random patterns.

'Some would call it a form of delusional behaviour, a precursor to schizophrenia.' Startled, I took a couple of seconds to see that he was smiling. 'Or maybe you just have a thing for faces,' he said.

He was messing with me and at the same time serious: *This is the rubbish we are dealing with.*

I remember looking back at him and starting to piece it together in my mind. What had led him here: the photograph on the shelf—a proud moment, a discovery and a prize—and then a realisation. *I was wrong,* he had said. And something else: *To hell with them…*There was an *us* and a *them*, and he was up against it. He was going rogue, and he was bringing me in; taking me on to his ride. That was the sense I got that day, that he was setting a challenge for me.

Go rogue.

Later when I read the transcripts, it was clearer. Early in his evidence they questioned his qualifications for his role at the School, pointing out that he hadn't worked directly with young people for ten years.

> DR J: That is right. My immediate experience related to developing drug treatments for children and young people.
> COUNSEL: Groundbreaking drug treatments—many would describe them in that way, isn't that so Doctor?
> DR J: Many would, certainly.
> COUNSEL: What would you say?
> DR J: I would say that I saw the results. I am still seeing them, and I warn you, we are yet to see them all.

In spite of the scope of that statement, there were no more questions about the drugs—nor was there any mention of the School being in some way externally controlled. When I came to read the transcripts, I was surprised by that. What happened at the School and how it operated was the subject of extensive cross-examination. On reading it, one would have thought that it was Dr J on trial—his vision and his methods, all under fire. But there was never any mention of two camps within a larger operation, and never, not in a single question or answer, was there any hint of the magnitude of it. Of course, the reason for this was simple. The judge and the lawyers and the bit-part players: none of them knew.

The revision of the curriculum started about five months in, when PW didn't show up to a tutorial. Ten minutes after starting time, in walked the Doctor, looking unusually dishevelled and hurried. With strands of loose hair falling over his shiny forehead, he kept one eye on the door as though expecting any minute to be interrupted. It crossed my mind he had been drinking.

'I'll be taking the class for a few days, people, if that's okay,' he said. 'I just wanted to bring you together.'

When I asked why, he replied with a cryptic smile: 'Strength in numbers.'

He smoothed the hair back off his forehead, pushed up his sleeves and sat on the desk in front of us. 'There is a piece of information I think you are entitled to know, so...Where do I start?' Picking up Rachel's headset, he searched our faces as though we could offer some guidance. There was something reassuring in his physical proximity, his physical strength. We leaned in.

There followed an explanation of what I had already been told: beyond our sessions with PW, the headsets were a device to record and monitor our neural patterns: the lessons, the music, the video games, the E-learning...all of it. Reports were kept and analysed.

'Your tablets are networked to a central database...Without your knowledge, I accept that. It amounts to poor practice, and I allowed it to happen.'

The last refrain he repeated: he allowed it to happen. It was his confession and he was seeking absolution. Rachel was not forthcoming. She called it for what it was: 'fucking sneaky' and 'for sure illegal'. Throughout the length of her rant—*what right do you have?*—I remained silent, and Alex laughed. He said it was the sickest thing he'd ever heard. Whatever the reactions, nothing seemed to have much impact on the Doctor's script, with which he continued.

'I would like to apologise personally for the invasion of your privacy. My only excuse is that I am required to work within certain parameters; these things are to an extent out of my hands...'

There followed some discussion of our contracts, the fact that his holding out on us constituted a breach on the part of the School, and an echo of the conversation I'd shared with Dr J during negotiations:

'Most certainly yes, you can leave.'

'What if we don't want to leave?'

'Then you stay.'

Rachel raised the issue of our status: students, patients, prisoners, guinea-pigs; or all or none of the above? Legal non-entity?

I listened, observed, taking the opportunity to mentally segue my narrative: *They wake in a room that is not a real room. They are not real walls. They are not real people, but ideas in the mind of a madman...*

The Doctor was patient with our questions and careful in his answers. The best he could do now was to ensure we were in possession of the right information. That was the next stage: the reports. He had taken the liberty of preparing reports for Alex and Rachel covering their time at the school to date and collating my weekly reports into a single document. He handed them to each of us and we started to flick through our bar graphs and brain scans. As the mood of the room internalised, we worked our way slowly through the pages—the process behind it forgotten and forgiven, the information like an opiate to be feasted on, devoured. Here it was, page after page, week after week: the blood flow in our brains, the working of our minds.

Alex pointed to the dates. The Doctor confirmed they could link activity data to a particular day and suggested we try an example using Helen's stories.

'So here, number twelve: the sea-god lesson. The next column is the number of the image in that lesson, with the length of time spent on the image and the area of dominant brain activity. For this example, Alex, it tells us you spent limited time on that first image, Proteus—a great deal more time on the second image.'

He flicked pages to check a label on that one: Boy with Growth. 'This was your area of dominant brain activity, in the cerebral cortex,' he said as he drew an outline around the area. 'Right here at the junction of the three lobes. This area of bright orange shading shows an extremely active neural network; this is empathy. At this sort of level, it would indicate an ability to mirror pain.'

Up until this point the Doctor's tone was perfectly clinical; he could as well have been talking to Alex about his digestive tract as the neural pathways that formed his psychic and emotional framework. But at the mention of the ability to mirror pain, Alex flinched, and the Doctor saw it. He paused and pulled his seat closer so that their knees were touching. It was a gesture of intimacy such as I had never seen in any of my sessions. When he spoke again, it was softer, murmurous, like a cone had formed around the two of them and he was speaking a dialect only Alex could understand. 'You remember, we talked about this—the risks; it is enough without theirs too. A gift, a curse...'

Alex nodded, squinting under the spotlight. The Doctor patted his hand and turned back to me and Rachel. We had found our corresponding pages. The Doctor looked over to mine and pointed out that there was no shading. 'The area failed to become active.'

'What does that mean?'

'In your case, we might want to fortify that response. To the extent that it is possible.'

Rachel let out a guffaw. 'We might want to make you a nicer person.' (I'd been having a rough few days. After an email from Mary I'd started to slide, punched the fridge, pushed over a whiteboard and banged Rachel's door again. She summed it up: 'You've gone to shit.' She'd been slow to accept my apology.)

Things got weirdly personal here. The Doctor seemed to consider Rachel's comment for a moment before flicking back and forward in my report to find where this particular network spiked. The only one that was even a little bit orange was the agar plate. It seemed I had more empathy with a plate of swarming bacteria.

There was another point of comparison between me and Alex in lesson nine, image one—Prince Sado, the terrible son who starved to death in the rice chest. Alex had an unsurprising level of empathy, 'whereas Daniel experienced an elevated level of limbic activity—that is, pleasure. Perhaps a sense he got what was coming?'

I nodded. The end result: no question. It was justice. The Doctor raised a hand in Rachel's direction as though to fend her off. 'There are reasons we empathise with different things. Our experiences, our circumstances...they can combine to make it hard for us to put ourselves in someone else's shoes.'

'And if we'd like to round it out—you, Rachel, for the most part in this whole part of the "boy with growth" lesson, show zero activity—with a theta burst here...It appears you were on some kind of shamanic journey.' Her face was blank. 'Or in a state of deep sleep,' he said with a rare, broad smile. 'One of the two.'

We ended on the high note, so to speak, of the music session. 'Wait for it,' the Doctor said, getting us each onto the same page: lesson seventeen, the Beach Boys, 'Good Vibrations'. Our colours were consistent across the board—not just the three of us, but everyone—Tod and the sisters and the back-row boys. That was a big deal for the Doctor. He was marvelling at the images like our brains had produced a multi-part harmony of their own.

'Look at the synchronisation here; it isn't just auditory processing—it's movement, attention, memory, all of it. The music fortifies the connections.' He pointed to the penultimate row of head shots. 'By the second refrain it is right across both hemi-spheres.' He smiled and put a hand on my arm. 'This is the jackpot. This is what it means to commune with your brain.'

After Dr J left, we decided to conduct a covert search for images of real brains, the gross stuff, Alex said: brain porn.

We found brains of all sorts, jellied and bloody like a foetus, or dried up and jaundiced (a cauliflower). We stuck mainly with the bloody ones, zooming in to get a close up on the capillaries, the folds and ridges of the tissue. There was a cool image showing the layers of brain pulled back in strips across the top of the head, ear to ear—the scalp, bone, dura, brain tissue—but our favourite (even Rachel only pretended to gag) was a picture of a head sawed in half to reveal the full monty, shiny and gelatinous. Tufts of long fair hair were still attached on either side of the scalp, and captured in the picture at the edge of the image was a hand in a bloody rubber glove. There followed a series of images of the slicing up of the brain—one captioned (seriously): 'The amygdala—that is your fear and anger.'

It is not very big, your fear and anger, tucked up there in your temporal lobe.

There was no end of interesting material here, an entire internet subculture, countless Pinterest pages, and why not? It was compelling stuff. Scrolling and clicking, from gruesome images to fun facts. Our top seven:

1. If you brush your teeth with the wrong hand you will increase your self-control (we agreed to try it but were unclear on how to measure results).
2. The brain has more fat than any other organ in the body (one for Tod).
3. Seven hours after his death someone stole Einstein's brain.
4. The cerebral cortex is 4 mm thick. The human brain contains 86 billion neurons which travel at 220 mph and charge 25 watts of power (*okay*, so that was my like not theirs; they had to force me off the 'interesting measurements' page).
5. The subconscious mind controls 95 per cent of our brain (I don't know how they know that).
6. You have 70,000 thoughts a day (ditto).
7. Lack of sleep leads to lack of growth.

None of us grew that night. Sleepless, we ended up in the courtyard where our brief conversation moved from a reprise of *What the fuck is this place?* through to bravado around *Who cares, all good*, into weighty silence as we pondered our individual and starkly contrasting neural activity. My sense was that we were each waiting to see if the others rubbished the whole thing, but nobody did. As the conversation trickled off and I took one last look at the stars, I decided to lead myself through the task of communing with my brain:

- Close your eyes.
- Picture the pre-autopsy brain inside my own skull.
- Now excavate, layer by layer, through the cerebral cortex into the deep limbic system, all the way to the brain stem.

I learned quickly that what the brain does when you try to focus it in on itself is deflect to other parts of the body. It arcs up. Out of nowhere there is pressure in nasal passages, a ringing in the ears, a gaseous gut reaction, then other shit comes in and eventually you just want to go to sleep, leaving the brain safely out of reach: job done. In short, the brain doesn't want you getting too close. I'm not talking about mantras and meditation; I'm talking about going in, feeling your way around. The pink clump, just a few centimetres in, so close yet so far away.

To reach my brain as I lay in the courtyard that night, I had to get tough and do what the bloody rubber glove had done: saw through my scalp and split my cranium in two, open it right up. It was a messy business and I didn't think it was what the Doctor had in mind when he talked about *communing*, but it was *my* way and it was getting me steadily further in. I ventured into new territory, going where no boy had gone, a journey into the centre of the brain, *over the ridges and folds. I discover the deadly molecule and blast it into oblivion and save all our innocent lives, then I arrive in the midbrain. This is the jackpot, the default network of humankind; it is lit up, a bright and rolling tunnel. I will reset it and be cured. We will all be cured. We are, each of us, miracles. I look down, not through a human eye. What sits in the cranium is a life source, an interstellar power...*

'Daniel, buddy.'

I opened my eyes. Alex and Rachel: one on either side. There is that time between night and day when the sun has risen and you can still see the stars in the sky. When you have everything.

I had a dream when I was five that next to the bins on the street I stumbled across a big Santa sack of good things—Chokito bars and ninja figures and fluoro soccer balls. Then I woke up, empty-handed. I hated myself all week long for not reaching out and holding on to that bag, convinced it could have travelled with me between worlds. I remembered that dream as events unfolded at the School over the next little while.

The shift in approach reflected in the revision of the curriculum and the introduction of a full disclosure policy was also the basis for contract renegotiation. My take was that the benefits all went one way: ours, but the Doctor was adamant that there were risks involved and in accepting them, we were doing our bit. He was right. I was in effect signing up to do something I'd sworn I'd never do: group therapy.

But that was not immediately apparent. For the next session, we met in the courtyard. There was a jug and glasses on the bench and a pair of mynah birds that flew away on our arrival. (The curra-wongs were coming less; the trees were bare and the ground had been swept.) The Doctor wore a pair of round-rimmed sunglasses and sat on the table casting his eyes around the upper level of the building, the framed glass and concrete.

'It *is* good, isn't it?' he said, and launched into a spiel about balance and symmetry, the recurrence of elements and the texture of the concrete and timber.

'The pears, they are the centre point. During the course of the day as the sunlight moves across the space, the elements orbiting around them—the pots and the glass and the corridor and class-rooms, and any time at all, the building frames the sky.'

There was more: the formwork above the glass—each section with the plugged holes, the different numbers (18 sections, 92 holes). That was important, that there was a gradation between the lower and upper level, that the form evolved. The variation in height and dimension.

It was hard to agree with him when he said it was important for us to understand all this, but what worried me was not the randomness of what he said (by now par for the course), but the fact that there was something nostalgic in his tone, like he was speaking of a golden time, past tense. At the end of it Greg appeared in the corridor alongside a stocky woman with a honey-coloured pony-tail, who was dressed in a man's suit. They walked around a few times, not speaking. We asked Dr J who she was and he said 'occupational health and safety'. When he left he seemed to time it to cross the corridor when they were on the other side.

Next time Greg took my measurements (another 1.3 cm), she popped up again. She didn't introduce herself, just looked at my numbers with a frown of concentration.

As I said, the group thing crept up on us.

It was raining so we went instead to Dr J's office. He patted his knees and launched into lecture mode. Recapping on the levels of activity in the various areas of the brain, he talked about how we were made up of different parts, different sub-personalities—and how each is a necessary part of a structure, how each plays a role in our self-preservation. Even the parts we don't like, he said, but he didn't want to start with them. To start, he wanted us to identify a part of us we liked well enough, or at least were okay with. Something we wouldn't want to change.

After a while Rachel said, 'Like what?'

'Okay, so for instance: Alex, the part of Alex that likes to dance.'

229

A silence.

'Okay, I'll start,' said Alex. 'The part of me that likes to dance. Your turn, Daniel.'

I mumbled something with the word fucker in it.

'It's hard,' Rachel said.

'Yes, it is,' Dr J conceded. 'We tend not to like ourselves. You were a good runner at school, how about that?'

She shrugged. 'I won races.'

'Okay, good. Sprints or distance?'

'Distance.'

'What makes you a good distance runner?'

'My legs?'

'Yes, what else?'

'I dunno. I wanted to win.'

'You are determined, and you go the distance. So there it is— the part of Rachel she doesn't want to change: the runner.'

And so we kept going with parts for a bit. I said I was pretty happy with my entrepreneurial side, and we all conceded our maths brains could stay. Rachel liked that she kept things tidy. That was about the sum of it. Rachel kept coming back to his idea we wouldn't be better off without the bad parts. That didn't make sense to her.

'There *are* no bad parts,' the Doctor said.

She said that was just bullshit.

'Each part is to be valued and understood. It is important that you understand that.'

She was getting impatient: 'So Daniel gets a gold star for banging down someone's door.'

His answer to that was there are parts that need to be promoted, and parts that need to be managed.

'Well, he better start managing it 'cause I've dealt with enough shitty people I can tell you and there is some bad shit going on with this boy and I am saying here and now that's fine if you want it that way but you leave me out of it. You leave me the fuck alone.'

It was difficult for me to process my thoughts at this time. I loved and hated what was happening. The fact she cared enough to string the sentences together was a minor triumph, but the fact we were in group—the group thing; like I said, it crept up.

The Doctor ran with it: 'Okay so let's stick with your example, Rachel…if that's okay.'

I don't know whose permission he was requesting. I never gave it. Droplets of sweat ran down the side of my body as he asked me why I banged on her door and I said I didn't know. He asked me if it was because I wanted Rachel to open the door and I said not really. Did I want to give her a message? I didn't know. It felt like he was picking at sores. It didn't feel possible for me to remain through another of his questions so I got up and walked out.

I went into the courtyard and waited in the rain. I thought someone would follow me out, but they didn't. I sat there alone, then went to my room and looked for faces in the shadows on the ceiling and wondered what they were talking about now.

Some time after dinner that night I saw the envelope slipped under my door. Another email from Mary.

> Dan no need to worry about me Ive got everything in place.
> They had a pest man do the whole building except for the ones
> he refused to step a foot in cant blame him poor bugger. Nina
> says he was one of them muslims but a nice fellow in spite of
> it. Nina walked me to the shops and I cooked us the sausage
> casserole and we sat on the walkway and ate it in bowls and
> watched the shenanigans. Nothing you haven't seen before

I didn't mind opening it and I didn't mind thinking back. The flats

231

without the tenants, before they came.

Before: Mary walks me to school and goes to work at the pie shop or the place they made jars and after school I go to Nina's and eat fairy roll and when Mary comes to get me she opens the door to our place and calls out 'we're here' like there is someone to tell and sometimes she brings leftover pies and we eat them sitting on the carpet while we watch movies or pick our favourite contestants on reality TV and when we finish we stretch out and I use a part of her as a pillow.

I didn't mind. The timing felt somehow deliberate. Like it was paving the way.

In our next solo session, Dr J took it up where we left off.

I didn't sit. I paced around, stopped at the photo on the wall and matched trees with their reflections, some blurred in rippled water. He asked me how I thought it went the other day.

'What did *you* think?'

'I thought it went very well.'

I laughed. 'Low expectations.'

'I didn't have any.'

'Well there you go.'

'Can we take it up again?'

'Take what up?'

'What we were talking about when you left.'

When I resisted it was only because it was expected of me: 'I don't think I was really talking about anything...I think you were just trying to make us fit into this bullshit theory of yours about sub-parts.'

'Sub-*personalities*.' He got up from his seat and came over to the wall and waited for me to look at him. 'The thing is, Daniel, I know and you know it isn't bullshit.'

I shrugged, asked him what they talked about after I left.

He paused, nodded, accepting the question as a way forward and positioning himself into his next move. 'Funnily enough, we talked about the photo you're staring at now, about where we'd put ourselves if we were in the frame.'

He wanted me to guess what they said. I thought about it and got it right both counts: Alex in the woods, Rachel climbing high up in the mountain.

'And you?'

I stared at the lake, at the section with the bracken floating on the surface of the water. I thought it would be the deepest and I imagined other bottom feeders. It is the only place they can live. All around the bracken, the lake reflected a dense canopy of branches so that the water was black and bottomless.

When he spoke his voice was gentle and quiet. This was his move. 'You don't need to tell me, Daniel. But you can.'

I did. I started.

I told him to ask the questions.

'Who is there?'

'The two of them.'

His lips are not moving but I can hear all his words like he is inside my head. *Filthy durry-muncher. Fat horse.* The days blur, the things he said, and did. The Doctor could read me: 'Just pick one, Daniel, one day, one thing he did.'

'He hated the stink of smoke on her skin.'

'Where is he?'

'On the couch.'

'Where is Mary?'

'Coming in from outside.'

Brian said she'd been smoking; she said no. He found her

packet and made her take one out. The Doctor asked where I was. I told him: I am listening from the bedroom. I get up and stand at the door. He has her by the hair. I don't come out, but I want to.

'So step through the doorway, Daniel,' the Doctor said. 'He can't get you here.'

You come closer and I'll drop her and kick her teeth out.

If she likes the taste of it so much...

It is slow. The boy watches. She swallows the paper and tobacco but spits out the filter. She is coughing, gagging, and Brian has gone. I get her water and she sticks her fingers down her throat.

Later, I said he had to leave; she had to kick him out. But he had said sorry and started piling crates and paying rent money. I said I'd move out, then; I'm not living here with him around. 'You can't,' she said. 'You've got nowhere to go. You don't have any money.'

She was wrong; I had money by then, but I couldn't tell her that. I slept a night in the spinning ball at the park. It was nice in the spinning ball. She said if he did anything again it'd be over. 'I promise.' For a couple of weeks it was best behaviour. He fixed the light in the bathroom and made burgers.

'What do you feel when you think about him?' the Doctor asked.

That isn't the right question.

He told me to start again and make it different, the way I wanted. But I shook my head. Why I couldn't do that is because what I remembered—the dark enfolding my core—was not how much I hated him, but how much I hated her.

Narrative Structure and Technique

The waterhole on a clear day, warm and still; their voices a background noise. The willow branches reflected on the water.

It was different from the lake in the Doctor's photograph. I stared at the prism of colour—the perfect reconstruction like a secondary existence. I picked up a stone and threw it and the image fractured. Only moments later, as the ripples faded, there it was again, re-formed, gloating—like the Terminator blasted in bullet holes, healing up to kill again.

When light hits a surface there are a number of possible outcomes: it is diffused and absorbed, it is transmitted through the surface, or it is reflected back. It is linear algebra, a pretty simple multiplication. Reflectivity is a ratio. (Although there are a lot of factors that mean that some days things just look different.) I could explain in a great deal more detail how this (reflection and refraction) fits in with electromagnetic theory—think of light as an electromagnetic wave and you are halfway there. The reason I won't do that is because I am like a dog whose chain has been yanked every time I pull that way. I bore people, often—the members of my family most of all. The reason I do this is that everything comes back to the spectrum in one way or another and it frustrates me (deeply) that people lack even a basic understanding of the concepts, despite the fact that our brains are wired to grapple with that and much, much more.

(It is said that my timing is bad and my subjects are not age-appropriate—that when she was twelve, for instance, my daughter did not need to understand how electromagnetic currents travel through her body. If she is to understand the hormonal cycle, I argued, the role of electromagnetic currents is both essential and unavoidable. I am told I picked the wrong moment because this was an important 'talk'. I also told her she would begin to have the desire to touch the opposite sex. Things got heated. The twelve-year-old left the table.

I am further told that smoking a joint in the back garden with the now-sixteen-year-old is not an appropriate father–daughter milestone. I counter that it is a critical moment of shared internal reflection; we are the better for it. And I maintain my stance.)

Refraction. On some level, I think that is what we were doing: bending light.

On our second attempt, we nailed it.

It was a dark and windy night. (The Doctor suggested that as a scene-setter and I ran with it.) *I enter stage right, the only door. The lights aren't on, but I hear a sniffle, a whimper. I am alert to danger, prepared.*

Then a perspective shift: it is Brian and Mary; they are in the kitchen. So that's it then, the three of us in place, three shapes in the dark. (In the flats, there were always hundreds of others around you but when it mattered, just a single, silent witness.)

It was a dark and windy night.

'I said that already.'

'That's okay. Keep going.'

They don't hear me or see me because I am prepared and I am like a shadow.

What I see: first, their shapes. He is holding her over the kitchen bench with her arm behind her back. The gas burner is on and there is a pot on the floor. The volume turns up and there is a different register of sound, low and high, animal, human...I move across the room. I am like a shadow, that is how.

'Go on, that's fine.'

I am there in the kitchen, behind him. I don't turn back. I form an intention. I lift the pot from the floor and raise it over my head and in a single, sweeping motion I crack it against the side of his skull, the thud of metal on skin on bone. It is a vibration more than a sound. The man falls forward against the kitchen bench as the woman becomes free.

His hand is in the fire.

We can smell his skin.

This time, *his* skin.

It was late in the afternoon, the Doctor and I standing in the gentle yellow light. He was close to me, close enough for me to feel the heat of him. I didn't move away, and I wasn't surprised at what he said next.

'But that isn't it, Daniel, is it?'

•

237

Over the years, Rachel has been careful in what she gives me, like dosing a sick child. But one time she asked to meet my mother. 'For God's sake don't take it the wrong way.'

She saw the burns. Mary held them up for her to see and told her that I saw how it happened. 'He saw a lot. He did his best.'

Like a shadow. That is her story now. We all have one.

But move it any further forward:

Mary places a hand on my shoulder and the other cups the back of my neck.

I flinch.

'I know you're angry with me. I know this is hard for you.'

You don't know the first thing.

Later she is holding my laptop. She is logged in, and she is shouting. 'Who is V? Who is X?' I lunge forward.

Hate is a substance that accumulates and hardens. When they were gone, it was just me and Mary. I don't know how to change that. Hate doesn't listen when you tell it to move.

Now I try this:

Around the bed there are four of them, two sitting down, two standing back. Hands tied to the bedposts, it isn't a girl. It is the right person this time. It is me.

May the blood of the lamb...

May you tremble and flee.

I dive down. Past the mathematician and the scientist, the husband and the father, until I am sitting on the kitchen floor.

It is a different day. Her head is in my hands.

There is an area in the brain known as the septum that sits in the midline between the two cerebral hemispheres. It connects into the hypothalamus, deep in the unconscious regions. The science is inexact, but circuiting between the two are the nerve cells that house our circuits of aggression, our biological roots of rage. Somewhere in that buzzing mess lies the bomb in the brain.

Her hand is resting in spilled milk and the blood makes pink swirls. I am looking at that because I can't look at her face. I am crying and she says she is all right. It will be all right, she says. I pick up pieces of broken plate and tell her I am sorry.

Tell me, Doctor, what part of me did that?

What I like to think about sometimes are the million points in the brain that never light up on any scan. It is true for every single person. In my mind, I connect us into one shared neural network— each of us forming such an infinitesimal part of something so vast and unknown that our imprint is invisible and our individual actions are wiped away.

Music: Sounds and Silences

I click on the names of strangers, the names of friends.

Case studies, all of us. A series of diverging and replicated experiences: metrics, not narratives.

Now I am starting to see that what matters is the purpose for which it is all collected: the proof point. What is the larger story they are trying to tell?

On one of our last nights at the waterhole, Alex told us about the day he first walked home from school alone.

He was eight years old. He and his father had just moved away from the city, and Alex had 'gone quiet'. At first his dad said that was okay; but it had been long enough, and now it was time for him to 'claim the place' and 'own his path'. The first step in achieving that involved them standing together barefoot in the bush behind the house, closing their eyes and imagining roots springing out from the soles of their feet into the ground, as far down into the earth as their minds would take them, and then permitting the energy to reverse and surge upward into their bodies and arms, to eventually sprout out through the tips of their fingers. In effect, to become trees. This, his father assured him, would foster their own growth and sense of belonging.

Step two was easier for Alex to grasp as a concept but a much greater challenge: to walk home alone from school. It was six kilometres, and his father calculated that if he maintained a steady pace it would take him about an hour.

He did not underestimate the size of the challenge for his son. In the lead-up to the big day they marked out the best pedestrian route (four backstreets, two sets of lights, one long winding road to the front gate), and on the day itself, he dropped Alex at school and handed him a printout of the directions. (Knowing full well the boy's chief concern was not getting lost, but getting home alive.)

What are you afraid of? his father would ask when he found Alex in various states of paralysis. And the answer?

Death. In his more fluid moments, he could put it into words. 'I am dying.'

The answer—*we all are*—did not, of course, cut it.

As Alex spoke, we didn't interrupt him, not even Tod. He traced his steps that day as though every tree and pothole were etched in his memory, starting as he walked out the gate of his school. By the first street corner his heart was pounding in his ears and his body was like a leaking tap—'I was sweating and crying and I kept needing to take a piss.' He started counting, like his dad had told him to. He got all the way to a thousand.

I could relate to his fear of the streets—like the bush to me, a minefield in the mind, a series of horror-flashes of what is real, what is imagined…The sound of a dog barking: yellow teeth puncture flesh. A roar of acceleration: body dragged into the rusted underbelly. Any sighting of people on foot or behind wheels: chloroform and knives and white vans—every bad story he'd ever heard about bad people.

And with each image, he was falling into the bottomless well of non-being, cold and airless, his mind a blank, his organs failing: something akin to that happened eleven times between Alex walking out of the school gate and turning into his street. With the stops and starts it had taken him almost two hours. His shirt soaked through with sweat, his head pounding, he was at the point of collapse. It wasn't until he reached the next door neighbour's house that he saw the figure standing at the gate. As Alex approached, his father motioned him through in a definitive gesture and commenced a series of deep breaths, continuing until Alex could repeat at least one, and then: 'After me,' his father said, as he began to pound his chest with both his fists, slow and rhythmic. 'Come on, with me…'

And Alex did what he asked. He pounded his chest. He lifted it up, to the extent that he could, and pounded it again, and again, until his father was satisfied the motion was driven by his heart and not his hands.

They sat on the front steps for a long time, the silence broken only when his father turned to look him in the eyes and said: 'You are good and brave.'

Alex leaned his head on his shoulder and fell asleep right there and then.

Four years later, when Alex's father died in front of him, he took his son's fear of death with him. Partly because whenever the fear crept in, his father loomed up in his psyche and no part of Alex would allow himself to be anything but good and brave. (Most times he conjured the image of himself pounding his chest in time with his father; once he even caught himself doing it.)

But another factor was more transformative. Death was now his most-loved father's permanent state of being—so as time went on, and Alex missed his presence more and more, he hankered to be closer to it: to find a deeper understanding, a kinship. He embarked on a comprehensive research project to consider death from every angle and resolved that there was nothing to fear because there was, in fact, nothing to come. That a decomposed corpse was simply a nutrient for the soil.

In time, it was Alex's continued existence that formed the subject of his dread—specifically, the uncertainty around the duration. For young people the term of life can feel like a life sentence. What Alex required was a way to exercise control. The basis of his second project was his need to know that in whatever circumstance he found himself, he could end it. He needed an exit pass.

He began to consider his surrounds, scoping heights and sharp edges, bodies of water. Imagining the shape it might take. When he was satisfied his death was possible in a practical sense, he could relax. In the idea of non-being he found his solace. Death was his friend and confidante—dare it be said, his soul mate.

And that was before he started the next project.

I am trying to think now when I sensed Alex was no longer marching beside us. He put on a good show, I can say that. Later I thought about his father at the gate and I realised that, day in day out, coming to lessons, walking us through his whiteboards—that is what he was doing: being good and brave. He was convincing enough to let us believe we were mapping a collective future, *marching with the fervour of purpose...*It was just a matter of time before he had to show it up for the made-up story that it was, before he had to show us what was real.

A couple of days in a row he said he was tired, and then he didn't show up for a session with PW and I remember I was more disappointed than concerned. It was the last day of an exercise to track gamma, and Alex and I were trailing way behind Rachel. PW had taken on a whole new aura around the three of us. Smiling, he'd shake his head and repeat, 'You guys...you guys...' Not dismissive, but in a marvelling kind of way, sometimes resting a hand on our shoulders.

And then: no Alex. No big deal. It wasn't like it hadn't happened before. When he came in to breakfast a couple of days later, it was to tell us he'd be skipping PW's sessions.

'I am doing more Doctor,' he said.

He kept coming to the whiteboard sessions, but even then, he wanted to work more alone (a seven-slide PowerPoint on hazardous waste in Honduras): fixated on a particular problem, more granular than ever before.

What 'doing more Doctor' meant—I learned this only on reading the transcripts—was that twice a week over two weeks he sat in a chair in his office while the Doctor collected a baseline of twenty-one sites of his brain. There was some argument in the proceedings about the need for this, given the precariousness of his mental state, the Doctor providing cogent reasons as to why observing the patterns of one's own brainwaves might produce positive clinical outcomes. There were pages and pages on the risk assessments that were performed or not performed and how the decisions were made—the decision not to medicate, the delay in treatment, and then back to the results of the tracking.

The overall theme of the questioning was that whatever he was doing, the monitoring and the feedback, whatever combination, whatever magic potion, it didn't work. The Doctor disagreed. It was during those sessions, he said, that Alex was at his most frank and open.

> COUNSEL: Could you give us an example of that, of something he imparted to you in one of these discussions?
> DR J: I can. He said he wanted to curl into a ball and enter into a state of non-being.
> COUNSEL: You mean die?
> DR J: That is what he meant, yes I think so.
> COUNSEL: And your response to that?
> DR J: I encouraged him to curl into a ball, and assured him he would not die.

Alex was not speaking figuratively.

Let me explain what it looked like in practice, on the concrete floor of the classroom, under the second whiteboard. One arm clutched at a knee, the other leg outstretched, a hand cradling his ear, eyes open, unblinking. It was a shape similar to the one I'd seen that day in his dance class, then with the teacher kneeling beside him. Because I'd seen it then, and because Rachel had pretty much lived it, we weren't overly alarmed. I did what the teacher had done, knelt down. I was nervous about touching him, but I did; I placed a hand on his shoulder and when he didn't flinch, I moved closer and put my whole arm around him. Rachel came down on the other side and held on to the outstretched leg with both her hands. It was an odd configuration, but it felt like what we needed to do for him to know we were there. There aren't that many of them, the times when what you do really matters, when you can change the course of things. We said his name. We said he'd be okay. We said we weren't going anywhere.

We are here. We repeated that a lot.

I lay down on the floor to get to eye level. It was what I had seen before, as he stared into a computer screen late at night, but when the noise came it wasn't something I'd heard before. There is a sound that is made when you rub your finger around the rim of a half-filled glass. It is like a musical note that is held. It is a sad song, low-pitched, clear and beautiful. It is the vibration of crystals transmitting into air. That is the sound that emanated from him now, the sound that had always been there, waiting. It was telling us something but we had no way to interpret it.

Rachel and I looked at each other in an unspoken pact: now that he had us, we would make it go away again.

It is what is known as the pointy end of the proceedings. Was the management and treatment of the children appropriate and reasonable in the circumstances? Helen K was recalled to give further evidence about the research project, how and why it came about.

> COUNSEL: So you embark into a universe defined by every-thing terrible, everything that might lead a young man to conclude there is no point in living.
> HELEN K: As I said, we couldn't ignore what was in his head...
> COUNSEL: What was in his head; yes of course, you took such good care of what was in his head. You support a course in which a boy with a history of chronic clinical depression is taken off his medication and you feed his mind with stories, depictions, of child sexual slavery and the public stoning of women...
> HELEN K: I did not provide him with those stories. Our focus was statistics and mapping.
> COUNSEL: No stories, no videos?
> HELEN K: That is right.

There were four pages of questions on how Alex got hold of the Yemen video. It was not through Helen. It was a USB drive on his computer. Before this, Dr J had been asked the same questions and provided the same answers. At no time during the proceedings did they get to the bottom of it.

If I could go in to bat for Helen for a minute—because I'm not sure she did such a good job of it herself—it wasn't that she didn't try to steer Alex a different way. He just always found his way back.

An example: a lesson like any other, we pulled out our tablets and headsets. The intro (a response, I assumed, to Rachel's request) was a few images: Hitler, Superman and shelves filled with thousands of brains in Petri dishes. According to script, we worked through how the Führer had used Nietzsche to justify mass extermination—taking ethics out of it and keeping the focus on excellence, seguing neatly into the possibility that we were all being drip-fed, our values manufactured in a meta world, the brains-in-the-vat theory. Like the Matrix. Our version of the world fed to us through neuro-electrical signals. (I'm not saying we started light, just that it was Alex who led us into the dark.)

We were getting into some mind-bending fun facts when Helen stopped to pose a set of questions, which she asked us to consider through a number of different lenses—historical, scientific, philosophical. These and subsets of the same: Who am I? What is time? Is it okay to grow brain-dead babies to harvest their organs? We embarked pretty merrily on that. Whether or not fish could reason morphed rapidly into whether it was okay to have sex with animals (animals more generally, not just fish).

247

Some questions didn't generate much heat: what happens after death is that we cease to exist, agreed. A little more on whether we should start putting terminally ill people out of their misery. Rachel came in hard here that we couldn't trust people to make decisions for other people. Alex? No surprises there: as soon as we're brought into this world we must have the right to leave it. And then a question of his own: should we have a right to give birth when we don't have consent of the child that it wants to exist.

So we just die out now?

He didn't seem opposed to the idea, and there we had it: the downward spiral, the millions of babies born into a core of pain and suffering...

'Okay, Alex,' Helen said in a last brave attempt: 'But is all suffering bad?'

'Maybe not,' he replied, 'but let me give you some recent examples of bad.' And none of us could stop him.

Perhaps I willed the distraction; anyway, at some point during that lesson I heard voices outside and I went to the window. It was raining, the view to outside skewered through the foggy glass and the rivulets of rain. The window looked out to the driveway. I rubbed the glass and pressed my forehead against it.

I could see someone standing at the gate next to a blue car, twenty or so metres from the building. It was Greg. He was facing the direction of the front door, shaking his head, talking to someone who was out of our view. Rachel and Alex came up behind me and Alex put his finger to the window, chasing the drops as they fell. I rubbed the glass again but when the other person came into the frame, we stood back from the window so as not to be seen. It was Tod. He walked right up to Greg. They were arguing again, their voices rising against the clatter of rain. It was getting hard to see.

At one point, Tod pointed in his face and I think Greg laughed and I remembered what Tod had done to his teacher. Whatever the reason he was taking Greg on, I was glad of it. A part of me wished he would lash out. He didn't. He turned back; Greg got into the car and drove away.

That was the same day I saw PW for the last time.

A couple of weeks had passed since Dr J had taken over his lessons when I glimpsed him sitting at his desk. It was otherwise empty, all his bits and pieces packed away.

'Hello, Daniel,' he said. His T-shirt was pale pink, a skeleton wearing a bandana. 'I think you've grown again.'

'Yep,' I said and pointed to the backpack on the floor. 'You leaving?'

He nodded. 'I am.'

He looked unhappy. I told him that.

He said, 'How have your classes with the Doctor been going?'

I sat down and walked him through what we'd been doing, my struggle with sub-personalities...He was shaking his head and smirking, then he started getting a bit weird, putting on an American accent and spinning lines:

'You too can improve your mind

'It's as easy as checking your pulse

'A window into your brain...'

It was sort of funny but not. He looked sorry when I asked him what he was talking about.

'I don't know. I actually don't know...' He went quiet for a while and when he started again he seemed to be making his best effort to explain: 'I had this girlfriend once,' he said. 'I thought she was perfect. And it went to shit. She wasn't what I thought. Same kind of thing. I loved this place. You hear what I'm saying? I just think I should get out of here.'

Neither of us said anything. I had a sick feeling in my stomach about what he could tell me if I asked.

'I saw his computer,' I said, 'when I smashed up the office.'

PW looked at me, waiting to catch on. I told him about the videos, the other children, the other places.

'How many were there? How many videos?'

When I told him, he nodded like I was confirming something for him, but when I asked who they were, he stopped, stood up and pulled his bag onto his back. I felt a sudden surge of panic. I didn't want him to go.

At the door he turned back and smiled and waved his hand.

'Should I be getting out of here too?' I asked. 'Honest answer.'

'Honest answer,' he said. 'I don't know.'

The bell sounded, now a kookaburra. Last lesson of the day.

I knew decisions were being made in distant places, and I knew that the basis of those decisions was not the fostering of our well-being—our education, rehabilitation, treatment—whatever you want to call it.

What we could never have suspected, and what seven days of legal enquiry never even touched on, was that at some point right around now, a set of circumstances necessitated a shift in the corporate objective: the endgame. It is concealed somewhere here in the database. I have looked, searched through subject headings, guidelines, operations. There is no manual I can find...But somewhere it is there in the missives between mothership and satellite, a change in direction: from the laissez faire—'let it play out'—to a more determinative outcome: to demonstrate failure.

Alex was Case Study #1.

QUESTION 3

Who, when, where, how...

Chemical Reactions: Combustion

I am running light-footed the way she told me to run.

I know where to enter, the path now well-trodden. I know it in the dark so it is easy in the day, but I watch for every rock and ditch and tree root. That is my focus, to get out the other side and not to fall. Low cloud skims the top of the trees and cocoons the bushland. I run with the thought I will get there in time because it is the only way I can run. I run with the lie.

The primary purpose of the inquiry was to address a subset of questions: to establish identity, date, place, manner and cause. When it came down to it, they could tick them off, like the symptoms of a diagnosis.

Alex P, sixteen-year-old Caucasian male.

On Friday 9 August, between midnight and dawn. (He had been in the company of student Tod M in the courtyard until 11.45 pm. I arrived at the waterhole after 6 am.)

In the area of scrubland known as the waterhole, falling within the parameters of lot 257: property of Mindsight, a subsidiary of Neuropharma Inc.

How is cause and manner.

While *cause* is a physiological concept (the reason the organs shut down), *manner* relates to circumstances, including the question of intent, or lack thereof. What was in the mind of the deceased? Evidence was called from a number of witnesses in an attempt to shed light. Dr J talked about his last one-on-one session with Alex. He recalled that they talked about the concepts of heaven and hell but 'noted nothing out of the ordinary'.

'You took notes?' the lawyer asked.

Mental notes, it turned out. Helen K concurred with the Doctor, stating that beyond the phosphorus experiment incident and injury, she did not see any evidence of a 'rapid descent' as had been put to her—more a 'plateau'. After a period of non-attendance, Alex was engaging in class. There was nothing in either his demeanour or behaviour that required an 'acute response'.

In terms of the *circumstances*, I begin on the Monday.

He was in the throes of it, no question. I liken it to the virus taking hold—swarmer cells colonising the amygdala, mutating into the prefrontal cortex. (If you want a case study of virulence, look no further than a major depressive disorder.) His response levels varied, depending on how close we were trying to get: he was either comfortably numb or holding himself still while we pushed pins in his eyes.

The lawyer framed it as a rapid descent, but that isn't my version.

On the Monday afternoon, when he hadn't shown up in the morning, I found him again on the floor between the whiteboards, sitting cross-legged, hunched over. He didn't look up as I came in. I slid down alongside him on the floor and filled him in on what he'd missed over the last few days—my session with Dr J, what Tod had been cooking, Greg's latest weirdness. He didn't give me any indication he was listening, instead studying the surface of the floor, a dark layer of scum that had congealed around the foot of a whiteboard stand, which he began now to scrape with his fingernail, ploughing the shavings into a single straight line. It was gross; I told him it might be toxic. He looked at me sideways—*like I give a shit.*

I moved around so we were face to face. 'Maybe you should be taking something, some kind of medication.'

He looked at me with gentle eyes. He reached over and held my sleeve and told me he didn't have a great record on pills. I persisted, said there were a lot of different kinds he could try. His focus returned to the shavings, which he was now rolling into a ball between his thumb and forefinger. For fear it was heading for his mouth I flicked it into the air.

'Okay,' he said. 'I will explain what happens to me when I'm on pills. They make me calm enough to just think "fuck it"...I think "fuck it" about a hundred times a minute. What is that, like a billion times a day, yeah? After a few days, it becomes hard not to listen.' He was looking at me now, seeing if I understood. 'Can I tell you something?'

I nodded.

'I tried it twice. I mean like really gave it my best—both times on different medication.'

Why was I not surprised?

•

I went to see the Doctor to raise my concerns.

He said if not pills, then what? I suggested maybe hospital; he rejected it outright: 'That isn't what we do here. Think it through, Daniel—you really want to hand him over to whoever's on duty in the nearest psych ward?'

'So you do nothing? He's tried to kill himself and now he is stuck in this place in the middle of nowhere...'

'He can leave here at any time.'

'He won't leave here.'

'So then he stays.'

Round and round. I didn't want to hear it. It got me thinking about my contractual rights—full and frank disclosure—so I demanded he tell me what happened with PW.

Pouring me water: 'He left of his own accord.'

'Why?'

'A difference of approach...'

'I liked his approach.'

'Yes, so did I.'

The explanation—when I pressed him for it—was that PW had 'an issue with management'. I asked him who the ponytail woman was and he said he wasn't exactly sure of her position title. 'She is the global head of something or other.'

'Global? So the videos on your computer, the other—'

He cut in. 'The School is part of a larger operation.'

'There are other schools?'

He flinched; I was getting warm but I didn't know why. I didn't know when to drill.

'There are twenty-six sites around the world,' he said.

'Including us?'

He shook his head. 'We are a sort of outpost. We are number twenty-seven.'

Even when I had the transcript in front of me in print years later, I skimmed the pages on the particulars of corporate structure and responsibility. They didn't give much away. Submissions were made in the absence of witnesses: corporate liability of the parent company went beyond the scope of the inquiry. The School had been repurposed as a research centre so there was no issue regarding its continued operation. At some point the lawyer referred to grounds for a civil action, but there was never anyone on Alex's side to take it up. In any case, my interest was not in the structure, but the other children.

'How many are there—other students?'

He took a long while to answer and seemed cautious when he did. 'They are not really students, the others. They went to court too, but they didn't have the same kind of option you did in this place. They are in custody, juvenile detention, or other facilities... And the sites are bigger. A couple of thousand all up, I'd say. That is how many.'

They are not really students...

A couple of thousand all up.

In digesting this I imagined a wide-open space populated with two thousand teenagers in different-coloured tracksuits; some of the faces I had seen, my boy in the yellow beanie front and centre. To get a sense of the scope I sectioned them in twenty blocks of a hundred, each block a square of ten-by-ten. While up until now I had them as part of our story, they now formed a narrative parallel to our own. Out of formation, I scattered them again across twenty-six sites, a shadowy and disparate backdrop of young people like us, but blank-faced, without purpose. Somehow, I already sensed it was a story no one was willing to tell. I felt sad for them, but separate. Sad was as far as I went.

'So what was the global woman upset about?' I asked.

He said it was a misunderstanding, about the meaning of a term in his contract. 'It was badly drawn.'

'You have a contract?'

'Yes,' he replied. 'I have a contract; we all do.'

He looked a bit weary and asked if that was enough for today. When I stood up, he smiled, and then followed me to the door, determined, it seemed, to end on a positive note: 'You've grown again, Daniel, did you know that?'

On the Tuesday night I was in the kitchen with Rachel finishing off Magnolia's Chinese chicken when Glen came to the door.

'Come. You should see this.'

We followed. When he stopped at the music room I hesitated.

'It's okay,' he said. 'They asked him in.'

Opening the door, I saw that the *him* was Alex and that he was standing against the back wall, eyes closed and swaying to guitar music, played by Imogen. She wasn't holding it like a normal guitar; instead it was almost vertical, the body resting on the chair between her legs as her fingers slid up and down the strings. The sound was Spanish, Latino…I shouldn't have been surprised by the way she could play; over the months I'd heard bits and pieces, but actually watching the speed and flurry of her fingers left me floored. The whole scene was a bit surreal. The corner lamps bathed the room in a pinky light, like dusk. Grace sat next to Imogen at the synth keyboard, watching Alex, waiting. When his arms came out to the side in a wave-motion she added sounds, first the ring of bells then birdsong, and when he ramped it up so did she, adding a set of eerie, robotic pulses. After a minute of that Alex dropped suddenly into a squat and sprang back up into a series of moves like the ones I'd seen before in the dance room—scarecrow, ragdoll, rubberman. Imogen improvised her way through it, ending up with a set of frenetic downstrokes that sent them all into the next phase. First a pause: Alex stopped, the music did too. He held his arms loose by his side, his knees bent, and just his head moving back and forth, slowly at first then speeding it up, unleashing. Grace throwing in a manic reverb of sirens and drills, Imogen some kind of mad, techno flamenco. At the top of the movement Alex surged into full head-banging whiplash then spun it into windmill, round and round and round...his sweat spraying into the air.

'He's going to break his fucking neck,' Rachel whispered, but neither of us moved.

What we were watching was high-frequency modulation mayhem, but in all its parts—sonic, kinetic—it was magnificent. (The sum of energies in the universe is unchangeable; standing that night amid a collision of a billion moving particles, I couldn't work out the maths on that.)

And then it crashed. Alex reeled back against the wall and fell to the floor. Imogen dropped the guitar. Grace finished off with an alien vocal, distant, solo...The show was over, Rachel and Glen and me not sure what we'd just witnessed—the nature of the frenzy, what it intended to summon—annihilation or release, agony or ecstasy—each of us sensing that somehow it was all the same.

The only sound remaining was the rasp of Alex's breath, the only movement the rise and fall of his chest. Should we clap or check his vitals? I didn't know.

That was the thing with Alex, I never did.

The ferns flash past me as I run, a cosmic green.

The chorus of birds is a vibration; the sound is a cry, crystals transmitted into air. You are good and brave, I repeat, more a plea than an affirmation.

You are good and brave.

•

On the Thursday morning, I saw the sleeping bags in the court-yard. It was a while since we had connected with Tod; he'd become moodier lately (Rachel said he was just up himself) and I was pretty sure he was fattening up again. But here he was in the kitchen, back at the stove, making poached eggs topped with haloumi and Swiss chard, and it turned out—so I now heard—that they had started up again in the courtyard, he and Alex. Neither was sleeping, and they were talking now about going back to the waterhole.

I couldn't sleep myself that night. I found Alex in the court-yard, alone. For a while neither of us spoke. It was my favourite kind of sky, a waxing crescent moon—a bare sliver just visible again, the rest of the surface faint and dark and hidden. It made me think of explorers and possibilities and new worlds. Alex was thinking about something else. He began in the middle of a thought, a ramble about the connections between people—the pathways—how some of us exist in a collective and some of us in silos. He talked about how his dad had been able to feel his pain.

'He said there are transmitters, vibrations; some of us close our eyes and hear it—the hum of human consciousness. That's how we know things we were never taught or understand things that have never been explained.'

It came across like a rumination on the parables, to which I posited my own explanation: 'Primordial knowledge.'

He nodded, considering that. 'The problem is that a lot of people switch themselves off.'

I assumed he must be referring to me and I said, 'Sorry if I do that.'

At this, his whole tenor changed. He almost jumped on top of me. 'You have no idea how far off that is,' he said. 'You are like a thunderbolt, man—no question, no one in contention. The most switched-on person I have ever met.'

It sounded so bulletproof. That afternoon I'd just got another email from Mary: *It isn't who you are*, she said…And part of me thought, maybe if I tell Alex who I am I can still be a thunderbolt.

Instead I deflected. 'Cool,' I replied. 'That's okay then.'

And I let him link us back to brainwaves and neural transmitters and the colours of the auras he could sometimes see around the back of people's heads. Eventually—around the time of the first birdsong—he rambled himself into sleep before I got around to asking what my colour was.

Our final lesson, Friday.

We put on our headsets and did as we were asked: ten minutes eyes open, ten minutes closed. The global woman appeared at the door; she entered uninvited and observed us without introduction.

'Ignore me,' she said. 'Pretend I am not here.'

That became harder when she proceeded to walk around checking each of our headsets. Up close she smelled of soap and I could see her eyebrows were just a brown pencil line. Dr J asked to speak to her outside.

In their absence, Alex paid no attention to the exercises set for us, but instead sat glued to the images on his screen—the bird's-eye view, four horizontal and eight vertical rows of blurred black and white brains resembling large single cells, or walnuts (whichever way I looked I saw faces). Within the shadowy interior were small patches lit up in blue and green: the level of activation, the oxygenated blood flow. Alex squinted as he moved between brains, then clicked into the next page. There appeared the electrical oscillations—pale jagged lines like children's drawings of mountains; they cut across each other in bursts and spikes, revealing the chaotic maze inside the scanned brain.

I watched him lean slowly into the screen, his face close

enough so that the light reflected on his skin, pale and translucent. I watched as he traced his finger over his mood state: a ten-second flow, a flat line on beta—the same way a week ago he had traced raindrops on a window…And in that moment, inside my own body, I felt the weight of what he saw and what he knew, and I realised maybe it is right, what his father said about connections. Maybe there is a pathway between us.

Maybe I can feel it too.

The Doctor's return, alone, only added further credence. When he needed to, the man could read a room. This was it, I thought: the domino effect of open doors, the universal algorithm of human connectivity…

He saw the boy's finger over the flat line and sat down next to him: 'Do you want to know about mine?'

Without waiting for an answer, he told us about the days when he questioned every decision he made, 'All the little meaningless ones—what socks to wear, whether to close a door behind me— because with every decision is the potential that it is the wrong one. What that means is that some days I cannot move. When you don't see me, Alex, it isn't that I have gone to the city or I am somewhere else. I don't turn up because I can't, because I'm unable to move from the floor of my bathroom.'

It took a while for Alex to nod, but he did, and as he did, he turned his tablet over on his desk. He then removed his headset, and without looking at the Doctor, he said: 'If it's all right with you, I am not going to wear these again.'

There was something definitive in his delivery. My take on it then was that he was over the worst of it; the fever had broken. You are well positioned to call me dead wrong, but that is how it felt.

Have you heard the story of the man who serves a twenty-year prison sentence and breaks out the day before he is to be released?

The next day Alex was gone.

On the other side of the bushland, the goat scurries away, his back legs disappearing behind a blackened hollow log. Images scramble like a song played backwards. Images of Alex and everybody who got it wrong.

Everybody got it wrong.

When I glimpse what is to come, I choke for breath, unable to propel myself forward.

There is the sound of a tractor in the distance...That is the reason I move. Because I am close enough for him to hear me. Because between us there is a pathway of packed earth.

I shout his name. I am screaming.

The morning air is misted, like a dream.

Friday afternoon, passing the dance room, I saw the global woman again. She stood at the door with Greg, her head cocked to one side, looking in to the room. I just caught what she said.

'You do what the Doctor says...You do nothing.'

At the sight of me, she moved on, Greg in tow.

At dinner, Alex was in the kitchen. I don't remember what we ate. I remember they talked about going back to the waterhole, he and Tod. We reminisced about the first time we'd got out there at night. I said I'd come and I thought I would, but later I stopped at Rachel's door and I knocked and she let me come in and lie on the floor and we talked until I fell asleep.

Some time after dawn, startled by something—I went to check the courtyard. The sleeping bags were there: two of them laid out, empty. I saw the kitchen light on. It was too early for that, but there was Tod, sitting at the table with a platter of food in front of him. Cut-up fruit and sandwiches, cheese and crackers and tubs of yoghurt, enough to feed a table but feeding only one.

'How did you open the door?'

'I found a way,' he said.

'You went to the waterhole?' I asked.

He said he didn't go. And before I even asked the next question he nodded, yes. Yes, Alex had gone. Alex had gone alone. He didn't look at me as he said it.

'Is he back?'

He shrugged.

The first thing to come into view is the willow branches. Then, over the rise, the unmoving surface. If the reflection was broken by the fall, it is complete again now, a grand sweep of dappled green. It is the simplest form of light–water interaction.

I see a part of him—pale flesh in shallow water, an arm; no, a leg—and then the rest rising above the surface on the rocky outcrop, captured in the act of pulling himself from the water as he has done so many times before. For a split second I believe it: he is climbing out. (It is a feat, what our minds are able to fit into those moments, the burst of thought: he didn't hear me, he is asleep, what I would sacrifice...) As I come closer I see what is really there. I see that his arm hangs down into the water, impossibly broken, and I see that his eyes are open. A picture I don't want to enter, a story I don't want to tell. But already I am part of it, the boy running to his friend, to save him...

The air suctions out of my lungs: like I have been hit and can't breathe back in.

I don't know what it feels like to have a brother or a son or a father, but I know that when I saw his eyes there was a severing of time in that moment—of life before and after.

●

His bedroom was empty, the bed made, a T-shirt folded on the pillow, nothing out of place. The screensaver was back to the waterfall, the sound on high, a trickling piano. The volume made me sit down at the computer and click into the desktop. Across the top of the screen were minimised versions of the whiteboards, not scanned but reproduced in adaptive graphics. Last was Rachel's whiteboard, the *Trajectory of Human Suffering: Solutions*. She had used the 'good news' board as a starting point from which to work backwards: improving trends in HIV, reduced malaria mortality rates, better schooling for girls in Sri Lanka. Then she moved on to dot points marking enablers for change: scientific advancement, international treaties...I had seen it before in the tutorial room; we had watched her sketch it out, Alex nodding along.

Back in his own room, here is what he had done: he had formulated the argument for the negative and added a second wheel, a second heading—*Barriers*—and circling around it, the list of them, all the reasons why the solutions were piecemeal, the human blockages to change, our human failings—'in no particular order':

- self-interest
- corruption
- ineptitude
- forgetfulness
- the forces of evil

Arrows linked back into *Fragmentation* and *Ignorance* and an NB: *We are not talking theory here.*

In his own quiet way, Alex had had the last say.

'You go,' Tod said when he saw me back at the door to the kitchen. 'You'll be faster without me.'

I turned, and ran.

The smell of mud. I plunge in, I am swimming, I swallow water...
When I pull myself onto the rock beside him I am coughing. I
look down. Cushioned against the green moss, his face is at an
angle to the surface of the water, as though he bent down to view
his reflection; to contemplate a plan. And there it is, the perfect
reconstruction of a perfect profile, disappearing as I pull him over
so that his eyes are looking at me and looking at nothing. There is
the beginning of a smile, like he knew how he would land and he
knew that I would find him:

Come on, Dan—you know me by now. This is okay with me;
this is good.

I nod back, and pull him into the water.

I did not leave Alex's body as I found it.

Instead I floated him across to the other side, dragging him
up onto the bank, all the way up to the place I knew he liked
to sleep, his spot, where there was grass to soften the bed and a
boulder the shape of a pillow—the same boulder the wombat had
dug his burrow behind—and I lay down beside him, and I put my
hand over his hand and remained that way because I felt sure he
wouldn't want me to leave him there alone.

There was a cut the length of his arm, a red, jagged line.

Waiting on the bank, we lay still, as we had done when things
went quiet and we let ourselves think. After a while, I couldn't
say how long—time was playing tricks—I thought I felt his hand
press up on mine. I sat up. I looked down for other signs but even
when there weren't any, I made the call: there was nothing to lose.
I leaned down over him and did what I could, pressed my mouth
to his mouth, cold spongy lips. I didn't remember what else, how
many chest presses. I wasn't listening for that bit. With each blow I

wondered if I was killing any last chances of him living. I wondered about that right up until I read the transcripts.

The answer was there, on the very first page.

Cause of death: transection of the fifth cervical spine *on impact*.

And manner: self-inflicted death with the intention to end life.

Social and Emotional Wellbeing 1.1

It was more than an hour before they found us.

I stared through tears at the sunken pit in his sternum, a blur of tattooed birds, the shape of their eyes more human than avian; I imagined him balancing at the end of the highest branch, raising his arms out to the side and high above his head, the moon casting light through the leaves and framing his silhouette against the sky. It struck me then, the significance of the detail—his bare chest: Alex had taken his clothes off and hung them on the rock.

The concept of intention at law has a broad sweep. When it comes to the killing of another human being, the law takes great care to distinguish the gradations of intention or recklessness or negligence. When the life we have taken is our own there doesn't seem to be quite the same rigour applied. The proceedings address a narrow set of questions.

When I considered all this at the time of reading the transcript, I thought it probably right that the level of intent in this case fell somewhere in the middle. The phrase I'd read once or twice in the newspapers—in describing some death or other—was *reckless indifference to human life*. As regards my friend Alex, it stuck in my mind as both so true and so utterly false.

What I have ended up with in the final round is another legal term. Alex took himself alone to the waterhole that night, he walked out along the highest branch of the willow tree and he stood upon it facing an uncertain depth below. In the lead-up, there existed a set of circumstances: at best, an absence of effort to contain the risk; at worst, facilitation. I have questioned who, in his final days and hours, played a part. Alex took off his clothes not because he intended to die, but because there was a chance he would survive; there was a chance that he would swim. It was a toss of the coin and, ultimately, it was his toss, I accept that. But that does not negate the responsibility of others.

You do what the Doctor says. You do nothing.

There is another term that has stuck with me. It is the doctrine they call *common purpose*.

They knew to bring a stretcher.

They closed his eyes and tucked his arms in by his sides and carried him back through the bush to an ambulance waiting at the top of the driveway. The others gathered there, all but the Doctor. All but the man in charge.

I walked back inside, through the waiting room, and opened the door to his office. Sitting in his wing-backed chair in the yellow light of the tulip lamp, he was dressed and ready, it seemed, for the remainder of this most terrible day—in his jacket and tie, his hair combed into its side part.

'Daniel,' he said in his quietest voice. 'Come, sit.'

I did not sit. I went to the window and pulled the curtain open and looked out to the group, some gathered at the back of the ambulance, some sitting on the ground, heads buried in their arms. I felt separate from them, separate from their pain, and from mine.

The Doctor came and stood beside me. When he put his hand on my shoulder, my legs went weak and I stepped back, away from him. I don't know what kept me standing; anger was the closest thing.

'You did this,' I said, my voice calmer than I thought it would be. His eyes looked paler in the light, the scar at the corner of his mouth a deeper purple, more prominent. 'You could have stopped it.'

'They are two different things.'

The veins in his temples surfaced as he clenched his jaw and held my gaze. There was a challenge in it. *Think this through,* his eyes seemed to be saying. But I couldn't think; I couldn't feel. I was watching this from a different vantage—this boy and man, their strange connection, and in the van outside, just metres away...

I took a last look at the ambulance before I walked over to the computer on the desk and tapped the keyboard. There they were again, the children, different ones, or maybe the same, hundreds of faces on a screen. I scrolled back and forward, clicking into other icons, finding graphs and numbers but not what I was looking for.

'Show me,' I said. 'Where are *we* in here?'

He shook his head. 'I told you. You are not in there. You are different. Daniel, please, you need to come sit.'

I looked down at my legs, my shoes and pants caked in mud, the scratches on my arms. But I didn't move. I didn't want to play.

'How are we any different? This may as well be a jail, out here in the middle of nowhere—part of some weird fucking experiment...'

He shook his head. 'This isn't the experiment, Daniel,' he said. 'I rescued you from that. You're not in there because you're here with me. I told you, you're different from them. You are lucky...' His voice started to trail off but came back stronger. 'You don't know how lucky you are.'

The words so jarred with my sense of what was happening that they broke something in me and when I reached the chair, I fell into it.

'You let him loose. You let him die. Is *he* lucky?'

'We could have given him drugs; we could have put him in a hospital. But you know yourself, he didn't want that.'

'You don't know what he wanted,' I spat back.

He leaned forward in his chair. 'What do you think I have been doing in here with Alex all this time? He sat where you are sitting now, or on the floor at the window...All our sessions, all the days leading to this. They all led to *this*...'

There was an emphasis on the last word, an inflection that attributed to it more than just acceptance, but something purposeful, something momentous. And it twigged.

'You think what happened, *this*...you think it is the right thing.'

He took a while to answer. 'What I think is that Alex was one of the most remarkable human beings I have ever met. I think that being the person he was while he was here—that is what he wanted. That is *all* he wanted.'

I got up, walked to the window. Outside it was just Greg and the ambulance now, everyone else gone.

'You don't know that,' I said. 'You don't know the first thing about us—about him, about me.' *After all this time.* 'You think

271

you do; you sit there and watch me move the pieces around. All your bullshit about contracts and stages and players and you still missed it, Doctor—you never worked it out...'

This was my only card to play. My proof, my truth, my story.

He reached over to the table and poured water into the glasses. By the way he looked up at me now—squarely, unblinking—I already knew I was wrong.

'You think I don't know, Daniel?' The voice quiet again, resolute. 'You think I don't know what you did?'

For a moment he let the words hang between us, until he could see the meaning sink in. 'I know,' he said. 'I knew it the first time she called here. I heard it in her voice, in her silence—the fear, the relief that her son was somewhere far away. And you, Daniel, every time we have talked about her it is etched across your face.'

When the tenants have come and gone, Daniel, when it is just the boy and his mother, what happens then?

My mind cast itself back to the session when he told me she had called, to all the sessions after that, hour after hour, and to what he was telling me he had known all along—how the tenants left and I banged on walls and kicked through doors...What happened then, the event itself—the day she found the files, my customer files, and said it had to stop. The detail didn't matter to him, only to me. My barricade of lies, how she wanted to tear it all down.

How light she felt, like a doll.

I don't see red. I see yellow and it is blinding. Sometimes I slump to the floor and make noise, however loud, for however long, and there isn't anything else but this...There is one way to be rid of it, different versions. This was my worst version. There was nothing to pull me back, just a long line of people with other versions of the same thing.

I held her by the neck, her back against the wall. She screamed when I let go and I hit her in the face with my fist and when she fell I kicked into her body and she turned her face at the wrong time and there was blood and milk on the kitchen floor. When I came back she was still there and I held her head in my hands. I held my mother's head in my hands. She asked where I had been, like it was any other day and I was any other son, and we talked about making a plan.

You can get to hell and back, Mary said, *as long as you have yourself a plan.*

I stepped away from the window, out of the light, but it was the fact of the matter, that all our days had led to this.

Sometimes we need to be seen.

In the waiting room outside the Doctor's office, I was startled to find the global woman sitting at the desk. Strands of loose hair falling from the ponytail, her fingers hovered above the keys of her laptop as though I had interrupted her typing. For a brief moment she looked at me that way, like I was an interruption, before rearranging her demeanour and closing the screen. Nodding to herself and softening the edges of her mouth, she got to her feet.

'I am sorry,' she said, without any inflection, any clue as to whether she meant it by way of condolence or apology. The only observation I could make was that she seemed somehow less bothered than she had been in the preceding days, less hostile. Looking on me now not as an object of annoyance or sympathy, but as an irrelevance. When she tucked the strands of hair behind her ears and sat back down again, my sense was that her job was done.

Outside, amid voices, an engine started. I strained to listen, to keep hearing the sound as long as it lasted until it died in the distance.

•

This isn't the experiment...I rescued you from that.

I had assumed that day that he meant prison: that is what he rescued me from. Now I have a better idea. I have read the transcripts, I know his story and now it is all in front of me. In his mind, he had taken me out of the asylum. By being there at the School, all of us, we formed the group they refer to as 'the control'.

A DIFFERENT SET OF QUESTIONS

Macroeconomics

A few years ago I came across a reference in a journal article to a study that commenced in the same year I was at the School. The article was entitled 'Crime Prevention in a Pill?' and the study considered the impact of drug treatments on underlying causes of delinquent and offending behaviour. It was a lifetime study based on a number of juvenile subgroups; by 'life' they meant tracking progress until age forty-five. There had been some promising early results with regard to attention deficit disorders and adolescent bipolar; the long-term benefits had been called into question.

I read the article during a period when I was not my best self. In no position to argue the point, I had given everyone a breather and gone to stay at the mountain house (shed, really), as I do from time to time. That is my solution; it does not receive universal approval. I explain that it is in everyone's interests; I take it too far and question why we insist on living as human tenements: there is shouting. I miss birthdays and award ceremonies and dental appointments. *If we all just got up and fucked off...*In reply, I nod and mumble and pack my things.

I read the article over again. I stared out from my narrow porch into the maze of silver-grey gums and thought about the School. Our little *juvenile subgroup*, our midnight sessions. Over the years I have spent many hours recreating the best of them in my mind. On bad days I draw a blank, but at least I can sit on my porch and let the vibration of birds and cicadas bang around my cerebrum and keep any unwelcome reflexive response contained. (I bought the place for next to nothing on account of the density of the tree canopy blocking the light; I don't mind a bit of dark, and the acoustics are bar none.)

What I had reminisced about less was my relationship with the Doctor. True to form, I maintained my rage, seating blame for Alex's death with him, partly because I didn't know where else to put it. Thinking about our conversations generally made me feel like there was a light shining in my face; that I had things—everything—to hide. At the same time there was this hankering sense of loss. When that became acute there were select parts I liked to replay. If I was careful, it helped.

There was a reference letter he wrote for me that was quoted by prospective employers every time I applied for a new position. That, of course, was welcome. And in a way, I always felt his influence. *Go rogue.* From the moment I left the university, from assistant to researcher to group leader, I made it my practice to reject labels and re-examine definitions, to be suspicious of universal truths and, most critically, to work outside other people's ethical frameworks. Heading the largest genome research group in the region, I am the stem cell man. (Now that I have equity in this thing, it is a very lucrative business. I can see how hard it must have been for the Doctor to walk away.)

He only once made direct contact with me: during the time of the inquest when I was on the other side of the world. I was twenty-four. The head of my department forwarded me an email that turned out to be from the Doctor, attaching the scanned brain-wave reports I left in my room when I walked out of the School seven years earlier. The three-line email itself extended an offer *for us to take up where we left off. To the extent that it is possible. I would like your brain on something.*

My response was to try not to think about what he meant. I printed off the email together with the reports and tucked them into a manila folder stashed in a bottom desk drawer. Later, I added my notes from the transcripts. Once or twice a year I pulled the folder out and closed it up again. A mental seal.

Rachel was different. They kept in contact. Whenever she brought it up with me, I did my best to shut her down. There was one time she dragged me into a project she was working on (I would have swallowed nails for her, and this time I sort of did). It was a stint at the Centre of Youth Development. For eleven months I matched survey reports with third-world satellite pictures and developed algorithms to predict juvenile health outcomes at the level of individual villages. Afterwards she hinted that it all had something to do with the Doctor—'his lifetime project'—and I said it was a shame he hadn't made it his project to save 'the life of one boy'. We were drinking tea at her kitchen bench.

Her eyes flashed with anger and she was about to say some-thing. Then she softened. 'I think he probably saved mine.'

She waited for me to look back at her.

'You tell me. Where would you be now if it wasn't for him?'

I cleared our cups and said nothing. On my way out to the car she called me an emotional amoeba. It was only when I was safely staring at the odometer that I was able to think about the cause of the blood rushing between my midbrain and ribcage. It wasn't her assessment of me, but her assessment of herself. *I think he probably saved mine.* I began to imagine the Doctor's sessions with the other students: what played out in parallel with my own as the Doctor delved and sidestepped and discovered inroads, as he paced and mumbled and pointed to contracts. What unfolded in each of them, and how it must have been as intricate and extraordinary as what had unfolded in mine. As I so often did, I landed back with Alex, his sessions, week after week—only now with the simple and inescapable conclusion that some of us, no matter what the effort, could not be saved.

By the time I arrived home, I'd began to feel an opening in my chest cavity, a sense of forward momentum. The opening was more a re-opening—*taking up where we had left off.* I pictured the Doctor's face in my mind, and rather than scramble to mute our conversations, I let snippets of them linger. I went on to script what we might now say to each other, and what he would see when he looked at me. It was something I had done in the months after leaving the School but it had started getting too glary. Now, all this time later, we were back in session.

It wasn't until I saw the article about the study and placed it on top of the other papers in my file that I re-read the email he had sent me—now more than fifteen years ago—and found myself drafting a reply. That took some time; in the end I asked simply if he was still there. I received an immediate response: the Doctor was *out of office*. Timeframe unspecified.

In frustration, I began adding to the file. I dug out information online about Dr J's early success. I searched his name, his university, his places of employment, but could find nothing about his current whereabouts. Finally I sent a message to Rachel, who was in the UK for a work trip. I didn't hear back.

Then two months ago, at a conference in Singapore, I was reading an American newspaper and there he was. That strange and wonderful face, his wide-set eyes staring out above a paragraph on page twelve. The once-celebrated neuroscientist, pioneer of groundbreaking drug treatments for millions of adolescents worldwide, was found in his home after a sudden heart attack. Aged seventy-six. Survived by his sister and his son.

I checked my phone. Text from Rachel: *He is dead.*

It took me some time to digest. For three days—the remainder of the conference—I sat in my hotel room with the television blasting and made my way through a lavishly stocked mini-bar.

There was no relief in the thought that my childhood secret was buried with him. I was back to where I started. Outside of victim and perpetrator, the story did not exist—which is what spurred me to put this together. Spreadeagled on stained hotel plush pile, I resolved to create my own record.

It was what happened next that shifted my purpose from a private to a public one; that raised a different set of questions.

I went back to the article and checked for links to the study. They were no longer there. It was only due to the persistence of a colleague that I was able to obtain a copy. The title was 'Drug Treatment and Adolescent Mental Health Disorders: Implications for Crime Prevention'. With a sudden sense of urgency, I flicked to the executive summary.

Across the globe, a total of more than 2500 young persons took part. The eligibility criteria applied to all participants across the twenty-six sites: each had been a resident of a juvenile detention facility for a period of not less than six months.

At the end of the summary there was a disclaimer. There had been a control group, but it had been disbanded. Buried within an appendix, another nugget of information. Instead of drug treatment, participants in the control group took part in an alternative program whose core components included, but were not limited to, therapeutic sessions, narrative therapy, neural monitoring and access to the natural environment.

The principal investigator of the entire study was a woman by the name of Madelaine T, global team leader at Mindsight, subsidiary of Neuropharma Inc.

A few days later I received a package in the post, addressed to my office. It was ten-year-old copy of the Mindsight Annual Report, no return address on the envelope. I checked with my helpful colleague and he knew nothing about it. Had I not seen the death notice, I might have assumed it was from the Doctor; as it was, the source remained a mystery. I flipped through. Towards the back there was a table headed International Network which set out research sites along with offices, contacts and locations, including Sydney, Australia.

It was only then, as I skipped to the final page, that I noticed the company logo: three blue capsules. In the place of the top half, a plant sprouting green leaves. I rifled through my transcript notes and pulled out one of my old brainwave reports from the back of my folder. There it was: the same logo. I placed them side by side.

I don't forget numbers. There were twenty-six sites; we were number twenty-seven.

•

It was not difficult to find.

The Mindsight address was a ten-minute walk from the Housing Commission flats where Mary and I had lived, long since torn down in the name of gentrification. The neighbourhood now was an incongruous grid of childcare centres, vegan cafes and nail salons.

It was a double ground-floor office in a multi-storey building: generously proportioned, with massive walls shrouded in plants and creepers—all good when it is thriving, but overall I'd think a risky business. I pressed a buzzer and waited. Eventually a young man opened the door. He wore loose jeans and expensive visible underpants and looked like he needed sun. When he saw that I was empty-handed he said I must have the wrong address. I looked at the logo on the opposite wall. This one was big. Three big blue capsules.

'No, this is the right place.'

He squinted, seemingly unaccustomed to visitors, but when I spoke again there was a noticeable double-take.

'My name is Daniel G. I was a student at the School...The facility...'

'Ah.' His eyes widened. 'Yeah, I know who you are,' he said, glancing now over my shoulder. 'You better come in.'

It was a single room with a closed glass door through to another office. Three desktops, state of the art: planet earth screen-savers zoomed in and out of oceans and land masses. Apart from two chairs, the room was empty. Underpants Boy took one of the chairs and introduced himself. His name was Jordan and he 'did the data stuff', he said. He didn't look much older than my gap-year daughter.

He pointed at the computers. 'This is the Hub.'

I walked over and tapped on a space bar. He did nothing to

283

stop me; just said, 'You need a password.'

'I don't suppose you're going to give it to me.'

He shook his head. 'He'll be back any second…Let's just wait.'

I didn't argue, surprised he was even this accommodating. I took a seat. How long had he worked here? He said four years.

Next question: 'Do you know who you work for?'

'Of course I know.'

'And exactly what they do?'

He seemed to contemplate that more seriously, but at the sound of footsteps he shrugged. 'I'm just the data guy.'

A figure appeared in the doorway, and my breath stopped. Thirty years on his face and thirty kilos off his frame, his hair now a sandy white. I think I mouthed the name rather than said it out loud.

'Tod?' He had thinned into an oddly handsome man.

'Daniel. Nice to see you.'

Stepping forward, he seemed genuinely glad. For a minute, I wondered if he was going to give me a hug, and for a second I almost wanted him to. It stirred good things, seeing Tod, a cavalcade of memories only jarring to a halt when the questions came flooding in, none of which I could find words to ask.

'You found us,' he said, putting a hand on my shoulder. 'Well done you.'

Time plays tricks.

No, it isn't *time;* it is the tyrant brain.

There was a clock on the wall of the flat and there were times when the minute hand refused to move. A temporal illusion, a dopamine funk…There are a lot of things said about time—that it is merciful, that it heals. The opposite is also true. The brain is your timekeeper, and it can be a vicious fucker.

Now it was playing a different trick. Tod was looking at me and smiling. He was asking me questions about myself like an old and dear friend. That slightly high-pitched voice. But something else was replaying, synced over his words. It was me. Asking the question I had asked in the kitchen that first morning, talking to the guy who could break eggs with one hand.

Why are you here? What was his crime? What happened in the courtroom—that is what I had been asking.

And his answer: *Same as you, same for all of us.*

But was it? Had he been part of *this* even then—not one of *us*? Standing in the office now, I was the boy in the kitchen needing someone to explain; I was the boy wanting to tear the room apart. In another stopped clock, I was still that boy, the moments linked in time to form a single unfolding event. Maybe that isn't the trick; maybe that is truth and the trick is putting things behind us in the first place.

Now as the first moments of the reunion passed into something less tingly, more stupefied, my questions took shape. The first one: *Who are you?*

Tod invited me to sit down at the centre computer. When he signed in, little green lighthouses appeared across the 3D globe. He reached over my shoulder and clicked on the single lighthouse in Australia, the middle of New South Wales. When the page came up it read: *Archived.* He clicked again.

'There you go.'

The School, the pear trees in the courtyard. At the first sight of it I felt a pang of something lost.

'The other sites were existing facilities,' he said. 'Detention centres mainly, a few reform schools. Ours'—he gave me a glance of pride—'ours was built specially.'

Then he nodded. 'Click anywhere on the screen. Go ahead.' And up came the search function.

He said he was going to explain something to me now and I said that would be a good idea. At this point he told Jordan he didn't need him anymore and the boy and his underpants headed into the adjoining office.

'They called us monitors,' Tod began, his voice fading, becoming a background noise as I moved through first response. On the other side of it, he was still talking.

'...part of our diploma...trainee youth workers—like a prac placement. The job description was to support kids and report back. I was eighteen, still a kid myself, and it wasn't much of a stretch. People can never tell how old fat people are.'

I had to think about that. And I had to slow it down in my head, process what he was saying.

'The brief made sense to me,' he continued. 'Kids like you guys were more likely to accept help from one of their own kind. The other centres had cameras, too. The Doctor wouldn't have them, though. He won on that, but us monitors—we were non-negotiable.'

As he went on he fell back into catch-up mode, embarking on career high points. The centre usually only ever kept the other monitors for a single 'cycle of students'; he was the exception, he said. 'It was because I got so close, you know...' What that meant for Tod was that they kept him on after we left, put him through his diploma together with an on-the-ground training program plus five years' field work in the Asia Pacific—a guaranteed minimum of six sites over four continents.

'Subsidised backpacking,' he said. 'Who wouldn't?' It was the old Tod: clumsy, over-eager, unable to shut up. 'I got into trekking—extreme stuff: long distance, high altitude...'

I didn't want to hear about his treks or his travels. What was flashing in my mind: our meeting that first morning and the midnight sessions. All the times he lay there next to us, listening.

'From then—from before I met you—until now,' I said. 'You've worked for them?'

He smiled, nodded. 'They don't have a lot of problems with staff retention.'

There was a note of bragging in it; I noticed he was wearing a very expensive watch. My chief thought—*you lying piece of shit*—I decided to hold on to. Not that it mattered now, but I found I was waiting for an explanation. Some clue to why he had thought it might be okay, the pretence, day after day.

This was the best I got: 'You have to know one thing, Daniel: I just played myself.' He leaned in like it was the part of the story that mattered the most. 'I mean, I really liked you guys.'

I must have gone into a zone for a moment. I heard him saying my name. '…niel? This would be weird to hear.'

I looked around at the computers. Fluctuating images on the screens. 'All this.' I gestured broadly. 'What is it?'

I got my guided tour.

First the baseline data—our vital statistics and juvenile justice records—then our treatment and progress. Tod moved aside to let me scroll through the student overviews, the grids and graphs. It was engrossing stuff; for a while I almost forgot he was there.

The final tab was labelled *Life-course*. When I clicked on it, a red box appeared: *Disbanded*. I recalled that from the study—the disbanding of the control group—and from the transcripts—the repurposing of the School into a research centre.

I turned to Tod and told him someone had sent me the annual report. 'Was that you?'

He looked perplexed, then annoyed. Shook his head.

'I know there's more,' I said.

Now he was shaking his head with a different look—the one that says: *you have no idea.*

There were eleven initial sites in the US. That grew to twenty-six worldwide—twenty-seven including us. The trial consisted of drug treatment for a number of mental disorders; it took place over a six-month period; the cohort were juveniles in detention facilities.

'The end-goal, as far as I could tell, was to make good citizens.'

Crime prevention in a pill.

He was hazy on how the School came into being. 'There was bad blood…In the end, the Doctor parted ways with head office and moved across the world. Got the School built, this office; established his program…'

'The control group. That meant no drugs?'

'Pretty much.'

'But we weren't in detention.'

'Depends on what you mean by detention.' He gave me that look again and shrugged. 'All that talk about contracts: *Take personal choice out of the equation and you end up with zero*, that's what he said. The guy was good, Daniel. Look at you. Look at all of you!'

He started the spiel: my career in science, how Fergus cornered a market and made his millions, the music mogul sister (just one; the partnership ended in tears—artistic differences).

'And Rachel, I mean she's like this special advisor on whatever it is…'

I rattled it off: Social Affairs and the Human Settlements Program.

'Yeah, I keep seeing her on TV.'

He fell silent on the obvious omission, our absent friend. Then he turned back to the screen and clicked on a nameless icon. There were our names and another set of indicators. This was the life-course data.

'But they disbanded it—didn't they?'

He paused. 'When we sought clarification we were told to continue monitoring you. They still wanted the data on the initial cohort; they just gave it a new title.' He clicked on another icon, top right of the screen. 'This is you.'

Here we were. Our biographical history data: all collected, so Tod explained, through adaptive multimethod fieldwork. It didn't take me long to tally the numbers. Out of 97 students:

- 94 completed high school
- 72 completed tertiary-level education, 24 to doctoral level
- 64 in the top tax bracket
- 58 had children
- 24 were married
- 11 had been prescribed medication for mental-health-related conditions; 2 admitted to hospital
- 3 were deceased
- 1 took his own life.

Impressive. But safe to say it wasn't the story they wanted to tell.

'None of the cohorts who took part in the actual drug trials ever came close to you lot at the School. Pick another lighthouse,' he said. 'See for yourself: income levels, education...'

I clicked on the globe and started searching. When I began to understand the scale of it, I suddenly felt very small. The first twenty-six sites were just the beginning. Every five-year period saw the addition of new trials. And it wasn't just detention centres. They were conducting the trial in youth shelters, hospitals, schools…

I interjected here—the schools and hospitals—'All of it, what is it for?'

He looked at me for a second like I was a simpleton. 'Drugs, of course. Drugs and data: what works, what doesn't. What sells.'

'There are governments overseeing this?'

He shrugged: not really. Private schools, private hospitals. 'All of the sites, all privatised.'

Three hundred and seventy sites with around ten thousand currently in trials. 'We're going back thirty years now. The tally for life-course participants is about to hit a quarter million.'

He nodded towards the glass door. 'Jordan in there,' the boy was now sitting outside the door swiping at his phone, 'his job is to conduct a meta-analysis of related clinical studies and link it all up. He is a very smart boy, you have no idea. "Brain the size of a small planet," Dr J used to say that. Jordan was the boy wonder; they'd sit in there for hours…'

He was going off-track. I tried, but it had never been easy to stop Tod mid-stream. 'I mean, he wasn't like that with me; I guess I didn't have the brains you guys did. He used to demand updates on you—the subjects you studied, the fellowships, every new position you held; any little thing you did was always a big deal in here. Rachel too. They were in contact—'

'She saw this?'

He shook his head. 'He brought her into the odd project, but she never came here. He didn't want her interrupted, the work she was doing.'

'And what about him? What was the Doctor's role in all this?'

'He ran his own ship. Or, I don't know, maybe they were the ship and he was the iceberg…' His voice trailed off. He looked a little glassy-eyed. 'He got sick a few years ago and went back to the States. To see his son, he said. You know, I didn't even know he had one, he never told me. He never told me any of it, what was happening with him and the company. It was a very toxic situation for a while. There were threats being thrown around; he got paranoid...'

I listened and I asked questions he couldn't answer, because he didn't know, because the Doctor didn't tell him.

What I was realising was that from those few snippets of conversation in our sessions all those years ago, I knew more about the Doctor than this man who had worked with him for thirty years: a photograph on a shelf, a proud moment, a discovery and a prize. *I was wrong,* he had said.

And the transcripts. He had seen the results. *I am still seeing them, and I warn you, we are yet to see them all.*

Tod slid over into a seat at the next computer. Nodding in a last-laugh kind of way, he proudly pulled out a business card: *Senior Data Strategist, Asia-Pacific Region.*

'There are seven data hubs,' he said. It felt to me like he wanted to brag again but thought better of it. He held the silence for a minute then leaned in. 'Can I show you something, Daniel?'

Tod tapped a drumroll on the desk and brought up a set of graphs and tables.

'This is our latest.'

Our latest.

Some of the fields had been emptied, and some were identified by code instead of name. But the common characteristics of the participants were clear. Age: 10–11. Younger than the other trials. And all of the children with early signs of attention deficit.

I scrolled down into the details of the trial and the monitoring. The focus here was the malleability of the pre-pubescent brain. The abstract listed a variety of drugs and drug combinations—mood

291

stabilisers, antipsychotics, anticonvulsants—as well as what appeared to be an algorithm for medication decisions. With all the acronyms on the main table, it was hard to make head or tail of it.

'CANDI—what does that mean?'

'Childhood and Adolescent New Drug Investigation,' he replied. 'These are pre-market...Before, they were limited to testing them on pigtail monkeys; this way they move straight into phase-three testing. The potential is massive.' He was falling into hard-sell mode. 'Within ten years we could be able to treat kids before the condition even develops. I mean, who doesn't want that?'

Tiny beads of sweat had sprouted on his forehead and into his hairline. I could feel my own breath becoming rapid, irregular. While he kept talking about the limitations of testing on monkeys—the challenge of matching cognitive development with the human brain—I drew my focus back to the screen, to the end columns. The first was headed AEI.

'Tod?' I interrupted him to point it out.

'Adverse Effect or Interaction.'

'And this?'

The column, in green highlight, was headed: Fiscal Impact.

Even to me, sitting at the screen with my old School friend Tod spruiking the wonders of human drug testing on ten-year-old children, the words appeared incongruous. In each of the spaces under the heading there appeared a coded hyperlink. I clicked on one.

The new page showed a set of calculations: a predictor algorithm involving length of treatment, cost and projected earnings. The big prize seemed to be drug treatment over a lifetime. The determinant was the age of first prescription. There didn't seem to be any ambiguity: the younger they started, the more chance you could drug them for life.

For a moment it felt as though I was staring at one of Alex's whiteboards—a new patch of lines and dot points, themes and subsets—and like Alex I was applying my own logic, desperately trying to make sense of it. My starting point was that there is a place where big ideas go bad, and that the amount of damage is generally dependent on two factors: the level of brain dysregulation of the people in control; and market forces.

Sometimes you get a perfect storm.

At the bottom left of the screen sat a cluster of lighthouses with a camera icon at the centre. When I clicked on the icon, each of the three computer screens around us suddenly came to life with a moving montage of video images. Surveillance videos like the ones I had seen all those years ago across twenty-six sites. Now there were more: thousands, not hundreds of kids...More dark-skinned than white; more third-world than first. Children of all ages in different places across the globe. Hospital wards and dorm rooms, classrooms and schoolyards. Children running and sleeping and playing, reading, eating, laughing, crying. Children doing what children do and taking what pills they are told to take.

When the screensaver returned, the little green lighthouses stared back at me, making funny faces.

'How can they run them all?' I asked. 'The cost...'

Tod smiled. 'That isn't the right question, Daniel. The question you want to ask is what are the earnings? I can tell you that: for the CANDI drugs that hit the market, somewhere around the GDP of a not-so-small country.'

The monster was emerging. A continuation of an earlier narrative, a single unfolding story: *The boy grows into a man of action. He infiltrates the mind of the beast and blows its brains into a million bloody pieces...*It is a process, a form of mental retaliation. I am not suggesting it is as good as the real thing, far from it, but at the moment you stand at the precipice of rage, about to freefall into vast valleys of destruction, it offers a subtle, critical release. *He picks up the monitors, holds them Hulk-like above his head and, with blood vessels bursting, smashes them through the glass wall and sends shards of shrapnel into every far-flung corner...*

Or something to that effect. It can take a couple of drafts.

'Daniel?'

I looked back at Tod and wondered what should happen to him in my story.

'Tell me about the woman,' I said. 'The global manager. Why was she there?'

'Madelaine. Hard work. That's where Greg is, by the way. He's her number two. Head office. Big role.' He shook his head. Shook it again when I asked what her visit had been about.

'There was some kind of blow up—you'll enjoy this—it was about growth rates. Across the primary sites they were pretty much zero, but you guys went through this group growth spurt. For some reason that was very bad news to them. She checked the numbers a hundred times, accused Greg of buggering up the monitoring. I was idiot enough to chime in about the importance of diet and she blasted me out of the office. For the life of me I couldn't work out why all the fuss about a few centimetres.'

'I can explain that if you want me to.'

The voice came from behind. The boy wonder had come back in and was standing in the centre of the room, arms folded.

Tod swung around, put his hand up. 'Thanks Jordan, I think I've got it.'

Jordan didn't move. I watched the crimson rise into his cheeks.

'I'd like to hear it,' I said. 'If that's okay with you, Tod.'

Tod looked at me, then back at Jordan. I had the sense now they were on different sides. The boy sat down cross-legged on the floor and rested his chin on his clasped hands. Somehow in just a few seconds he had claimed the room—sunlight streaming through the window and illuminating his backdrop, the wall with the logo, the giant capsules with their shiny green leaves.

'The reason Madelaine was there was that they couldn't keep you guys in the study with the sort of progress reports that were coming through. She was there to find a way to take you out of the comparison—out of the equation. The death of your friend Alex gave them that. The methods were disregarded on the basis of unacceptable risk.'

And her job was done.

'The height thing,' he went on. 'It was a deal-breaker. The adverse impacts of the CANDI cluster across the sites were coming through...'

'Okay, that's enough.' There was a note of panic in Tod's voice.

The boy raised a hand with an authority beyond his years, and started again: 'The impacts of CANDI: weight gain, metabolic changes, neurotoxic effects. They were bad news—very bad, actually—but head office was finding ways to tick the boxes, enough to maintain sales. The growth thing was a whole new factor. While you kids in the control were having your growth spurts, the drug-therapy kids were going in exactly the opposite direction: stunting, skeletal growth abnormalities, suppression of bone mineralisation, decrease in bone growth. Fat you could fix, but short was short.'

He glanced at Tod—who, I noticed, was listening to all this like he was hearing it for the first time—but the boy was not speaking to him. He was speaking to me and he was speaking with purpose, the purpose of one tasked with the transfer of information.

'What did they do about it?' I asked.

He paused to give the answer the gravity it deserved. 'I found a study conducted with macaques where they packaged a growth hormone into the drug to counteract the side effect. It was quite successful; the problem was that the testing wasn't conclusive for humans.'

A couple of years back he had discovered records of the same drug combination used to treat early adolescent bipolar across ten trial sites in Southeast Asia, including a hospital and two schools. 'Three hundred children aged eight to eleven...I can't find any trace of the results,' he said. 'I'm guessing it didn't go well.'

'So, what then?' I asked.

He shrugged. 'They move on to the next lot. None of this is one-off. This is global, Daniel, business as usual. This is what they do.'

He was staring at me now, his pale grey eyes drilling into mine, and I saw it in them, *the fervour of purpose*—the lifeblood. 'It is all about the end-goal,' he said. 'That is how they justify it. A world without pain.'

At some point while he was speaking, another image of Alex came into my mind. He was indicating to me his first whiteboard: cocoa farming, child slavery, the red country with the black spot— *to make the chocolate bars for the kids in the yellow countries.*

'And the Doctor?'

'The man who didn't sleep,' he said with a doleful shake of his head. He got to his feet, walked to the middle monitor and clicked back into our study. The montage of images appeared, ending with the courtyard—the section where Helen used to set up our experiments.

We ground ourselves on assumptions. When they are proved false, we are left with a different set of questions.

What I was looking at was not a research centre. It was exactly what the Doctor had always called it: a school. Designed to educate—as the Latin root would have it, to lead forth. And this was no archive, either. I was looking at a live feed.

'He reopened the School as soon as he could,' said Jordan. 'He needed more cohorts, more evidence. More lives well lived…That is where I came from.' He looked at me, smiled. 'You and I, we are alumni.' And when the smile faded. 'The Doctor did everything a man could do. I'm guessing it killed him.'

He turned back to the screen, scrolled down through several disclaimers to the bottom of the page, a link to the landing page for current programs. 'This study is currently recruiting participants,' he said.

And there, another list of names, another set of futures.

The videos were still playing on the outer two screens and there was an echo ringing in my ears like a chorus of voices.

'I sent you the report,' the boy said. 'That was me.'

'I don't understand,' I lied. 'What do you want from me?'

'I want what *he* wanted. What he wanted from you all along.'

To take up where we left off.

I would like your brain on something.

Not just mine.

I bundle this folder up now and add one final record. This is my file. Within it is everything I told the Doctor and all that I left out; at least it is as far as I can go. I answer the questions as best I can.

Time gives us different versions of ourselves. My best one was born the night Rachel sat between us in the courtyard and told us her story. It comes and goes, dependent on whether she is close by or far away. Over the years I have tried to make her understand that. Now I am trying to make her understand something else.

I sit on my porch and wait for the sound of her car. On the third day of messaging back and forth—*it needs to be in person*—I hear it, rising above the chorus of cicadas and magpies. *Hallelujah*.

She climbs out of the car. 'What is it, Daniel?'

So I tell her. About Mindsight, about Tod, about the Doctor and his protégé. She doesn't stop me at any point in the story—not even for Tod—but looks back at me and listens like it is the most important thing I've ever said. We stay on the porch through the night, side by side, glimpses of moon through the inky canopy—a final midnight session.

First we determine size and scope and then we create a second whiteboard. *Solutions*. She nods and turns to face me. Voltage transmitting cell to cell. We ask, the way Rachel always does: what now?

The beginning is a sandstone building with a curved, concrete structure and a core of natural light. Purpose-built. It is a school. There is only one, but there are more students: the alumni. Next is a database and a boy to grant us access. Between us, we set a new proof point. One case study at a time.

Already there is a different story. The first thing is to tell it.

ACKNOWLEDGMENTS

Many thanks to: Jo Corrigan and Malcolm Knox for their comments and insights, Richard Bandler for helping me with my brain, Mum and Matt for their loving support, Lyn Tranter and the marvellous Mandy Brett, and Peggy Dwyer—again—for her generosity every step of the way. I am also indebted to Gary Greenberg and Dr Allen Frances whose investigations into the diagnosis and treatment of mental disorders in *The Book of Woe* (2013 Scribe) and *Saving Normal* (2013 Harper Collins) proved invaluable.